T0378739

HIGH FINANCE

HIGH FINANCE

a novel by

KEN MILLER

ULYSSES PRESS

BROOKLYN, NEW YORK

Text copyright © 2025 Ken Miller.
All rights reserved. No part of this publication may be reproduced, stored in a retrieval system, or transmitted in any form or by any means, electronic, mechanical, photocopying, recording, or otherwise, except for brief quotations in reviews, educational works, or other uses permitted by copyright law.

Published in 2025 by
ULYSSES PRESS
an imprint of The Stable Book Group
32 Court Street, Suite 2109
Brooklyn, NY 11201
www.ulyssespress.com

Library of Congress Control Number: 2025936723
ISBN: 978-1-64604-865-6
eISBN: 978-1-64604-866-3

Acquisitions editor: Claire Sielaff
Project editor: Kierra Sondereker
Managing editor: Claire Chun
Copy editor: Renee Rutledge
Proofreader: Beret Olsen
Cover design: Abbey Gregory
Artwork from Shutterstock.com: picture frame © Oliver Hoffmann, photograph © fotoak, phone © pterwort, smoke © Vladfotograf, cigarette © Achira22, room with windows © VideoFlow, skyline © Gorodenkoff, desk © rtsimage, computer © Stokkete, man in chair © LifetimeStock, parquet floor © New Africa, stack of paper © New Africa, newspaper © Joice Brinkerhoff, glass tumbler © Volodymyr Burdiak, decanter © OddMary, rug © Ground Picture, paper ball © pics five, ashtray © gracethang2, ashes and butts © APPOLLOMAN

Printed in Canada
10 9 8 7 6 5 4 3 2 1

Disclaimer: This novel is a work of fiction. All the characters and events portrayed in this book are fictitious and any resemblance or similarity to any real person, living or deceased, or any real event is purely coincidental.

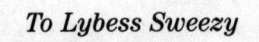

To Lybess Sweezy

CONTENTS

"The Lehman bankruptcy was the financial equivalent of 9/11."

—PAUL KRUGMAN
Nobel laureate, economist,
and *New York Times* columnist

"It was the biggest financial shock since the Great Depression."

—BEN BERNANKE
Nobel laureate and chairman of the Federal Reserve from 2006 to 2014

CHAPTER 1
THE STREET

That Lehman Brothers was going to end up as his best shot was a secret Jed had tried to keep from himself…and from the junior Lehman partners he'd met in earlier interviews. At the outset of his search, he, like all of his fellow members of the Harvard Business School class of '77, had an avalanche of alternatives. For Jed, his sector was always going to be finance, and most particularly, investment banking…where the money was. He'd gone to the Caterpillar, Inc., interview, only to hone his interviewing skills. He knew that climbing the corporate ladder in the industrial sector was not for him and that Cat's headquarters in Deerfield, Illinois, a half hour north of Chicago, would be as acceptable as Pripyat to a Chernobyl native. Forget about it! New York, the capital of capitalism, was where the big bucks were.

If one of the old-line WASP investment banks would have had him? Whoosh! But at First Boston? Well, after prying out of him that he'd joined Zeta Beta Tau, a Jewish college fraternity, the interviewer stared at his nose until he'd hidden it behind his hand. Something felt off at White Weld as well, and there too, he wasn't invited back. The almost Jew-free Morgan Stanley had risen to first choice for a couple of weeks. He had made it through their two sets of early screenings, and when they'd invited him to lunch, it had begun promisingly. Although everyone present seemed to be a junior or "three sticks," he was charming them right up to the best cup of coffee he ever had. But when he'd stood, the napkin he had tucked under his belt turned out to be the tablecloth. The crockery flying in all directions ended his chances there with a definitive clatter. So, fine. So, no Morgan Stanley.

Which left the ecumenical but predominantly Jewish Lehman Brothers. With scant job openings this late in Wall Street's hiring season, if he didn't receive an offer from them he'd be forced to return to Caterpillar on his hands and knees, and what? Learn golf, join Ravloe with its all-you-can-eat buffets heaped with schmaltz herring and kreplach, play poker with high school buddies who were running their fathers' hardware or house-painting businesses? The half-life of his own father's failures was ticking in the background as he tried to imagine the conversation with Amanda about Caterpillar's collegial family culture and the allure of Chicago's Art Institute.

Maybe God loved him after all. Lehman was a money machine. If he could get them to extend an offer, he would show those Morgan Stanley jagoffs (who were barely able to contain their laughter while they rushed him out to the reception area)! Fuck them anyway.

With Amanda still asleep, Jed examined the mirror one last time, giving final approval to the fit twenty-five-year-old with a full head of curly hair. His girlfriend's note taped to the apartment door annoyed the hell out of him as he fumbled with the locks: "You've got this!" In fact, he did not have it. At this moment in time he did not have anything, save for the Harvard MBA, which, among his competition, was like having a neat haircut and a shined pair of shoes. She knew zilch about what he was up against. All the way to the Lex, he worried that she'd jinxed his final interviews.

Emerging from the subway at the base of Trinity Church, Jed joined the herd sweeping north past the old Broadway graveyard toward Wall Street: late-to-work secretaries scurrying in their high heels, young bankers loping with long brisk strides, traders in white jackets pausing to buy a *Daily News* on their way to the New York Stock Exchange. At Wall he turned east into the blindingly bright autumn sunrise. Using his hand as a visor, he found the William Street sign and took the right.

At One William, the eleven-story triangular Lehman building with its bold little cupola, surrounded by modern skyscrapers, dominated its corner with ferocious understatement. Jed felt the doorman's eyes as he entered the neo-renaissance landmark. Wiping off a bead of perspiration, he presented himself to one of the two attractive young women seated behind an immense rough-hewn wooden desk that looked at least a century old.

Once seated, he was in a position to observe the scene more carefully. Runners, secretaries, delivery boys, bankers. "Congrats on the Hess announcement," he heard one young man say to another, who answered, "Don't jinx me, Himmelstein! No deal's done till it's done." It seemed to Jed as if he were watching a choreographed play, one in which each actor feared losing his role to an understudy. And above it all hung three framed daguerreotypes of men whose eyes seemed to be assessing his worth. He could only assume these were the original Lehmans. Bearded and bow-tied, each resembled the shrewd dry goods merchant he had been. "You...you would be lucky to have me here," he declared under his breath, all too aware that he'd not yet made the sale to either them or himself.

Soon after a grandfather clock with a long pendulum struck eight, his minder, a junior partner named Diamond, came rushing to collect him. He was portly, shorter than Jed's five foot eleven, and gussied up in a double-breasted suit with matching bow tie and handkerchief.

"We're late." He hissed like it was Jed's fault and led him over to wait for a manned elevator that would probably stop at every floor.

"We could walk," Jed suggested.

"Are you kidding? He's on nine!" Diamond replied dispositively, as if they would have needed several more weeks at base camp to prepare for the ascent.

On the way up, Diamond whispered his only briefing: "William Sawyer is the head of the oil and gas business, the firm's biggest profit center. Came to New York from the Louisiana bayou without a pot to piss in."

Sawyer's assistant was away from her desk, so Diamond led them right into a large office where a heavyset man in his fifties was stroking golf balls into a device that popped one back to him if it fell into its hole. Tentatively clearing his throat, Diamond announced, "This is Jed Czincosca. Did well in math, just graduated from the Harvard B school."

Sawyer, clearly annoyed to have missed his ten-footer, concentrated on another ball, neither looking up nor speaking. Jed glanced at Diamond, who was biting his cheek. "We can come back if—" Diamond ventured, prompting, at last, a response from Sawyer, who remarked in a Southern accent: "In my opinion, Harvard is bullshit." Diamond pulled anxiously at his collar, Jed swallowed, and Sawyer maintained the focus of Nicklaus surveying a putt at Augusta. Then, after what seemed enough time to have played nine holes, he straightened up and glared at the interviewee. "Tell me one goddamn worthwhile thing you learned in that institution of so-called higher fuckin' learning."

Jed, vetoing "regression analysis" and "branding semiotics," went with "how to deal with people from all walks of life."

"Is that right?" said Sawyer. Leaning his weight on his putter, he resembled a circus elephant balancing on a stool. "So, Harvard taught you how to handle a low-life hick like me?"

Jed waited for the laugh, but Sawyer remained stone-faced.

Jed lowered his eyes. "I doubt anyone handles you, sir," he finally ventured.

"Good answer," said Sawyer, returning his attention to the putter. "Nice to have met you."

After a mumbled "Thank you Billy" from Diamond, Jed scuttled out the door in his wake. "I've got to run to another meeting, so I'll just drop you off at Frankenberg's and pick you up around 11:45," Diamond seemingly decided on the spot. "That went well."

That went well? Hiding his incredulity, Jed composed himself and entered Frankenberg's office. Frankenberg was around the same age as Sawyer, and his shelves displayed Lucite mementos of acquisitions by GE, Sears, and IBM, capital raisings for Exxon and General Motors, as well as photos of him with Presidents Nixon and Johnson. Clearly, he was as important as Sawyer, but success hadn't settled in his midsection and jowls. There could be no doubt that Frankenberg was aware Jed was standing there, but he did not look up from his writing.

Eventually, Jed cleared his throat. Frankenberg affected to be startled. "Oh," he said in a display of sub-off-off Broadway acting, "What can I do for you?"

"I'm Jed Czincosca," Jed replied, "here to interview for an associate position."

"Ah," Frankenberg said, "well I'm sure you're good or you wouldn't be here. Is there anything I can tell you about Lehman Brothers?"

"Um…Perhaps you could share with me a lesson or two from your many years in the business?"

Frankenberg slowly took him in. "Sit down," he finally said, and Jed collapsed gratefully into the nearest antique American chair. As his fingers sank into the upholstered armrest, he remembered the red BarcaLounger his dad had salvaged from a curb in a rich Chicago suburb.

The older banker entwined his fingers, touched the steeple of the church he'd created to his lips, and cleared his throat: "Don't trust your clients or your partners."

Before Jed had an opportunity to respond, a liveried retainer appeared with a carafe and four Wedgwood cups. "Coffee?" Frankenberg asked. "By the way, call me Allen." Even as Jed began to relax a bit, he noticed that his hand reaching for the cup was shaking. "When you come to work here, I will teach you more about each of these precepts," Frankenberg said.

When! Jed was ecstatic.

"I suppose," Frankenberg continued, "it's 'a bit previous,' as that redneck prick Sawyer would say, for me to go too far into this, so I will confine myself to remarking that some of the bankers here are less than exemplary human beings."

Jed glowed in the warmth of Frankenberg's fraternal candor. "Could you…I mean what—?"

"What I am saying is that some of my partners have criteria for talent which would not be tolerated in a true meritocracy. Figure out who they are and avoid them."

When Frankenberg turned the subject to finance, Jed was delighted to understand at what he felt was a sophisticated level. Allen (as Jed had gingerly begun to think of him) mentioned that he was orchestrating the hostile takeover of Avis Car Rental by ITT covered above the fold in that morning's *Wall Street Journal*. Then he segued smoothly into a discussion of world events and their possible effect on markets. Jed's occasional "I couldn't agree more"-s allowed him to experience the moment as a "conversation." He was startled when Diamond burst into the room with a "Sorry to interrupt, but we're late for your final interview." Bidding Frankenberg a hurried farewell, Jed pursued the fleet-footed Diamond in a mad dash up two flights for their appointment with the firm's president.

Dodging analysts tearing down the stairway with armfuls of prospectuses, they arrived, breathlessly in Diamond's case, at the executive waiting area in front of Hathaway's capacious office. Soon after, Hathaway's younger assistant, the one farthest from his office door, had invited them to take a seat. Diamond began to fidget and look at his watch.

"How am I doing?" Jed asked in the hopes that making conversation would calm Diamond's infectious anxiety.

"So far, so good I guess," Diamond replied unencouragingly, before adding, "But rumor has it we lost a few mil on the forex market overnight, so the boss's likely to be in one fuck of a bad mood."

"Any tips?"

"Yeah. Don't fuck it up."

Several minutes later, they were shown in at the same time as a Black man of fifty or so, who was dangling a battered wooden box. Hathaway welcomed the three of them with a "Hi, Johnny." Diamond handed Hathaway Jed's folder, inclined his head respectfully, and backed out of the room.

Hathaway extended an arm to one of the three chairs opposite his desk and returned to some document he was studying. With Jed looking on, the shoeshine man opened his box into a makeshift seat, installed himself at Hathaway's feet, and began applying himself to the task of bringing a preternatural sheen to Hathaway's shoes. After drumming his fingers and looking out the window like he was alone in the room, Hathaway rotated the plush old chair he was sitting on in Jed's direction, causing Johnny to scramble into a new position. "So, Mr. uh... Czincosca," he said, civilly enough, against the background of Johnny's spraying and rag-snapping, "you want to work at Lehman Brothers? It says here that you've met Lemle, Brownstein, Smythe, Diamond of course, and both Frankenberg and Sawyer. Who did you like the least?"

"The least?" *Oh my god, the least.* "Well, sir,...Mr. Sawyer is a most unusual personality." This response elicited a raised eyebrow from Hathaway.

"Unusual in what sense?"

"I...I only had a moment with Mr. Sawyer," Jed stalled, "but it was clear that he has very strong opinions." *I should have chosen a more junior guy like Lemle, damnit.*

After another one of those interminable silences that Jed had begun to think of as the Lehman power pause, Hathaway remarked, "Well, you're quite the diplomat, aren't you?" And then he sat there. Immobile. Staring deep into Jed's eyes. It took all of Jed's willpower to accept the apparent brain scan without looking away while conveying the right admixture of deference and a confidence he did not feel. And when Jed mumbled him a "Yes sir," Hathaway stood, extending his arm again, (this time) for a peremptory kiss-off handshake. Over Jed's shoulder he yelled toward the door, "Get me on with Rubin!"

Jed was waiting at reception, only appearing to read *Fortune* magazine, his mind awash in whatever chemicals anxiety produces, when Diamond came to collect him. "How'd it go, Zinc?" Diamond asked, meting out the moniker that Jed hoped would stick with him throughout a long career on The Street.

"I…I'm not sure. I was only with Hathaway for a few minutes. But it seemed like forever and I—"

"Yes, Pete can be…imposing. C'mon and you can meet some of the guys in the bullpen."

After what seemed hours of exploratory probes under the guise of friendly banter by those he hoped would soon become his colleagues, Jed was ushered to the William Street exit by a young man whose name he was unable to recall. In the uptown subway, packed as tightly as the mosh pit of a Pink Floyd concert, he was thinking so deeply about what he should have said to Hathaway that he almost missed his stop.

When he walked in the door that evening, Amanda was already curled up on their Sears futon. She had let her black hair down, freeing it from the bun she wound it into each weekday morning. She had changed into sweatpants. He could tell she was in a good mood because she was laughing at something in *The New Yorker*, and she jumped up to give him a hug. She knew how "on" he got for these interviews and wisely waited for him to change into some loose Levi's and take a few puffs from the roach on his bedside table before asking, "How'd it go?"

"I...I think OK," he said, inhaling some more pot. "Toke?"

She waved it off, sitting back to hear his description of the day. And when he was finished, she leaned over to kiss him. "If they're any good at recognizing talent, you're in," she assured him cluelessly.

"No deal is done till it's done," he informed her.

Amanda was smiling expectantly, and he rummaged through his discursive thoughts to figure out what she was waiting for. Finally, she relieved him of the task, "I think I am going to get the editorial assistant job at *Gourmet*." He had forgotten to ask about her interviews.

"I knew they'd love you," he recovered. And after the briefest of hesitations, she curled up against him on the couch.

Many years later, Jed would look back on that night in the cheap Fifty-Second and Second Street studio apartment, darkening as the sun disappeared until they could only see the glow of the jay, as one of the happiest of his life. They were in the early phase of their relationship, and their indistinct view of each other in that unlit room was a metaphor for all the possibilities ahead.

Once he began his work in the beautiful old building, Jed was quickly schooled in the exigencies of the elite fraternity he was pledging. Nights, weekends, holidays—important in the lives of mere mortals—meant nothing next to the insatiable demands of the brothers. He came to think of himself as Zinc, just as the other associates accepted their handles. Pigliucci was Pig, Weisenfeld, the obnoxious suck-up Yale grad, was The Weasel, Levin with the prominent red birthmark on his cheek was Lobster, and soon just Lobs. They gossiped about the partners, for whom they had developed their own taxonomy: those who yelled at you were Screamers, those who threw things were Hurlers. Jed worked more for Diamond and Frankenberg (neither a Hurler nor a Screamer) than others; he did some balance sheet analyses for Hathaway (Screamer), and he tried to stay away from Sawyer, who was said to have thrown a golf ball through one of his office's landmarked windows. But Jed couldn't avoid doing a spreadsheet for him now and then. Their dialogues filled him with dread, lingered in his mind.

"On the price per barrel, did you use West Texas Intermediate or Brent?"

"I used the price that you told me to use, Billy."

"That doesn't answer the question."

"OK. I don't know."

"Too real world for you? Barring a miracle, guy like you? Won't ever give enough of a shit to find out."

Probably Sawyer disliked him just because he saw Jed as Frankenberg's boy, but rumor had it that Sawyer told anti-Semitic jokes, and his antipathy seemed to intensify with time.

"I been pondering," he drawled one day after Jed had been at The Firm for almost a year. "Goldman's drug testing their employees. Think we got any users 'round here?"

"No idea, Billy," he managed before fleeing to the men's room.

Sawyer's harassment notwithstanding, Jed was a superstar. It had become apparent that, even in a highly numerate culture, Jed's facility with numbers was extraordinary. Zinc became the element added ever more frequently to the enzymes of Lehman's deal teams, especially when the key issue was bidding strategy in corporate takeovers. No one could touch him on deconstructing the financials of "The Target." No one had as deep an understanding of its hidden liabilities, its profit margin potential, or how it manipulated its financial reporting.

By the time Jed received his first bonus, he had been taught to worship at the altar of discounted cash flow analysis, which places the least value on events further out in time and the greatest value on The Present. The evening he received that $85,000, the largest payout in his class, he sailed home with a cashmere sweater for Amanda and a suggestion that they save the white bean and duck leg cassoulet she had so assiduously prepared. This deserved a night out. At the restaurant, he noticed she'd hardly touched her duck terrine.

"You know, that's the chef's specialty," he told her. "That's why I suggested it. Frankenberg comes here with his wife."

"The piece I've been working on is about French cooking in New York," Amanda replied. "Of course, of course," Jed said blankly and buried himself in his swordfish.

The following Saturday when he arrived at 4:17 for the 4:15 showing of *Network* they had planned to see together, his exaggerated heavy breathing when he burst through the entrance did not buy him absolution.

"We only missed the trailers," he chuckled sheepishly as they settled into the two remaining seats in the top row of the balcony.

"I like the trailers," she whispered across the young couple holding hands in the seats separating them.

As he segued from deal to deal, he tried not to calculate when he would make Partner. The prospect of finally owning part of The Firm made him almost giddy. (Even if one of his father's harebrained schemes had succeeded, they would never have been worth a miniscule fraction of the Lehman enterprise.) And he had less and less patience for Amanda's need for attention. Except for sex he didn't need much of hers and, truth be told, not even then. His bouts of depression brought on by slights at work, real or imagined, were usually manageable with a joint and a few shots of vodka.

But then, his ascent hit a snag in the Ripkin deal. Ripkin, The Firm's biggest fee payer, was battling City Investing for control of Associated Leisure. Frankenberg was running the show at Lehman, and he had been relying more on Jed than on Lemle, the director who was ostensibly Jed's senior.

The female *Wall Street Journal* reporter who'd called him (not Lemle) had a husky voice and a Southern accent uncannily like Sawyer's, but so sexy! "My sources tell me you are the one who's closest to Allen Frankenberg, so I wondered if you'd be willing to confirm what we already know—"

He imagined a beautiful belle, early in her Big Apple career, impressed—as anyone would be—with the responsibility he'd been given on a billion-dollar deal. "Shoot," he ordered, a man with little time to spare. Sitting in his cramped, windowless office, he was conjuring a woman with blond hair, a seductive smile, and a full chest, one who looked nothing like Amanda.

"Well, I am sure you have seen the Thunderbird Properties bid that just crossed the tape."

"Um—"

"The one for $27.50?"

The analysis he'd given Frankenberg before they launched their $25 per share offer had shown the company to be worth between $32 to $35 to City after the efficiencies that their client could wring out.

"Who's impressed?" he asked in a deep, confident voice.

"You mean you're working on a reply bid?"

"I'm afraid I am not prepared to comment on our strategy at this time. Maybe when it's all over we can get together for a drink and a post-mortem."

When Jed picked up *The Journal* the following day, he was delighted to see his name and his "Who's impressed?" quote on the front page, along with another one he sort of remembered having said: "We are confident of our ability to provide financing at any level that Ripkin Global might require."

But it quickly became obvious that he had made a colossal mistake. It was bad enough he'd focused attention on himself. But even worse was the implication that Ripkin Global was planning an increase in its bid. While the Ripkin stock slid, Sawyer told any partner he could collar that hiring Czincosca had been an error. "He's history, if I have anything to say about it."

When Jed arrived home after an unusually brutal day of snarky comments at the unusually early hour of 7 p.m., he had no interest in food. While he finished smoking a mammoth blunt and consuming half a bottle of Stoli, Amanda attempted to pull the story out of him. She tried massaging his neck, but he had become nonverbal. The next morning, he was in no condition to work. She called in sick for each of them, fed him chicken soup, put some Mozart on, and rolled him some joints. By Friday she got him into the shower. After applying a little soap in the right places, she led him to the bedroom and nursed him to full life. That weekend the phone, atypically, didn't ring. Lehman Brothers had been momentarily transmuted into a living organism, holding its breath, awaiting a verdict.

On Monday, in his best suit, Jed went straight to Frankenberg's office to face the music. "Allen, I—" was all he managed before Frankenberg deadpanned, "You're fired." And after a charitably short beat, "Or you would have been if you weren't so damned talented."

"I—" Jed stammered, unsure how to express his appreciation.

"Forget it," his rabbi said. "Did I ever tell you about the time I fucked up a key calculation on a General Motors deal?"

The fact that Frankenberg was able to prevent his having been shit-canned increased Jed's standing with his peers. He applied himself with renewed zeal to the needs of The Firm, volunteering to participate in campus recruiting. This was the kind of extra commitment that would win him kudos, and it had the added benefit of enabling him to bring in a coterie of loyal novitiates. He was the initial sponsor of Fitzpatrick, a Baker Scholar from Harvard, and Smithson, a Penn graduate with a double major in law and business. Then, after hours of interviews at the Stanford Palo Alto campus, there came Breedlove, a geekily brilliant PhD candidate in mathematical aerodynamics.

"So, tell me about yourself, um.... Oscar," he'd begun.

"I'm hungry," was the surprising response.

"Would you like me to order you a burger or something?" Jed decided to roll with it, thinking his reply generous.

"Not that kind of hungry, Jedediah," Breedlove had snapped. "You asked me to tell you something about myself, didn't you?"

Insolent bastard! Jed didn't appreciate the implication he was slow, and where did he get off calling Jed by his given name? Although annoyed, he forged ahead, intrigued. "Hungry, how?"

With no further prompting Breedlove recited his personal odyssey: a broken home, poverty, a long list of academic honors and victories in math competitions, concluding with a phrase Jed would never have dared use in his Lehman interviews: "I want it all. Money, power, glory."

After Breedlove answered some math questions so dazzlingly that Jed felt jealous, Jed decided to invite him to New York. It was unlikely this young man would get through the selection process, but after a long, unproductive day, Jed figured *Screw it, at least it will show I can think outside the box.*

By late in his second year at Lehman, Jed felt he had found a way to handle the pressure. Broken deals and criticisms required "sick days," but if he could make it to the weekend, dope, Stoli, and sex in proportions appropriate for the exigencies of the precipitating factor allowed him to manage his return to functioning verticality.

Unfortunately, the sex part with Amanda shriveled a bit with the arrival of their firstborn, Peter. He was a beautiful boy with his mother's high cheekbones and a dimple in his chin that scrunched mischievously when he laughed. He was inquisitive, inspecting thoroughly all food, toys, and fabrics in his vicinity. However, now it was not just Amanda that Jed kept waiting but Petey, who needed, according to Amanda, "more of his daddy." But, when Jed managed to carve out a whole Saturday morning of free time for Amanda, who used it to change Petey's diapers, feed, hug, and read to him, Jed couldn't help but think, *Why do I even bother to come home?*

One late Friday afternoon toward the beginning of his third

year at the firm, Jed stopped by Frankenberg's office to deliver a Has/Gets analysis for Bendix. The industry pioneer was one of Jed's top accounts, and he was helping the company plan a clandestine sweep of ASARCO mining shares in the open market. Frankenberg looked preoccupied.

"Continental Insurance needs a billion or so to hire more agents and expand into new markets," he told Jed, putting the Has/Gets in his briefcase.

"Sounds great."

"But they can't take on more debt without getting downgraded by Moody's and S&P," Frankenberg explained. "And if they sell common stock, they dilute the ownership of their existing shareholder base, maybe hurt the value of management's options."

"Can I help?"

"I need a security that looks like debt to the tax authorities but is counted as common stock by the rating agencies."

Jed understood the alchemical challenge. "By when?"

"Before the Commitment Committee meeting Monday afternoon."

"Let me have a go at it, Allen," was the response that led to a late-night evening at the office. He tasked Fitzpatrick with an analysis of Continental's debt deals and Smithson with the yields and payout ratios on their shares. Breedlove drew the short straw: a complex cost-of-capital analysis.

As surprised as Jed had been when The Firm hired Breedlove, he was almost as amazed that Breedlove had convinced someone to marry him. "A biotech research assistant at Rockefeller University," Breedlove had said, showing him a photograph of a woman with a butch haircut and coke-bottle-thick eyeglasses. She was pregnant. "Nadia got us tickets for the Colombia Chamber Orchestra at Lincoln Center tonight," Breedlove lamented.

"Think of the money you'll save on dinner," Jed told him.

From home Jed poured over the Internal Revenue regulations,

SEC rules, and Moody's precedents. He called every hour or so to harass, or as he thought of it, to "guide" the team at the office. When he showed up in person at 4 a.m., the three associates were slumped at their desks like plants someone had forgotten to water. But in the Miracle-Gro of Jed's presence they snapped to. Breedlove lied for them all, "Hey, Jed! Great that you're here!"

"Yeah, right. Let's see what you've got."

"So, what I did was, I assumed—"

"Did I ask what you assumed? Just hand it over," Jed interrupted, blowing Breedlove up at the launch pad. Reviewing the analysis did not appease him. "Motherfucker! You're what? Going to solve the whole problem single-handedly?"

Breedlove had integrated the work of the other two and laid out his own annoyingly thought-provoking but flawed solution. "I ask you for a fucking cost-of-capital analysis, but no, you decide to come up with your own genius answer. Your assumptions are crap!" Jed blared, tearing the work in two and stomping on it. "You've got some pixie dust that can make Continental grow at 6 percent? A magic potion to make a 3 percent preferred trade at par? We've wasted four hours on your bullshit."

Breedlove stood motionless. "Jed, I....I wasn't trying to do your job. Was just—"

"Ha! Do my job?!" Jed shrieked, looking like he was about to achieve liftoff before he composed himself. "OK. Out! Take the rest of the day off."

Poring over data through the next several hours with the now-cowering Fitzpatrick and Smithson did not produce the solution he'd promised Frankenberg. Each fix of one problem caused another to pop up. In need of some sleep, Jed wearily headed home in one of the cars the dispatcher summoned from the line waiting on Hanover Street.

There is no solution, he thought, as he shut the blackout curtains against the early morning sun. But when he awoke Saturday afternoon from a dream about griffins and other mythical amalgams, he heard himself exclaim, "Yes!"

Dressing hurriedly, Jed went over the attributes of the security they would create, double-checked the numbers, and called Frankenberg with his elegant solution—a hybrid perpetual preferred stock. Based on Jed's inventive reconciliation of an obscure Section 163 tax regulation with a Price Waterhouse Opinion Letter and a Moody's decision about one of Continental's competitors, Frankenberg was able to shepherd a $1.2 billion convertible preferred "stock" issuance through a successful public syndication. In essence, Continental would go on to save $40 million a year in taxes, The Firm would earn $30 million on the trade, and a whole new line of business had been created. Jed was a hero.

He made partner soon after his thirtieth birthday and was named head of the newly formed Structured Finance department. In no time he assembled a team of highly paid ninjas operating with impunity in the no-man's land where tax, accounting, and rating agency rules met. His bonus that year was $2.3 million: half cash, half Lehman shares. He used two million of the cash to buy another slug of shares at 20.33 percent under the market. Finally, he had the toehold he'd worked his ass for: his first serious ownership position in The Firm! And soon anyone who needed to sell Lehman shares knew he was the go-to guy. With no difficulty at all, he set up a line of credit at Citi to buy at every opportunity.

The more Lehman stock Jed owned, the greater his commitment to The Firm grew. As his investment increased, so did the frequency of his Stoli/pot binges, and the more frequently they occurred, the more nudges Amanda gave about the family's need for a "relaxing vacation." A week here and there at their second home in Quogue was not what she had in mind. Her nagging after the birth of their second son was becoming unbearable to him, as apparently as his bouts of depression were to her.

Finally, one Saturday evening, the issue over vacation was resolved. He had been reading to Petey, who was six, and Robby, who was almost four. *Tiffky Doofky* was a story about a dapperly dressed canine garbage collector seeking love in all the wrong places. Amanda entered the room just as Tiffky found his true love in Estrella the snake charmer.

"Stay, mommy," Petey begged. She sat down on his bed.

"Do ducks really know the future?" Petey asked, referring to the prediction by Madame Tarsal, the fortune-telling mallard who had foreseen Tiffky's happiness.

"Only talking ducks," Jed said.

"Daddy, story," Robby requested, around the thumb in his mouth.

Jed and Amanda looked affectionately into each other's eyes over the bodies of their sleepy children. "Once upon a time," he began, "Tiffky and Estrella had a litter of two beautiful puppies. Tiffky was a complicated mutt, and happiness was hard for him. He loved the puppies like crazy, often bringing a special something for them that he'd found in the garbage."

"Woof," Robby said.

"But he was crazy focused on one thing."

"What, daddy?" Petey wanted to know.

"Owning the dump, or as much of it as he could get his hands on—"

"Do doggies ever go on vacation?" Petey interrupted. He had obviously been pre-programmed by Amanda. In a heartbeat Jed went from angry to resigned to magnanimous.

"I don't know," he smiled, "but how would you boys like to go on one?"

After they arrived at the eighteenth-century Hôtel de Crillon on the Champs-Élysées, Jed retrieved the joints he'd snuck into the au pair's luggage. He surprised Amanda with a day of cooking classes at Lenôtre. He allowed Petey to call room service, and when the tray of *croque monsieurs*, their translation of Petey's "ham sandwiches," arrived on an ornate silver cart, the boys were delighted.

The second day began well enough in the hotel's sun-drenched breakfast room. Jed and the boys were enjoying croissants and cups of *chocolat*. Amanda was happily torturing with her French a stranger at a nearby table when the waiter handed Jed a lovely little envelope with a polite "*Pour vous, Monsieur.*" Jed tore it open, and then he tore it up. Instantly he yelled the guy back.

"Waiter! Check."

Amanda's reparative attempt, "*L'addition, s'il vous plait,*" annoyed the shit out of Jed.

"What's wrong, honey? There's been an international incident?" she asked, reaching for his hand in the taxi to the Bois de Boulogne, a large park in the 16th arrondissement.

"No, goddamn it. But with Audit now reporting to Sawyer, I might as well work in the Soviet Union." In the cab, while Jed stewed in his angry juices, Amanda proceeded as if it had become her most urgent life task to teach them all French.

"Bridge is *le pont,*" she explained. "The word for tree is *l'arbre.*"

But even when they arrived at the park, Jed couldn't let it go. "Every time my guys make an outsized gain, Sawyer sends his tools in to review trades, interrogate everyone."

"Jed. Relax. You've got nothing to hide." She looked at him for affirmation, but he averted his eyes. "C'mon, we're on vacation," she coaxed.

"We're on vacation," he mimicked in a high-pitched voice. "How do you say in French 'Fuck the Internal Audit Department?'"

She could hardly bear it. "How 'bout I translate 'I'm married to an obsessive who thinks of nothing but business?'" she yelled once the boys had skipped ahead on the sylvan path.

They were arguing so heatedly they almost didn't hear the splash when Petey pushed his younger brother into the Lac Majeur. Jed ran up to a scene of rowboats gliding across the water, a family of ducks struggling onto shore, and Petey screaming, "Over there!" His older son pointed to a place where Jed saw bubbles breaking the surface. He plunged in, felt around, and finally making contact with his son's body, hauled him up by his shirt. Though the water was too deep for Robby, Jed was able to stand, and he carried his youngest son back to the shore. For a terrifying few seconds, Robby stared at his father unseeingly, but when Jed slapped him on the back, he gasped and started coughing. Amanda wrapped her arms around the boy.

"It's okay, it's okay," she assured Robby in a frantic voice while Petey stared at the ground.

"Jesus, Petey. He's only four!" Jed raged, shaking the contrite six-year-old so hard that even Robby was reduced to tears. Since Robby was crying anyway, Jed let him have it too: "Stick up for yourself, goddamn it!"

At the hotel, they showered and dressed for their long-scheduled dinner at the exclusive Taillevent, and as they closed the door to their suite, they heard the au pair's attempts at peacemaking about who pushed who at the Lac Majeur. When, implicitly having buried their earlier near-lethal argument, they arrived at the restaurant, the snooty maître d' studied the reservation list forever, finally smiling as if he had resolved a knotty problem. "Monsieur Zeencoska, you will follow me if you please," he said and led them to their table, pausing briefly by a large cage of live game birds. "We can prepare him any style," the maître d' said, gesturing at the quails, snipes, and woodcocks.

The sommelier appeared as two busboys in Taillevent uniforms were helping them push in their chairs. To show him who was boss, Jed rejected his suggestion of a full-bodied Côte de Beaune, choosing instead a ridiculously expensive '74 Napa cabernet. A server with a "Taillevent" emblem on his tuxedo arrived to offer them a complimentary *amuse-bouche* before the waiter with a waxed handlebar mustache arrived to take their order.

"Would Monsieur-Madame permit a suggestion or two?" he said unctuously.

"Why not?" Jed answered over Amanda's "*Mais, oui.*"

The waiter then rattled off a list that seemed to delight Amanda. She chose the Rémoulade de Tourteau à l'Aneth and the Tournedos de Boeuf Rossini *avec* Pommes de Terre Anna.

"And for the gentleman?" he inquired, turning toward Jed.

"Do you have, like, a green salad?"

Following a pause—a long pause—the waiter conceded: "I ask the Chef shall he prepare for you the *salade verte.*" And then, with ill-concealed disdain, "Will that be all, or will Monsieur be having a *plat principal*?"

Flushed, but pre-ballistic, Jed took a deep breath, "OK, I'll have this one," he said, pointing to the Selle et Cotes d'Agneau Dorees à la Sarriette aux Saveurs Meridionales.

Over the hors d'oeuvres, Jed was enthusing about a block of Lehman shares he'd just bought from a desperate partner who needed cash for his father's brain surgery, when he noticed Amanda wasn't listening. Probably she was off in some kind of culinary nirvana with her unpronounceable complexity of an appetizer. "I'm what? Boring?"

"Boring is not the *mot juste.*"

He frowned. "Well OK, what is the mo juiced?"

"The *mot juste* means 'exactly the right word.'"

"Uh huh…What is the right word?" He clutched the sides of the table.

"Narcissistic? Solipsistic? Self-absorbed? It's multiple choice, and there is more than one correct answer. Actually, if you want to, go with "Other." I am all ears."

"OK, Amanda," he said, twitching with anger. "Other! Other, as in, other worries than how good something looks, tastes, sounds, feels! Other as in working constantly to create security for us. You think I can flip a switch from win or die to all lovey dovey? Do you have any clue about the shark tank I swim in every day? Let me tell you something about sharks: They stop swimming, they drown."

"I had no idea I was living with a world class ichthyologist," said Amanda, placing her chin on her hand and looking at him with fake adoration. "Do say more."

"You know?" he said through gritted teeth. "This whole thing has just not been working."

"What whole thing?"

"Our m…Maybe we should just—"

He was interrupted by the arrival of her Tournedos and his Cotes d'Agneau. The steam and fragrance that arose between them upon the simultaneous revelation of their exquisitely presented dishes gave them each pause. Silently, they began to eat. In their most intimate moments, he had never witnessed a look of such sheer rapture on her face. And his lamb! It had the texture of meat but was melting in his mouth. The sauce, built on a base of butter with a hint of champagne, was ambrosia for a god, making him younger with each slowly chewed bite.

When he acceded to Amanda's "You have to try this" as she held out a forkful of her beef Rossini, sheer delight shamed him into a ceasefire. She looked beautiful in the candlelight.

"I am doing my best," he muttered.

"Mmm," she said, and they laid down their forks.

CHAPTER 2

CAPITALISM 101

ROBERT ISAAC CZINCOSCA, JED'S FATHER, WAS INCAPABLE OF WORKING for anyone but himself. How he rose from Private to Private First Class in the US Army remains a mystery. After he came home at the end of World War II, he got in "on the ground floor" of the Maidenform Brassiere Corporation, which had segued from supporting the troops through its parachute harness business to supporting women's breasts. As Robert told it, he secured the job on the strength of an intro from an Army buddy along with some stories about his helpful risk-taking during the London blitz.

The newly returned veteran took his hiring as evidence of his sales ability, and a sense of kismet from having landed a job so quickly carried him for the first few months. But he could not even bring himself to say the word "boss," and he bridled when he had to fill out a customer call report.

The week after he quit his Maidenform job, he announced, to Jed's older brother, Lenny, "It's time for one of our father/son excursions." Robert always insisted on keeping his plans a surprise, so neither his wife, Ruth, nor the boys knew what excursion he had in mind other than that it would be "outdoors." Robert had been hyper in his immediate post-bra week, slamming the icebox closed, waking up at five-thirty to chastise the milkman for banging the back screen door, and frequently leaving the apartment to run never-specified errands.

Lenny was uncomfortable handling his father alone, but Jed, age seven and almost four years his junior, had been judged too young to be included. During the night, a snowstorm of typical 1959 ferocity had dumped twenty-six inches on the streets of Chicago. The sound of cars passing below the frosted windows of their third story walk-up was more muffled than usual. The snow had stopped, but a few flakes drifted down from roofs and trees.

After Lenny had put on his snowsuit, his mother jammed his gloves on, wrapping his muffler so tightly around his neck that he gagged. Then she fumbled in the trunk the Czincoscas shared with the Levys and Cohens on the landing outside their front doors for Lenny's Mickey Mouse cap. She pulled it over his ears and pronounced him adequately bundled for an extremely cold winter day in the Windy City: "*Genug*...enough." Then, as she turned to give her husband a hug, Ruth's hand brushed the flask in his back pocket. She looked as if she was about to say something Lenny's father wouldn't like. Instead, she turned back to Lenny, who felt her dry lips on his forehead. Jed had been sentenced to a half hour in their shared room for screaming about his exclusion and leaving a mark when he hurled his Superman doll at the wall.

As Lenny and his father walked downstairs, Lenny began sifting through some clues his father had dropped about where they might be going. Was the boy to look forward to a freezing afternoon of catching no fish through the ice at Jackson Park Pond? But despite hints about how many fish they'd seen there last summer, Robert had a different plan in mind.

Lenny had never been to the basement of their apartment building, and the roar of the furnace was deafening. They bypassed the chute where the coal was delivered, and Robert flicked on a light. He grabbed his son's sleeve with his left hand and two large pails with his right; then, he pulled the boy along, and they headed straight to the source of the noise. Releasing Lenny, Robert picked up a nearby shovel and filled one of the buckets with furnace ash. When he stepped back and nodded at the empty one, no words were required, nor would they have been hearable. Once Lenny seemed occupied, Robert reached behind him and took a few pulls from the pint he thought the lad didn't know he was carrying. Even after putting the Mickey ear flaps up, Lenny was sweating by the time he finished his task.

The Pontiac Robert bought on installment for two hundred bucks from Feldheim's Used Wheels, the family car forever, had a trunk large enough for the two heavy buckets. They wedged the buckets in with boxes of merchandise Robert was supposed to return to his recently former employer. Lenny closed the trunk after stealing one last look at the drawing of a pretty woman in a short skirt and brassiere who was smiling flirtatiously as she laced up a shoe with a blade under it: "I dreamed I was ice-skating in my Maidenform bra." After a few minutes of digging the car out, off they went.

As they turned onto Luella in a better-off neighborhood than their own, they saw a wasteland of little snow mountains with door handles, antennas, and snow-covered mirrors peeking through. But they also immediately spied their first potential "client," an older man in a black suit and tie sitting at the wheel of a stuck Chevrolet. He was hitting the steering wheel with the heel of his hand, and it looked like he was swearing. Fumes were coming out of the Chevy's tailpipe in gray puffs as he gunned its engine, and the two entrepreneurs probably would have smelled burning rubber from its back wheels if their windows had been open. "Think he's an undertaker?" Robert chortled.

The father and son team stopped in the middle of the otherwise deserted street to reconnoiter and didn't have to wait long before the "prospect" stepped on the gas again. Through their car's closed windows, they heard the muted squeal of his Goodyears in the inversion they'd created. The prospect's car rocked as the driver's rhythmic pumping failed to achieve escape velocity. Robert beamed as if he'd just been chosen by one of Arthur Godfrey's talent scouts.

"Get out," he ordered.

"And what?" the boy asked.

"And help the man."

"Help him how?"

Robert looked annoyed, like Lenny was being purposefully dense. "OK. On this first one, I'll show you the ropes."

So, they exited the warm car to a blast of arctic air, and he knocked on the guy's window. The guy rolled it down. "My son," Robert chuckled ingratiatingly and nodded downward, pointing at the boy with his head. "My son can help you out of this pickle." He nudged Lenny, who smiled on cue.

The guy didn't quite smile, but he seemed intrigued. "He doesn't look big enough to—"

"Guaranteed results or your money back."

"How much?"

Getting the picture, Lenny piped up, "Whatever seems fair."

"Fine, kid. Work your magic."

Robert and Lenny walked back to their car. Robert opened the trunk, handed Lenny a bucket, and lifted his chin toward the back of the guy's Chevy. Lenny dragged the bucket there.

"Throw some ash under the wheels," Robert instructed.

"I'll get my mittens dirty. Mom will kill me."

"Take 'em off."

"It's fifteen degrees outside."

"Don't be a weenie."

So, Lenny took the mittens off, and Robert told him how to spread the ash. His hands were probably red by the time he finished, but there was no way to tell under the soot. The boy hated to think about what the inside of his mittens were going to look like, but he wasn't about to touch that fender with his bare hands. Father thumbs-upped the guy to step on the gas, they both leaned into it, and the car was free! And Lenny fell into the ashes he'd just laid down. *Mom is indeed going to kill me*, the boy thought.

Robert pulled him up and nudged him forward as the guy

stopped in the middle of the street. Rolling down his window, he gave Lenny a "You'll go far, kid" and five dollars.

Robert and Lenny were both exultant. "Clever, that 'whatever is fair' thing," Robert whooped. Lenny had rarely before felt the sheer joy of his father's unconditional approval. And better yet, he would have a great story to lord over Jed with when they got home. They moved on to their next customer, a woman with a toddler in the passenger seat (another five), then a Motorola repair man (three bucks in quarters), and finally, a doctor on a house call (seven).

"Mitchell's for ice cream!" Robert hollered when the doctor had driven away. Adding it all up while they parked, Lenny had twenty dollars in his pocket. After a slight delay while Robert checked something in the trunk—code for a clandestine swig—the two installed themselves in one of the empty booths, each of which had these new little jukebox machines. Robert splurged on three songs for a quarter. The lesson was about to begin. "You see what I'm saying?" he started, as The Platters began crooning in the background. ("Oh, oh yes, I'm the great pretender...")

"I mean...what, um—"

"So look, you see how easy it is to make a buck on your own? Your mother? If I let her make the decisions, I would still be working for someone else." A pimply high school age boy in a white sailor hat with Mitchell's embroidered on it came by and wrote down Robert's order for two scoops of chocolate-chip ice cream with hot fudge. Taking his cue that a little extravagance would be OK, Lenny ordered a banana split with extra whipped cream. Robert was so relaxed he wasn't drumming his fingers on the table but not so relaxed as to be slurring his words when he gave Lenny the headline. "You do not have to kiss anyone's heinie in life, my boy. The way to become a man is do what I did to Bert Stockton."

"Who?"

"Stockton, the guy who started at Maidenform two lousy years before I got there. Thought it was his right to order me around."

"Did you punch him in the nose?"

"Not literally. But listen, if I told him once, I told him a thousand times, my name is Robert, not Bob, so when he's, 'Bob, I want you to be at Marshall Field's at noon today. Oh, and Bob, be at Carson Pirie Scott no later than two with the samples for Mr. Valentino,' since he isn't talking to me, I don't really need to say anything. But I want to make sure he gets the point. So, I'm, 'Listen close. On the off chance that we ever run into each other again, be sure to let me know how it worked out for Bob, whoever the hell he is.' I slam the door and skip out for good."

"So, um, was he sorry to see you quit?"

"That's not the point, damnit!" He shook his head in resignation; Lenny was his son, and there wasn't anything he could do about it. "Check, please," Robert called to the server. And they made our way home in silence, composing their respective reports for Lenny's mother on the way.

Over the ensuing years, Lenny's father started and sold or folded many businesses. Sometimes the selling and the folding were indistinguishable, as when he would hand over the keys to one of his "enterprises" in return for the "buyer's" willingness to take over the accounts payable. But the pattern—or the "syndrome," as Lenny's mother called it, even back then—was always the same. He refused to think about his next business until he had disposed of the previous one. When those "upstream mergers" were especially brutal setbacks, his MO was to head out for a long walk with a pack of Lucky Strikes and a hip flask of White Horse scotch. Thus would begin a "strategic planning period," the only measurable output of which was a stream of cigarette butts and empty bottles.

Lenny got an inkling of how hard these reversals were on his mother one evening when he was twelve and his father was "away with the boys," celebrating a "cash-out." He was helping his mom dry the dinner dishes. The nearly finished book of crossword puzzles she likely wanted to get back to was on the counter. Jed had walked up a flight to watch *The Cisco Kid* with Barbara Kelly, whose family had the only TV on their block. Lenny and his mother had been half listening to the *Amos 'n' Andy* show on WEBH, but when Andy began to sell Amos on his latest crazy scheme, Ruth turned Andy off mid-sentence.

"I knew he knew," she mumbled.

"Huh?"

"I knew he knew where that Bisquick box was. Before your father walked out on his last steady job, I put the cash I saved in a 'secret' place. But he knew where it was." She took a step toward the sink, dried her hands, put the dish towel down, then picked it up and dried them again. "The amount went up and down depending on rent payments, medical bills, stuff like that.

Even in a bad patch I tried to have enough cushion..." She let the water run, filled a glass.

"...to cover one of his self-destructive tailspins. But right before he walked out on Maidenform, I had five hundred seventy-five bucks in there, enough for three months' food and rent."

"Un huh," Lenny responded. She didn't need much encouragement to go on.

"I should have put in less. Maybe he wouldn't have quit."

"Mom, it's not your fault. He had to pursue his dreams."

"His 'dreams,'" she repeated, vigorously re-wiping the already clean table. "The man gets so depressed—" And she trailed off before continuing, "And then—" she teared up, "So the worrisome thing—"

Their moment together was interrupted when Jed burst happily into the room, announcing, "Barbara showed me how to pee!" Barbara was a pretty redhead with mischievous green eyes. She was a couple years older than Jed. Lenny had once overheard her say to Jed, "You have the cutest curly hair!" What the hell did she see in his little *pischer* of a seven-year-old brother?

"What does that mean?" their mother inquired. "This is a special skill that Barbara knows the secret to?"

"Yes! You have to shake it gently before and after."

After dragging Jed to the boys' shared room to a chorus of what'd-I-do's, Ruth headed directly upstairs to see Mrs. Kelly, and Jed missed quite a few episodes of *The Cisco Kid* until the family's own Motorola appeared a few months later. During that period, Lenny often locked the bathroom door to fantasize about what Barbara and he might do together.

On an April evening a few years later, the whole family was watching an atomic explosion on live network television when the doorbell buzzed. The four trooped downstairs to retrieve five heavy cardboard boxes, each containing ten Jiffy fire extinguishers. Tearing open the first box, Robert was so enraptured Lenny wondered if a real A-bomb explosion in the neighborhood would have distracted him. He turned to Jed as he exclaimed, "You and I are going to make five times on this deal." It was Lenny's turn, not Jed's! And Jed was still in the doghouse for his Barbara Kelly adventure, but it was clear Robert was still blaming his oldest son for the Burial at Sea fiasco.

Lenny's job had been to dial up East Coast boat captains who might be willing to "enter into a joint venture with huge upside." From a phone book in the main library downtown Lenny had ferreted out a boat owner in Port Clyde, Maine, who didn't hang up on him. He secured the man's agreement to throw a body overboard. But as weeks went by without Robert having produced any corpses, it became increasingly clear that this project was a bust. In the "unwind," Robert lost a few hundred dollars in long-distance calls, newspaper advertising, and Bangor/O'Hare airline tickets. He never explicitly blamed Lenny for the write-off, yet the boy was made to know he'd let his father down. Jed was happy to remind them all that he'd had nothing to do with this one by appearing to stand up for his big brother. "It was just bad luck that the guy Lenny begged into saying yes was short on patience."

Jed's use of the verb "beg" was intended to remind their father that Lenny had zero sales ability…that Lenny was incapable of hiding his doubts about the products and services he was supposed to move. And, yes, Lenny had been almost crying when he neared the end of his prospects list. Jed must have heard Lenny use the word "implore." Robert had tried to teach Lenny, to no avail. ("You're doing them a favor. Not the other way around.") In Jed's case, no lesson seemed needed. He came out of the womb as a postdoc in sales and marketing.

When it came to the Jiffies, Jed left each morning after breakfast with a full box in his red wagon and returned in the afternoon. He usually sold at least three. He had a sweet smile, and he bragged that if could convince a neighbor to invite him inside, he would make the sale nine out of ten times. Apparently, the fires he started in living room ashtrays, though frightening, were easily extinguishable. In his third week of trooping around the neighborhood, Lenny was walking home around 2 p.m. following a couple of enjoyable hours in the library when he saw Jed talking with Abe Feldheim, the "rich kid" in his class whose father owned the used car dealership where Robert had purchased the family Pontiac. Lenny stopped to hear what they were up to. Neither Jed nor Abe acknowledged the older boy's presence, but they didn't seem to mind. "Think of it this way, Abe. You make some easy money, you save some lives."

"And what do I have to do to earn this no-sweat hundred and fifty bucks?" Abe asked suspiciously. He knew his schoolmates all thought he was a doofus, but he let his guard down to Jed's simulated sincerity.

"I am picking up IOUs by the handful from folks who love the Jiffies but don't have cash on hand to pay for them," Jed's earnestness almost convinced Lenny.

"So?"

"So, all you have to do, see, is buy them from me at a huge discount and sit there as the payments roll in."

"Fer instance, what's huge?" Abe was sure he was being shrewd.

"I move twenty extinguishers on credit, pick up IOUs for $200, sell them to you for $150, and you pocket the difference."

"What if they don't pay?"

"Not a problem," Jed had an answer for everything. "If they don't pay, you take back the Jiffies. Mrs. Baumgarten? The orthodontist's wife? She's got two young kids in the house. What's she gonna do? Let 'em burn to death?" Jed's proposition most likely sounded a lot to Abe like the collection part of his dad's business, as Jed surely surmised from watching Feldheim's repo goons pressure their father on the Pontiac debt. It was an especially bright, sunny day, but you could almost see the light bulb going on over Abe's head.

"You think I'm a dummy? Make it $125."

Jed looked somewhere between shocked and insulted, but then he seemed to regain his composure. He furled his brow, stared at a crack in the sidewalk. Finally, he looked up with a pursing of the lips. Then, with what was clearly, to Lenny at least, fake ambivalence, he held out his hand to Abe. "OK. We've got a deal."

By the end of the summer, Jed had sold all the Jiffy's, some for cash, the rest on his "No Money Down" plan. His only problem was explaining to their father where the missing seventy-five dollars went and how the enterprise had cleared over 1.4 times the original investment. "Dad, if we could do this every couple months, we'd be making over a thousand a year from this one business alone." Jed was a maestro at ingratiating himself to their father. And Abe? After a few attempts to collect on the receivables he ended up with twenty fire extinguishers and a $125 write-off.

As Lenny moved on from eighth grade through high school, he started to argue openly his father. Their exchanges over family dinners became ever more bitter. "What're you, against God?" Robert asked (he thought rhetorically), when President Eisenhower added 'under God' to the Pledge of Allegiance.

"Yes." Lenny left it at that. His father was too dumb for a sophomorically precocious sixteen-year-old to educate. And Lenny attacked his father's business ideas with growing conviction, to the point where one night Lenny actually said: "That might be the stupidest idea I have ever heard. Please pass the potatoes." Robert was planning to open a "bar" where customers could buy doses of fresh oxygen.

"Don't speak to your father that way," Ruth dutifully intoned as she passed the bowl to Lenny.

When Lenny turned toward her, she rolled her eyes. Lenny took this as a green light and went all in. "Seriously? C'mon, you really think people will pay for oxygen when it's everywhere for free?"

Jed attempted a "May I be excused?"

"Eat the rest of your hash, young man," Ruth snapped.

"You never get it, do you, Lenny?" Robert asked, shaking his head with melodramatic frustration. And he turned, after casting his eyes to the heavens, or, more accurately, the crack in the chandelier, to include Ruth in his cosmic rebuke, "Who puts food on this goddamn table?"

"You do, dad. May I be excused?" Jed wasn't asking their mother this time.

"Yes!" Robert shouted without even looking in Ruth's direction. "How's a man supposed to succeed when he is surrounded by skeptics?"

As Jed was making a break for it, Ruth looked her husband acerbically in the eye, her face flushed. And then, her voice dripping with unprecedented sarcasm, "I just want to say for the record how very grateful we all are for your business successes…when they do occur."

Wow! She might as well have said, "It's nice when a mark wins at three-card monte." Robert looked at her as if she'd slapped him.

"You'll see, Ruth," he said to her in a low voice. Lenny felt like an extra in a scene they'd previously performed in his absence.

The night Lenny told his mother that he was choosing Colgate, in Hamilton, New York, over the University of Chicago, her face caved and her lips trembled as she struggled to find the right words. Lenny had dreaded this moment. "U of C has a better reputation," Ruth managed.

Lenny nodded agreement.

Ruth turned, dabbed her eyes. "I am afraid...we will see less of each other."

"I know that, mom. I don't like it either." Lenny moved his chair closer to her, wrapping his arm around her shoulder and resting his head in the crook of her neck the way he used to when he was a child.

"Then why? I want...I want you to do what's best for you. But please. Help me understand." Her voice trailed off and they sat there in silence. Except for the drip of the faucet that Robert had promised to fix.

Lenny cleared his throat. And then cleared it again. "Mom," was all he could get out before he too began to tear up. "I'll visit you every chance I get. It's just that, it's just that—"

"Robert never understood you," she conceded.

"He seems to understand Jed OK."

"Yes, they're peas in a pod. But then...so are we, *mein schatz*, no?"

Lenny gulped. She'd never before acknowledged their special bond.

Lenny could only imagine how conflicted Jed was about his big brother leaving home. He would probably miss Lenny's presence while nevertheless basking in his new centrality. When Jed had been little enough for Lenny to goad and tease him, Jed had studied and even seemed to admire Lenny's technique in getting their mother to deflect the blame onto his innocent self. *So*, Lenny would ask himself in years later, *don't I deserve some credit for his success on Wall Street?*

When Lenny came home freshman year for Thanksgiving, Jed was delighted to inform him that their father had put Jed in charge of Corporate Development. This boiled down to helping Robert implement some increasingly harebrained schemes. Like the one they heard their father toying with one Friday after Thanksgiving. Jed and Lenny had returned from Bertollucci's, where Lenny had taken him for a Coke. Afterward, they tiptoed past the living room and paused to eavesdrop on a conversation between Robert and his pal, Max Levy, the recently retired Metropolitan Life agent who lived across the street.

"You know, Max," Robert began, "lots of people will buy a puppy for their kids at the beginning of the summer, and then, come the winter, the dog can't be outside as much and is a huge pain in the ass."

"Yeah, so?"

"So, we could rent folks puppies for the summer and pick them up in the fall."

"What do you suppose people would pay for this?"

"Don't know yet—but think about it. They would have from, say, October through April without needing to buy any dog food and stuff, so there's lots of profit margin here. I read that the average family spends $2,400 during the life of a dog."

Then, after a brief silence, "Uh, Robert? I see two problems here. One, what about the kid who kinda grows to like the dog? And two, what the hell are we going to do with all these dogs?"

This time the silence was so long the youths threw in the towel. When they returned on their way to raid the icebox, the men's creativity, at least one six-pack later, had taken Robert and Max to a new level.

"How 'bout this, Maxie?" neither son had ever before heard their father giggle. "We have all winter to train the dogs to use a human toilet. Think what we can charge year two after we've taught them to flush."

The brothers rushed to their room with potato chips and other snacks that were never supposed to leave the kitchen. "Jed, bring me five toilet-trained collies by next Friday," Lenny commanded in his best imitation of their father's voice. And the boys had a good giggle of their own.

By Lenny's sophomore year Jed was proud to let it drop that he had become their father's Junior Partner. One of the more astounding developments, at least to Ruth and Lenny, was that Robert's Oxypure bar on Rush Street was a success. People were paying two dollars for a five-minute pick-me-up and three for a ten; just before Lenny's return for a long weekend the July of his junior year, Jed had written Lenny that their father was clearing $200 a week, and in the cab from the airport, Lenny braced himself for an insufferable onslaught of I-told-you-so's.

Ruth had rushed home late from an appointment, and she found Lenny staring in wonderment at their completely renovated kitchen. New countertops, a new stove, new dishes. The icebox had been replaced by a GE refrigerator. Immediately after their warm hug Lenny asked his mother, "The oxygen business is doing this well?"

She gave him a long look before finally answering, "Ha!" She was wearing a calico dress Lenny'd not seen and a gold-toned Bulova wristwatch with some tiny, embedded diamonds. Her hair was in a pixie cut, which made her look ten years younger than her forty-nine.

Lenny was never sure in those days why his mother always seemed so busy. Whatever she spent her time on, cooking wasn't it. However, Lenny's return from college was always a special occasion, so she would not be heating cans of Broadcast Corned Beef Hash or serving three cans of Chicken of the Sea tuna with one of Campbell's Mushroom Soup and calling it tuna casserole. No, Lenny's welcome home dinner was to be cow's tongue, cucumbers with onions in vinegar and sugar, and mashed potatoes with, as always, an abundant supply of Wonder Bread and margarine. The spices were salt and pepper.

Lenny might have gotten through the meal without fireworks, but his father seemed determined to set them off. Robert was already frowning as he sat down, and he lowered his chin so as to look censoriously through the upper part of his bifocals in Ruth's direction, "Nice dress. Seems we've got money to burn." When he then segued into predictable bragging about turning air into cash, it became intolerable. Moreover, Lenny was bubbling over with new knowledge from Professor Foley's class in radical economics and turbocharged by the left-wing zeal of Alice Chowdhry, his fellow acolyte and first-ever girlfriend, who Lenny was dying to sleep with. Yes, it was time for his father to gain, from him, a perspective on the evils of capitalism. "Do you have any idea what Marx, Engels, or Trotsky would have to say about your petit bourgeois oxygen business?"

Robert understood enough to get that he was supposed to be insulted. "Did any of those guys know from making a living?" He glanced at his wife, though without any reasonable expectation of support.

"They knew important truths. More important than exploiting others to feather your own capitalist nest."

"*Our* own nest, Lenny. And think of it as creating jobs."

Ruth began gathering up the dishes. Robert used his little finger to extract a piece of food from his teeth.

"No! Think of it as impeding mankind's leap from the animal kingdom into the domain of human freedom!" Lenny declaimed with callow conviction, putting his napkin in its ring.

At that point, Jed attempted what Lenny assumed would be the first of several "may-I-be-excused"-s, but to Lenny's amazement, their mother granted Jed manumission on his first try. Maybe she was worn down by the cumulative effect of two boys' incessant champing at the bit, but it was particularly galling to see her give up so easily. An excessively upbeat "later" aimed in Lenny's direction was all Lenny heard before the door slammed.

"Where's he off to, mom?" Lenny asked as Ruth and he brought the dishes into the kitchen. Jed hadn't offered to help clean up.

"He has a new friend he's been seeing a lot of."

"What's his name?"

"Maria."

"Maria?" *Damn!*

Chubby Checker's scandalous new release, "The Twist," was on the radio. "Who is Maria?"

"A young woman he works with. At the Chinese restaurant."

"When will he be back?"

"I don't know. That's your father's department."

As the song on the radio switched to "Itsy Bitsy Teenie Weenie Yellow Polka Dot Bikini," Robert wandered in for a beer. "No idea," he smiled, winking at Lenny as if they shared a secret and their dinner altercation hadn't occurred.

"What do you mean no idea?!" Lenny was speaking way too loudly.

"It's a good bet that he'll be home to shower before the milkman gets here."

"They're sleeping together?! That son of a bitch," Lenny exclaimed in a jealous outburst.

"Don't talk like that in front of your mother," Robert said over his shoulder as he left with his beer.

When the door between the kitchen and the rest of the apartment stopped swinging, Ruth wiped her hands on her apron and turned toward Lenny, waiting while the refrigerator juddered through the end of its cycle. "It won't come as a surprise to you that your father and I have had issues over the years."

"You argue a lot."

"That's a symptom. Not what I'm talking about." Her eyes were moist, and she reached for a Kleenex. "In the early years after you were born, he had two near-fatal accidents driving drunk, and I was worried to death."

"Because you loved him."

"Yes, I still, then…When I fell for him, I was living at home. I was an office manager for a dull Gary, Indiana, dentist. Robert was on fire with one of his schemes and I…he was going places—"

"So, you fell for him. And you got married and had me and Jed."

"Yes. And, well, naturally I didn't want to see anything bad happen to him, but also, I was especially worried, after I quit my job to take care of you little *bubbeles*, that he might leave me with no way to make ends meet."

"Well, at least you can relax a bit now that he's been so successful."

"So successful," she repeated quietly. Her brow was furrowed, and she turned away to look at the lilies of the valley on the Metropolitan Life Insurance calendar, which was still on May though it was a month and a half after Memorial Day.

"The Chinese restaurant," she began again, "the one where Jed works. It's owned by a wonderful man named Sam Pang. Around the time you started at Tilden High School, I stopped by to welcome him to the neighborhood. If you made allowances for his English, you realized that he was extraordinarily accomplished, intelligent. He told me about his life in China. A merchant, he was, before he fled. Had owned a very profitable liquor business. Not as profitable as the department store we lost in Dresden, but still…We talked about his plans...He cared about me—"

"Oh my god, mom, are you telling me that you and this Chinese guy are…"

"We're…helpmates," she interrupted.

"Helpmates?? What does that mean?"

"When we get together, we discuss business." She looked like a kid who admits to stealing a piece of bubblegum when she's pocketed a whole pack.

"But—"

"Enough already."

End of conversation. Lenny thought about this exchange but

never discussed it with Jed or their father, nor did he broach the topic again with his mother. He graduated Colgate, finished a two-year Peace Corps stint in an Indian town called Sangareddy with a useless competence in Urdu. It took him six years to earn his PhD in economics from the University of Michigan. Graduate students are supposed to be a depressed lower form of life, but all it had required for Lenny's naturally sunny disposition to shine was finding something he was good at, and getting into a relationship with Neera Agarwald, a third-generation Indian American grad student. Neera was beautiful—and it didn't hurt that she was remarkably uninhibited in bed.

In the summer before Michigan granted Lenny his doctorate, he came home from Ann Arbor for a long weekend. The plan was for the family to have dinner together on Friday and Saturday. Jed was 22, working for some mutual fund in the Loop and living in a furnished apartment near the University of Chicago with, as he put it (having discovered that astrology was helpful in getting laid), "a beautiful Capricorn." There was room for Lenny on Jed's couch, but Lenny opted to sleep at home in their childhood room. The soon-to-be-Dr. Leonard Czincosca's attitude toward his father had softened over the years. Now an adult, he had become more able to see his progenitor as the vulnerable, well-meaning human being that he was. So, it was a fireworks-free Friday dinner with the family. Saturday promised to be the same, until Robert put down his forkful of tuna casserole to announce, as if he'd just had an epiphany, "You know? Tomorrow? I feel like Chinese. What say we all go to that Pang guy's place for dinner?"

Lenny and Jed searched their mother's face for a clue. The family almost never went out for dinner, and as far as either son knew, their father didn't especially like Chinese food. Ruth stared at Robert like he'd suggested a family skydiving expedition. Then she composed herself, "Great idea, Robert. I won't have to cook. But why don't we just get it delivered? It's so much more *gemütlich* at home."

"I think not," he declared, and that seemed to be the end of it. But Lenny and Jed heard raised voices from their bedroom later that evening. The next night, sure enough, the four of them found themselves walking over to Pang's Peking Palace. As they approached, they saw one red neon sign in the window featuring four Chinese characters within a large gabled pagoda. Another, somewhat less visible through the humidity on that part of the window, said: "Authentic Chinese Food. We Deliver." Two dragons, facing each other over the front door, guarded the entrance.

"How you've grown," Pang said to Jed in much improved English over that which Jed remembered. Pang looked to be a good fifteen years younger than Robert. He was about Robert's height, wearing a clean white dress shirt, slacks, and a well-shined pair of loafers.

"These people have a reservation," Pang explained to the line of eight or ten standing near the entrance. "Welcome, Ruth…and family," he said in a pleasing baritone, gently touching Ruth's elbow, guiding her with the remaining Czincoscas, a waddle of ducklings behind her, to a corner table. Once she was seated with her back to the wall, the rest of them took their seats. Robert glared at Pang as he sat down.

The tablecloth was plastic but clean. Pang personally brought the obligatory sweet and sour dips along with some fried wontons and egg rolls, which he told them were "Complimentary. In honor of my former employee." Jed was seated next to his mother, and Pang winked in their direction. Jed smiled knowingly at the clanging coming from the back and exchanged pleasantries with Pang. Each of the fourteen or so other tables was filled with noisy guests at various stages of dinner.

The room was too brightly lit. Chinese-style paper lampshades with red tassels hung from the ceiling, and some whiny Chinese music was repeating itself in a loop. Robert complained about the table, which needed a shim to fix its wobble, and when Pang kneeled to insert a few napkins under one of the legs, Robert leaned toward him to growl, "The music is too loud. How about turning it down?"

Ruth jumped in, "How's business, Sam?"

"You know, " he replied, and Lenny couldn't tell if that was his way of saying "not bad" or if she really did already know the details. Robert, who may have picked up on the ambiguity, seemed intent on making a scene.

"I can't believe the guy gets away with $6.95 for chopped chicken, some celery, and a few cashews," he complained before Sam was out of earshot.

"C'mon dad," Jed attempted, "this isn't The Palmer House."

"Right. But these people...these people come here and take what they can."

Ruth pushed her chair back sharply until the wall stopped it. "Robert, Sam has been doing business in this neighborhood for more than twelve years. If he wasn't giving fair value, he'd be out of business."

"Oh, Sam is it?" father shot back. "Did he give *you* fair value?" and he slammed his fist on the table so hard the soy sauce fell over. The black puddle spread across the table and began dripping onto the floor.

"*Shoyn genug*, Robert! Enough!" Ruth said, knocking over the toothpicks as she grabbed a few napkins from their black metal holder and bent over to soak up the sauce.

Lenny looked on while Jed, who had no idea that there was anything more than a casual relationship between Pang and their mother, struggled to understand, "Dad. What are you talking about? What's eating you?"

"Ask your mother," Robert suggested, crossing his arms and scraping his wooden chair around to stare away from us out the window. Lenny caught Sam looking cautiously through the slats of the plastic strips separating the dining area from the kitchen side. Jed and Lenny turned inquisitively toward their mother, who sighed and put down her chopsticks.

"Boys," she admitted, "I do have a long-standing relationship with Sam Pang."

"Hah! It's time to fess up, Ruth. Let's just get it out there," Robert demanded, swiveling noisily back to the table. The diners at the closest table were pretending they weren't paying attention.

"Well," Ruth acquiesced, "after I got Jed the job here..." As she paused to gather her thoughts, Lenny noticed Jed's eyes open wide with surprise. It had been a key part of his brother's self-narrative that he had just walked in and talked his way into his first steady job.

"Sam, unlike your father, seemed to appreciate my intelligence and analytical skills. He had a lot of practical experience, and he knew who to trust in Chinatown."

"That's the cover story," Robert interjected.

"We built a business together. I own part of this restaurant and the Beijing Kao Ya at 24th and Stewart. We are thinking of opening one in Gary near where I grew up. We've done very well."

"How well?" Jed asked. Robert pulled out an unfamiliar silver hip flask and without even trying to hide it took an extremely long swallow.

"My share throws off around $40,000 per year," Ruth admitted without affect.

And now it was Lenny's turn to be shocked. He had thought only his father was a confirmed capitalist. The title of his doctoral thesis was "Stealing Surplus Value: The Microeconomics of Worker Exploitation by Small Business in the United States of America, 1864–1964." Jed and Lenny wordlessly shared the realization that mother's stunning business success, in and of itself, was a humiliating diminution for their father, who indeed appeared shocked by the amount.

"Forty thousand, Ruth? No kidding? That's...that's more than I—" he shook his head. He stood up, wrestled his coat on, and shambled out the door without a word. Jed stood up to go after him.

"Leave him," Ruth said. "He'll go drink it off somewhere."

Soon after that evening, he sold the oxygen business for a modest gain, after which, according to Ruth, he rarely left the house. He made a few desultory moves in the direction of starting another business but was frequently drunk, Ruth reported. When his life finally ended in a car crash on April 14, 1976, it wasn't a total surprise. He was doing sixty-five on I-90 heading toward Gary, Indiana, in broad daylight when he swerved off the road, hitting a culvert head on. An empty bottle of White Horse in the car and his blood alcohol level left little doubt that he had achieved a desired result.

At the funeral, Ruth dabbed away a few tears, but she seemed more remorseful than grief-stricken. Jed and Lenny kept surveying each other and thus each succeeded in not crying. Jed composed himself and spoke with loving humor about how much fun he and father had had working together. *Jed looks like mom*, Lenny thought as he watched his brother at the *bima*, but Jed's speech patterns, his intonation? If Lenny closed his eyes, he could hear their father giving his own eulogy. Standing to take the microphone from Jed, Lenny looked out on the sea of friendly old Jewish faces through a film of tears. Lenny could almost see through the eyes of the mourners how much he himself resembled his father Robert in bearing and facial expressions.

"Not every business dad started turned to gold," Lenny said. "But some of them worked, and to Jed, mom, and me, he was a big *macher.*" Lenny could see his mother put a handkerchief to her eyes. He was on the right track. "Our arguments, which did take place from time to time, taught me a great deal. In fact, I got my doctoral thesis out of it."

Others rose to praise Robert for his imagination and his creativity...and to thank him in absentia for the one still-surviving business, an add-your-own-fixings hot dog stand, which continued to provide jobs in the community.

Mercifully Rabbi Bamberger's only allusion to the circumstances of Robert Czincosca's death was an opaque reference to Maimonides, something about "dying by thine own hands," so the ceremony was rather conventional. Sam Pang attended in a tailored dark blue suit, and at the reception afterward, Jed and Lenny were standing close to their mother when Pang came near and murmured in her ear, "It's over, Ruth. He wanted this." And then, having stood there awkwardly with those words hanging in the air, he thought to add, looking at Jed and Lenny, "I am sorry for your loss."

"How sorry?" Jed stage-whispered to Lenny as he turned toward the Rabbi's twenty-eight-year-old daughter, who looked stunning in the light from the stained-glass window. Jed and Lenny left the funeral service, dazed, to go their separate ways but agreed to meet for lunch in New York toward the end of the month, when Lenny would be East for an interview with the NYU Economics Department. Jed had finished his first year at Harvard Business School and was dating a classmate from Manhattan whom he described as "a beautiful Aries *shiksa*." Jed knew the city better than Lenny and chose the Oyster Bar under Grand Central Station.

On the appointed day, Lenny cabbed in directly from La Guardia and arrived in time to meet Jed outside the entrance after a near sleepless night.

Entering the cavernous underground space, the two looked out at what seemed like several hundred tables covered in red and white checkered tablecloths. The sound of waiters screaming, plates clattering, and people laughing, conversing, and sneezing bounced back and forth off the tiled walls and the granite floors. As soon as they were seated and got a waiter's attention, they placed their orders and joined the yelling like fans at a concert who must stand on their chairs simply because everyone else does. They tried to stay away from politics; Lenny had become a leader of the Union of Radical Political Economists. The group was known throughout the US as "Urpies" and had members on the faculties of many leading college campuses.

Jed fancied himself an enlightened capitalist, an oxymoronic phrase in Lenny's opinion.

"How's Neera?" Jed asked, not caring much about the soon-to-be-PhD in molecular biology Lenny had been living with for four years. Jed had only met her once, and it had been a disaster. He had mistakenly called her Nisha (the name of a previous girlfriend with whom Lenny had enjoyed a brief fling), and Neera came away from the encounter convinced that her lover's money-grubbing capitalist brother had written her off as a transient experiment. Now Neera had only five months to go before their son would be born, a fact she had asked Lenny not to mention.

"Fine."

"You'll make an honest woman of her one of these days?"

"Probably not, if by that you mean marry her." The couple was planning to live together but shared a rejection of bourgeois norms. "And how's *your* love life?"

Jed welcomed the change of subject and proceeded to describe the promiscuous life of an eligible young Cambridge bachelor. He would have gone on, but Lenny managed to interject.

"Sounds lonely," Lenny said when Jed paused for a swallow of beer, and then, helpfully, the smoked trout, Manhattan clam chowder, fried clams, and double-decker platter of iced oysters arrived.

"Talked to mom lately?" Lenny inquired between bites of the delicious trout.

"Did you ever wonder how dad found out about mom and Pang?" was Jed's reply.

"I guess she got a little sloppy with her secret toward the end."

"Or not," Jed answered.

Lenny stopped with a mollusk halfway to his open mouth. "Ah," he recovered. "You mean dad got suspicious. Rummaged her drawers. Found a note from Pang or something."

"That is one possibility," Jed inclined his head quizzically, daring Lenny to be the Watson to his Sherlock. They both found it weird to be discussing the most confidential matters at the top of their lungs. Nevertheless…

"What are you suggesting?" Lenny screamed a bit louder than the peripheral pandemonium might have required.

"Maybe, in the end, she'd just had enough," Jed yelled back. "Set up the whole restaurant scene."

"What??!" Suddenly Lenny was furious with his brother.

"Look," Jed shouted, "she was clearly *schtupping* Pang. She knew about dad's insecurities…All she had to do to get him gone was make sure he learned about it."

Lenny pushed back his chair. It was either that or push Jed's chair over with him in it. Their mother would never kill their father on purpose, nor would Lenny off Jed, although the thought had occurred to him sporadically from the moment he first laid eyes on the newborn Jedediah. "Fuck you!" Lenny exploded. And he saw the couple at a nearby table stare at them before returning to the safety of their menus.

"Calm down, Lenny," Jed soothed. "It could have been subconscious. You know…"

You can love someone without liking them, Lenny reminded himself. With the help of a great psychoanalyst who had once shared this dollop of wisdom, Lenny had gotten over the loss of his only-child status. He took a couple of measured breaths. "Look, Jeddy," Lenny said, and as soon as he'd belittled Jed with the childhood nickname Jed hated, Lenny felt less angry. He sat back down and reached for the last oyster on the platter. "It wasn't her fault father was a fucking manic depressive!"

And now it was Jed's turn to be hurt because in regard to temperament, as the two both knew, Jed was virtually a clone of their father. "Maybe he wasn't a great man, but he was a great guy," Jed said defensively, and he began to cry, covering his face with his napkin. Lenny watched, unable to bring himself to stand and put his arm around Jed's shoulders.

The wide concourse outside the Oyster Bar was busy with commuters already heading back to Connecticut. In one spot, the columns that hold up the arched ceiling form a whispering gallery so that if two people stand on opposite sides, their backs to one another, it sounds like they're speaking right into each other's ears. Jed's Aries had told him about this, and the brothers had agreed to try it when they made the date. At the exit, they wordlessly split up and headed to the columns on either side of the wide corridor.

"You're not him, Jed. You're not father," Lenny told the granite column.

"I know, but what if—" he whispered from across the crowded concourse.

"You'll be okay."

CHAPTER 3

TEMPORARY EMPLOYMENT

THE NICE THING ABOUT WORKING AS A TEMP, SHE THOUGHT, AS SHE SPRITZED the bamboo palms, watered the aglaonemas, and pinched a dead leaf off the philodendron, is the complete lack of accountability. When she finished at five, her life was her own. Each evening, upon returning to her Flushing Meadows rent-controlled apartment, she let down her hair, offered the plants a few words of reassurance, and took a hot half-hour bubble bath until all her follicles, every pore, and each cuticle was purged of the air conditioning, office germs, and subway smells.

Every few days she got a new boss, usually with expectations so low he would be shocked if she showed the slightest initiative or intelligence. Such recognition was always unwelcome. It made her feel discovered, violated, as she imagined a well-educated prostitute would feel when a customer asked, "What's a smart girl like you doing in a place like this?"

After her bath, it was time to microwave one of the meals she had prepared over the weekend and do a crossword puzzle or listen to NPR. Then she was ready to watch TV and go to sleep over one of her landscape architecture books. When she was in a particularly good mood, she would put her routine aside to chat with a phone solicitor for, say, the Patrolmen's Benevolent Association while she did her nails.

Sometimes her sister would call from Vancouver. Lizbeth favored weekends and holidays for her "reach-outs," so Deborah wasn't surprised when she picked up on the night of July 4, 1981, to her sister's "Hi Deborah!" As a kid, Lizbeth had been on the morose end of the spectrum; how did she get so OTT cheery?

I am not lonely, Deborah bolstered herself against the expected onslaught when she heard the familiar voice.

"How's life?" her sister asked. At twenty-six, two years Deborah's junior, Lizbeth was proud of her own life. Her husband was enjoying an early success at Deloitte Haskins & Sells. She had a boy—two, and a girl—four. Both were happy and well-adjusted, and with sweet Canadian accents.

"How are Bruce and the kids?" was Deborah's reply.

"Fine, thanks for asking. What have you been up to?" Lizbeth loved to rummage Deborah's existence for clues of emptiness she might use to generate advice. In Lizbeth's view, it was time for her sister to "get on with it" and stop "wallowing," as she loved to put it, in the ruins of a failed marriage.

"I was reading a book." Silence. "About a man named Olmstead."

"That's nice," Lizbeth said. Deborah heard her disappointment as she continued her probe for more than the thin gruel she'd been offered. "And how did you spend the day?" Lizbeth had concluded that her own success in spousal choice gave her standing to be the dispenser of wisdom.

"Oh, let me think. Did the laundry, a crossword puzzle, some cooking for next week, listened to the BBC—"

"The BBC! Yes, this is going to be the wedding of the century!" Lizbeth interjected. "You are as pretty as Princess Di, if only you'd take an interest."

Bloody hell! How could I not have seen that coming! "She remains for the moment merely Diana Spencer…but I shall be sure to watch. Maybe I can pick up some tips for when I bump into a prince on the subway sitting on few million quid," she said, struggling to conjure an end to the conversation.

On those occasions when a fellow worker asked her to a weekend party or a bar for a drink, the thought of meeting an eligible bachelor brought her ex-husband to mind, and she invariably decided in favor of an evening at home with Johnny Carson. Michael's principal qualification had been his colorable claim to financial independence as "an established food critic"—all her father needed to hear. "Good luck, Duckie," he had said, employing her childhood nickname, "I wish you the best."

The three London years when Michael persisted in his dead-end job as a restaurant critic writing for a British public that couldn't afford to eat at the places he reviewed were bad enough, but soon he was critical of everything. Starting with her cooking, he moved on to her various other perceived shortcomings. He seemed to have discovered that she was "too tall" for him and soon formulated other issues with her looks. Worst of all, he treated her like a pet he was once proud of but which no longer shook hands or rolled over, and he would not countenance her "humiliating" him by getting a job to supplement their meager income. Worst of all, his obsession with that character, the French food genius, Yves-Claude Le Fournier, was exclusionary and intolerable, an obsession so strong that when Le Fournier moved to New York, it had actually pulled the young couple out of London.

At first, she'd tried to resist the move. "That's not a job!" she'd said when he told her of his plans to freelance for the *New York Post*. "That's a hobby!" If pressed, she would have readily admitted it: She had ceased to be considerate of his feelings.

"Bloody hell! What do you know about jobs? You fantasize about work the way normal people fantasize about sex."

"Oh, now I'm not normal? And sex? Ha! If you fantasized about it, maybe that would be a step in the right direction."

He was quivering with anger, but all he could come up with was, "Bugger off, Your Bitchiness," as he stormed out of their East End flat.

She had nourished the hope that things would improve in New York. But there Le Fournier and Michael continued the culinary explorations that her husband's occasional income could barely support, to say nothing of their frequent *degustations*—the wine tastings that had him home past midnight. "Pairings," choosing the right wine to match the cuisine, were among the essential lessons his gifted French friend was teaching, along with the importance of texture, visual presentation, blah, blah, blah.

When she took her first position through a temp agency, Michael could hardly object. The alternative was eviction. "My plants," she said. "Think of it as what I must do to pay the water bills." But his pride was hurt.

Throughout the growing tension between her and Michael, Lizbeth had been a Greek chorus of one: "This is clearly not working out." Although the sex had transitioned from obligatory to nil, she rarely felt the loss. But their final battle made her wonder. She was looking in a catalog at what Columbia University offered in landscape architecture around twelve-thirty one night when she heard his key in the door. "Need I inquire where you were?" she heard herself ask.

"No, you needn't, because you profoundly do not care."

"That's not true. I'm a curious type."

"No, you're a jealous type."

"Jealous?" Her eyes widened.

"Yes, jealous. Every time I am out with Yves-Claude, you act like I have been cheating on you."

"Oh my god. It never occurred to me."

"You know, Deborah, you are so… you are so—"

"Say it! Bloody say it! Say what's on your mind!"

"I dine with one of the great culinary talents of our generation, and this beautiful man and I, we share together the most profound sensual experiences, but the whole time, the whole time, I can see you here, your lips pursed in disapproval."

"Great culinary talents," she couldn't restrain herself.

"Yes! And speaking of talent, what about mine? You think Yves-Claude would share these meals with just anyone?" he shouted, he thought, rhetorically.

"No," she said. "Just anyone who would pay."

"Screw you, Deborah. You care more about your fucking plants than you do about me."

"You're right, frankly. My plants don't try to make me feel stupid and ugly. They like my touch." And seizing on the nagging insight which had been creeping up on her: "Let me ask you, Michael—or *Michel* as I know The Great One affectionately calls you—is it me, or do we have perhaps a broader problem?"

"Why…how dare—? *You* are the broader problem. He's…It's you. It's no more complicated than that."

"Great. Good to know. I will tell all my American friends that my former husband disliked me for who I am and was not, in any way, shape, or form, a poofster." And she turned off the lights, leaving him in the dark.

"You don't have any American friends," he shouted after her. And that was that.

As the well-educated daughter of British civil servants, she had no trouble, with the help of her agency, working most weekdays. But when Lizbeth appeared for a surprise just-us-sisters visit, Deborah took a few days off. They stayed up all night the Tuesday before the royal wedding, drinking Pimm's with all the trimmings and watching the live coverage on Deborah's little Zenith TV. They followed avidly the discussion of Lady Diana Spencer's gown with its eight-meter train, her tiara, her French perfume, the history of her glass carriage. But soon after the vows that transformed Lady Diana into Princess Di, Lizbeth spoke up, "You need more connectivity."

This comment, made over an empty bag of Cheetos as Princess Di waved from her glass carriage, suddenly had a certain resonance. Perhaps if she were to allow herself to be engaged in a steady job with its concomitant office politics, she'd at least have the distraction of something to gripe about…a harmless way to be connected to others. But the temp agency kept calling, and she remained set in her ways.

Finally, though, toward the end of one Friday in late '84, she accepted that her period of temping must end. She had spent the day in a small accounting firm performing the most menial tasks at the brusque direction of a mousy neurotic who actually wore a green eye shade, suspenders, and a string tie. When he sent her back to resharpen the very pencils she had just handed him, she thought *Enough!* A real job…maybe more pay, some healthcare benefits?…Of course there'd be that slight loss of… of what? The only loss she could calculate was that of her anonymity. For the first time in her working life, she would be more than just a social security number. She would be Deborah. Or maybe even "Deb." But she was ready—ready to trade in what's-her-name for a US version of the Deborah Cunningham she had been when Michael had liberated her from her parent's home in Gibraltar seven years earlier.

As was typical in her life, there was never a real choice, no fork in the road, no path not taken. Although she had many interviews, the only situation that appealed to her was the first place the agency sent her. It had an electricity like none of the other offices where she'd worked.

Her interview with Rebecca Schwartz, the efficient, pudgy but very buttoned-up head of Secretarial Personnel, a thirty-something brunette with a short, low ponytail, set the tone.

"Miss Cunningham, I have your typing, dictation, your references, and see no problems with your skill levels, assuming of course that the references check out. I expect your passing our drug test will not be a problem." She looked up from the papers she'd been consulting, and, seemingly satisfied with Deborah's unperturbed demeanor, continued. "So, what we are interested in today is whether you'd fit into the Lehman culture."

"And how will we know that?" Deborah asked, lingering on the "we" a tad longer than necessary.

"We won't," her interviewer responded. "But we can make an educated guess. The stakes at Lehman Brothers are high. Everyone here is high strung, and I don't think I would be telling tales out of school if I were to say the executive whose assistant position we are trying to fill is the most…well let me put it this way, your potential boss has high standards. He runs Structured Finance, one of our most important profit centers. His previous assistants have lasted six months on average."

"I see."

"Well, you really don't see, Miss Cunningham. But I see no harm at this point in allowing you to make his acquaintance. His name is Jedediah Czincosca. He liked you on paper well enough; please be in his office at 7:45 sharp tomorrow morning." And with that, she stood, gesturing toward the door. "Good luck. I will let you know if it works out."

"Let's give it a punt," Deborah replied in her best British accent. "It was a pleasure to make your acquaintance," she said, certain that if she did get the job, this woman would be no friend.

Czincosca did not, at first, look up from his desk as the woman Deborah presumed was his temp du jour showed her to one of the three seats across from him. He was in his mid-thirties, she judged. Not bad looking. Short, curly hair. Light, thin eyebrows. Darkish complexion. An expensive-looking necktie and a pinstripe suit, tortoiseshell reading glasses through which he was peering at some documents that seemed to annoy him. Finally, he tore a page into several pieces, signed another with a Montblanc pen, removed the glasses, and, raising his eyes, acknowledged her presence for the first time.

He looked her over frankly, saying nothing. While his lingering gaze was not lecherous, it certainly established that he was a powerful man assessing her not just as a potential employee but as a woman. She waited, her hands folded in her lap, without fidgeting. "So, you're interested in this job?" he asked, apparently not displeased by her appearance. Blond hair in a tight bun. Aquiline nose, blue eyes, thin lips, ears on the petite side. Her bosom was obvious, neither hideable nor flaunted. She had chosen a turquoise blue blouse, demure, but not so as to obscure her corporeal assets, and a navy-blue skirt, just long enough to be business friendly.

"I am interested in *a* job, Mr. Czincosca." Cheeky won't hurt with this chap, she wagered. He sucked in his cheeks, weighing his response, when she continued. "I understand that you set high standards, and, in principle, it would please me to attempt to live up to them."

"Tell me a bit about yourself, if you don't mind. Your life today."

She complied, revealing she was single but not that she was divorced, exaggerating the pleasures of being an expat in New York. "And," she concluded, "I attended a wonderful lecture at the New York Public Library this past Saturday…free to the public, on trees in the Serengeti." *He may as well know from the outset that I've a brain.* Then, she paused and leaned forward slightly. "I hope you will not consider it too bold on my part, Mr. Czincosca," she said, "But I wonder if I may inquire as to what you are looking for in an assistant and, if you would, a smidgen about you…as a person."

Czincosca seemed taken aback. But then, smiling with the forbearance of a generous monarch, gifted her his response, "Well, Miss…" he glanced down at his papers "Cunningham… am I pronouncing it correctly?"

"A little less 'ham' and more 'um'; 'Cunningum' if you will, Mr. Czincosca. And you're nice to ask, but please do feel free to call me Deborah."

"Yes, well…in answer to your question. I like to think of myself as a creative type; this gives me license to be rather disorganized." He paused as if seeking approval for this offering of self-deprecating humor. "That's where you, I mean, that's where my assistant comes in. My assistant has to keep the trains running on time."

"Might I request an example, Mr. Czincosca?"

"Well, like, right before you came in, I was looking everywhere for my wallet and when you leave, I must run to the airport."

"Where do you usually put your wallet?"

"In my overcoat, but it's not there. And it's also not in my pants or jacket pockets, nor, as you can see, is it on my desk."

She stood up, walked across the office to the chair where his overcoat was draped. "I've looked there already," he said.

She got down on her hands and knees and peered under the chair. "It must have fallen at an unusual angle," she said, handing him the missing item. "Taken a bad bounce."

Tucking it into his back pocket, he seemed more pleased than embarrassed. "And in answer to the second part of your question, Miss Cunning…Deborah, I am the father of two boys. I like to get home, when possible, to have dinner with them. I have a brother who is a professor. I was raised in Chicago. Both of my parents have passed away."

"Who looks after the children?" she asked.

"Oh! Yes. I have a wife. We have been married for six years." The omission clearly discomfited him. "Here," he said, turning around a picture of a smiling black-haired woman with a lacrosse stick over her shoulder. "It's been a pleasure," he said, striding across the room to grab his coat. He paused at the door to allow her to precede him. He seemed to stand around 180 centimeters. "The job is yours if you like, Miss Cunningham," she heard him say as he rushed away. "Let us know."

After she began working for Czincosca, as in the earliest days of her marriage, she was initially quite eager to please. Memos dictated at 9 a.m. appeared error-free on Czincosca's desk before ten. Appointments were promptly made and confirmed with a neatly typed "itinerary" as she called it, setting forth relevant particulars (including floors of buildings and secretaries' names). Back then, her enthusiasm level was so high, she had to concentrate on not skipping or running to the copying machine.

Despite her negative first impression of Rebecca Schwartz, she took the precaution of stopping by the personnel office at the beginning of her second week to thank her for her support.

"Oh. It's you," Rebecca said without affect. "You've arrived."

"Yes. And I am so pleased to be here," Deborah replied, still standing in the doorway. "Well, you didn't seem to need much help from me in getting hired, did you?" And then pointedly looking over Deborah's figure, "I am sure your looks didn't hurt with Jed," she added with transparent ruefulness.

"I am certain I would not be here without your support," Deborah said and, producing a fake smile, excused herself with a "Thank you so much."

Her new boss seemed nice. Although clipped and intense when he asked for something, he did so with an entitled politesse, which enabled him, just, to skirt the imperiousness of so many of those petty tyrants she had encountered on the temp circuit. Most of his demands were not directed at her but rather to a group of eager young men who vied for his attention and attempted to intuit his desires. Usually, he would meet with four or five of them at a time in his office. Although a team leader invariably handled most of the interaction with Czincosca, it was not atypical for a younger banker to burst forth with an attempted contribution. She came to understand that this was a perilous move. If her boss was pleased, the speaker left his office with a proud glow, but a frown from Jed meant a ruined day if not week, with team leaders and associates piling on their own exaggerated criticisms.

Initially she could not but be impressed with the sums involved. She learned that a $300 million financing was a small deal, but a billion-dollar maneuver could be "meaningful" to the firm. Lawyers, she gathered, were either rainmakers who could bring her boss some business or supplicants who wanted business from him. Auditors, with few exceptions, were seen as ignorant bean-counting dweebs. While a few of these professionals—she could name them after her first two months—were good at generating new business, mostly they didn't even try, which consigned them to a lower phylum.

Within the firm's pecking order, junior gophers ("analysts") were nonentities, foot soldiers to be thrown into battle at all hours of the day and night. Associates, similarly expendable, were routinely castigated by the vice presidents who themselves were the butt of constant criticism for the slightest flaws in their work product, haircuts, or speech peculiarities by the partners. But a handful of senior partners had important relationships, which gave them the stroke to demand the attention of Czincosca's group for their clients' problems, and they were the ones who had to be serviced. From these troglodytes, Czincosca's junior professionals hid, cowering behind whatever rocks they could find. A request by Czincosca to devote a few hours' work on a project for the trog who ran the Sydney office might become a multi-month waste of time (a "circle jerk" she heard it called) on the other side of the world or even a path to career extinction.

This had famously happened to the Structured Finance group's only permanent vice president. Deborah was told that his ex-wife liked to joke that her alimony had been paid in frequent flier miles. When he failed to storm out (as his wife had) following his year in the sky and a pitiful bonus, Kelly had become the "go-to guy" on hopeless dead ends. Associates made sport of his eating habits (gross), his hair (thin, receding, but constantly and futilely manipulated to hide a bald spot), and his mustache (Maalox). Occasionally they left fake notes for him, forging Czincosca's signature: "See me immediately."

Deborah barely noticed when her new colleagues began calling her "Didi." She was too busy marveling at the lengths the analysts and MBAs would go to get on a "real deal." Not within effective fawning distance of Czincosca himself, they prostrated themselves before the assignments coordinator. Since their résumés were available to her, she was particularly amazed at their behavior. Why bother to get all A's, Phi Beta Kappa, and magna cum laude in college, serve as a lieutenant submarine officer, and kill yourself for a couple of years at Harvard Business School to lead a sleep-deprived non-life in New York City and then shamelessly elbow colleagues aside for the right to work on other people's problems? Perhaps the sleep deficit served to remove any inhibition—which she assumed they must have had at one time—against ass-kissing. The contrast between their frenetic striving and Czincosca's apparent self-confidence deepened her respect for him and her pleasure in the decision she had taken to begin a real job.

From the very first day with Czincosca, she had discovered an uncanny ability to vibrate in harmony to his moods. She was the cello to his violin. But occasionally he seemed unable to read music. The amplitude of his mood swings was wide, and she was always on the alert for opportunities to prevent a mangled movement from transforming into a botched symphony.

The worst times were those when something minor went wrong on the same day he had some contact, any contact, with a partner named Sawyer who ran a competing profit center. Like the Friday, her fourth week on the job, when the deli put banana peppers instead of the plain yellow ones on his tuna sandwich. She was managing this OK with some humor and some black pepper from the kitchen until Sawyer's office called, and after that conversation, there seemed little she could do. He had his head in his hands when she entered his office.

"Do you wish to talk about it?" she asked gingerly. No response. She walked toward his desk, wondering if she should say anything else, and was standing there when the phone rang. He looked up. His eyes were red. She decided to pick up the phone on his desk.

"Oh, Mrs. Czincosca," she said. It was only the second time they'd spoken. "I'll put him on."

"Tell her I'll call her back," he said through the hands now covering his mouth. When, to the obvious annoyance of the wife, she had done so, he spoke.

"Please sit down.... Talk to me."

"With pleasure, Mr. Czincosca."

"Deborah, I think I need to leave early today. I'm not feeling too well."

"Do you have a headache, Mr. Czincosca?"

"You can call me Jed now. And...yes...a headache. You could call it that."

"What else could you call it...Jed?"

He stared at her, and his eyes, a mere four feet away, were overflowing with pain. "You could call it depression," he said. And when she waited he added, "Maybe you could call it stress."

"Forgive me for saying so, but there are ways to relieve—"

"I know them all. And frankly use them each in various combinations, but—"

"But what, Jed?"

"But sometimes they just make it worse."

"It?"

"The stress!" he exclaimed. But when she recoiled at his surprising vehemence, he quickly apologized. "I didn't mean to—"

"Look," she said, "I am here to support you and to help you."

"Win, succeed—" he supplied, cutting her off again.

"Yes, but—"

"I don't want to die," he said, hiding his head in his hands again, leaving her wondering why this wasn't a non sequitur.

"You'll feel better after a nap," she said soothingly.

"I need to close the Ripkin deal, finish the IBM subordinated convertible preferred."

"A nap. You'll feel better," she repeated, giving him his overcoat. "Let me walk you to the elevator." She handed him his briefcase. She pressed the elevator button. Probably he saw her, but his eyes were focused into the middle distance.

Other than Sawyer flare-ups with their concomitant meltdowns, out-of-town trips were the most recurring sources of tension for Jed. He was invariably anxious about departures, and in the hours prior to blast-off, she always felt the pressure rising. The town car downstairs could count on not less than a half hour of wait time, since getting to a flight early was for wimps.

Even many years later, she still flashed back to one typical separation scene that she remembered with the vividness of a bad exam dream: Bleary-eyed young desperados were throwing together slide presentations that had just benefited from senior input not available at 4:30 a.m. when they were putting to bed the previous "final" version. Motherwell, Czincosca's senior lieutenant, was looking at his watch and inquiring about transportation and accommodations in LA. Meanwhile she was trying to keep up with Jed himself, who was giving new meaning to the term "lateral thinking" as he free-associated through details they had gone over before.

"Did you talk to Leach's office about getting together on Tuesday?"

"His secretary said she'll get to us."

"Actually, Wednesday would probably be better because I told Accounting I'd work with them on budgets in time for the Thursday management meeting. Have you seen my cell? Did Susan ever call us back? I need a haircut."

As she handed him his airline ticket and tried ineffectually to body-language him out the door she replied, "I'll set something up with Mr. Leach for late morning on Wednesday, or maybe sandwiches in his office. I saw you put your phone in your briefcase. Susan got the draft and is sending it back with a few changes. It will be here by the time you return. I'll get you a trim for Wednesday after work."

As promptly became clear, mentioning the sandwiches—a new idea—was a mistake. Czincosca stopped his forward movement. Motherwell, who was tapping his feet with hummingbird frequency, made bold to observe that traffic can be heavy at this time of day.

"I've been to La Guardia on a few other occasions," Jed shot back at him acerbically, then turning to her, said, "I don't know about sandwiches. Hmmm. Perhaps just a meeting would save time. No. It wouldn't. I've got to eat anyway. But make it my office. He'll come. We're having a great year this month. Ha! And while you're at it, why not invite Smith? His revenues are way down. We can do his budgets at the same time. If the stuff from Susan arrives today, messenger it to me at the Bel Air. And make the haircut for Monday after work. I want to look sharp for Mr. Huge and of course for my esteemed colleague."

At this point Motherwell had a quite unpleasant message to deliver about the airport from which their flight was to depart, causing Czincosca to exclaim, "Freakin' JFK!?" What are we just standing around for!" He grabbed his briefcase and, followed by Motherwell, another vice president, and two bag carriers, ran out in the direction of the elevators. She would have a good forty-five minutes until he called from the airport, but she could look forward to a largely uninterrupted six hours after that.

Something about her first bonus subtly changed her attitude toward her job. It was her misfortune to know that bonus was Latin for "good." And she began to think more and more about what "good" meant. In what sense had she been good, by whose standards, and how good? By the numbers, thanks to checks from Lehman and Czincosca, she had been 6.9 percent better than inflation. She still had only saved seven months' worth of her modest overhead, although this was the largest amount she'd ever had in the bank. Unfortunately for her sense of well-being, she now knew a lot about how well her coworkers lived. She began to admit to herself that her Flushing Meadows apartment had a lousy kitchen and was too dark even on a sunny day. The plants could be a lot happier. Czincosca spent more in half a month than she in a year but had already saved so much that he could live a long and luxurious life without working another day. As a boss, he still looked comparatively OK, but when had she begun making comparisons? For every positive descriptor of Czincosca, she could suddenly, it seemed, think of a negative:

Self-assured/egoistic

Well-groomed/vain, obsessive about his personal appearance

Intense/moody

Focused/largely ignorant of anything but business

Nice to subordinates (compared to other movers and shakers in the firm)/calculating

Ambitious/ruthless

One part of her job was becoming a real nuisance to her. Once she had gained Czincosca's trust, he asked her to help with his personal family matters. This put her in much closer contact with Amanda, a woman whom she suspected had never had to work a day in her life, one who seemed to resent the time her husband spent in Deborah's presence and who in little time began treating Deborah like her own household help. Amanda had no compunction about seeking Deborah's attention to the most trivial matters, ones a woman with nothing to do other than be present for the children's meals, school meetings, and doctors' appointments (some of which the nanny took care of) might reasonably be able to handle on her own. Her saccharine faux declarations such as "I-would-be-so-terribly-grateful-if..." only exacerbated the chronic aggravation. And Deborah saw the charges for the mani-pedis, the scrubs, the hundred-dollar lunches, and the tennis lessons. When she showed Jed the $100,000 donation that effectively bought Amanda the chair position at the Food Bank for New York City, he shrugged: "marriage tax."

Then too, there was the seemingly omnipresent Rebecca Schwartz. Even though, under Jed's protection, Deborah was almost untouchable, Jed could not shield her completely from the Personnel Department, where Schwartz had been promoted to the top job. Deborah found her quarterly "reviews" demeaning, but when Jed acceded to her request to seek an exemption, he had come back with the disappointing news that the reviews were "mandatory." Schwartz reveled in her victory. Typically, her Head of Secretarial would review the assistant to the chief of an important profit center, but, perversely, Schwartz told Deborah in the immediate aftermath of her defeat: "I have decided to handle your situation myself."

"My situation?" She could barely contain her outrage.

"Yes. As I feared from the outset, we have a culture issue with you."

"You feel I am too cultured?"

Now it was Schwartz's turn to vent: "You are making my case…And by the way, I think we need to discuss your appearance. Your job is not to look great for your boss."

"Yes, we really should discuss my looks the first chance we get," Deborah said as she stood and stormed out of the conference room. It was that or manslaughter. When she got the negative review from Personnel, she showed it to Jed.

"What Schwartz is saying is that my bonus from The Firm will be negligible."

"I will make up the difference and then some."

"I am so sorry that I've never been able to abide this woman."

"Don't worry about it. Cost of doing business."

Perhaps it was due to Schwartz's suggestion, but occasionally Deborah did feel from Czincosca an interest in her person that went beyond the professional. Like the time one Thursday evening in her second year when he asked her to stay late to help meet a deadline he normally wouldn't have worried about for days. "I was just thinking, Didi." He had never used that name before, and he was standing way too close. "What is your astrological sign?"

"Surely you jest," she answered, cutting off, she hoped, any further such initiatives.

That was as close as he came to a "move," but from time to time she did feel his eyes on her, and because she screened all his calls, she could not but suspect that the sanctity of marriage was not one of her boss's core values. "Put her through," he often directed when a woman with no apparent professional connection gave Deborah only her first name. There was a female lawyer at Covington & Burling who lasted almost a year. And she noticed that Jed stayed a bit longer in Los Angeles than business seemed to require, often after accepting a call from one "Maria."

By Deborah's second year, Czincosca's humor had come to seem more puerile than witty, its casual cruelty, like everything about him, serving his Machiavellian purposes. She had to admit, if only to herself, that not only did she like being in his presence less but had actually come to look forward to his business trips. On those days, she could chat more with her coworkers, who fell into two occasionally overlapping categories: those with ambitions and those with husbands. Roger, the gay temp who had rotated around the department for a couple of months before Didi had anything to do with him, was in the former group. He wanted to be a clothing designer with a focus on men's accessories. He was viciously irreverent about the pretensions of the "so-called professionals." Referring to Czincosca as "The Bitch Queen," he did a hilarious mini-skit of her boss falling asleep in front of a mirror after a whole weekend of primping.

Roger was the one who got her to give up her nightly routine. She couldn't believe the invitations she said yes to, but bowling with a bunch of his friends was a scream. Soon she was ice-skating indoors in ninety-five-degree weather and on the lookout for new jokes and excursions to share with Roger. The shooting gallery with those big earmuffs and real pistols was her idea. She had her first real American friend.

One of her boss's better buddies was Tom Levitt, the chief financial officer of News Corp. At often more than $30 million in fees a year, News Corp was one of the firm's more important clients, and when Jed wasn't out of town or in the office, he was likely to be over there working on one of their financings. Every six months or so Levitt would be feted at some exclusive corporate boondoggle involving private jets, special seating, and scads of celebrities. In between parties they got together to sample the cuisine of the finest Manhattan restaurants, like Le Bernardin, The Grill Room at the Four Seasons, or Le Coq Foutu, with Czincosca usually picking up the tab on the theory, supported by both of them, that this was an ordinary and necessary business expense.

When she first met Levitt in person, Didi was shocked to discover he was only a little over five feet tall. She had to laugh at her own surprise. She knew immediately that it had not been his booming telephone delivery but rather the enormity of his billings that had caused her to assume he was a large man. The Levitt misconception revealed to her the extent to which she was being subsumed in the firm. She had come to notice that when she said "we," she was frequently referring to Lehman Brothers. Nevertheless, she knew with ever greater clarity that she must not spend the rest of her life there. Strangely, even as the breadth and depth of her social relationships expanded, she also realized she was lonely. *In fact*, she said to herself one night after bowling with Roger, *I am as lonely as I have ever been in my life.*

It was in this time frame that she first encountered Billy Williams, the courtly sixty or so receptionist at News Corp. His trim build seemed that of a former athlete who still cared about his personal appearance. His smile, which flashed from beneath a neatly trimmed mustache, was mischievous and unsubtly flirtatious. As she asked to be shown to the office where Czincosca was working, his brown eyes caressed her breasts and hips. "*How forward*!" she thought as he carded open the door to the executive suite and extended his arm to indicate her destination. He left his station to show her the way, and she was piqued that he had manipulated her into walking in front of him.

She was pretty sure this fellow would still be at the reception desk when she had completed the departure ritual (which Roger called "kissing off the BQ"), and sure enough, he was.

"I'm Billy," he told her, smiling boldly.

Did I ask you? she thought as she tore hastily toward the exit with Billy in her wake. A down door was opening as she arrived at the elevator bank, and she side-stepped a man in a suit to enter. She turned to give Billy only the most cursory of nods. "Didi," she conceded, just before the door closed.

A week after their first encounter, she picked up to hear his voice on the phone. His "Didi, this is Billy" sounded so self-assured. Like she was pining for his call?

"I'm not going to say, 'Billy who?'"

His chuckle was melodious, grateful. "When can I see you again?"

This is what she meant about the directness of American men. There was no subtle lead in, no playing around, no flirting. Just goals, objectives. If she said yes, would he move right on to "Can we have sex?" She decided to put him in his place. "Why not? I'll let you know when I next plan to drop by News Corp."

Again, that sweet laugh. "No, I'm talking 'bout getting together for, you know, dinner, maybe some jazz."

"I'm not a big jazz fan," she told him.

"But you do eat dinner, I imagine. I mean, you know, from time to time?" He chuckled a bit more tentatively.

"Look, I'm swamped right now. It was nice of you to call."

"Well, if you don't mind, maybe I'll be nice again."

And he was. After a couple more not-unpleasant calls, she agreed to meet him at a tiny club with only six or seven tables in a basement off MacDougal Street. There was sawdust on the floor, a slightly elevated stage, and rickety wooden tables that didn't match. She nursed a scotch while he told her a few stories about the signed photographs of Ornette Coleman, Charlie Mingus, and Lester Young on the wall.

They were exchanging a few basic facts about themselves when a group consisting only of bass, drums, trumpet, and a female piano player walked onto a small stage and began tuning up.

They played a couple of numbers, and Deborah's mind began to wander. *What was I thinking? How can I end this dead-end date without being rude?* she was asking herself. But then the piano player began to sing. Her songs were about everything under the sun, but from her first number, Deborah felt her at a primal level that no music had reached before. Halfway through her third song, Deborah was beyond "hearing" as the music, caressing her, flowed over her skin and entered through her pores. The words were hot, and the vocalist was exhibiting half-moons of sweat under each arm. Beads of wetness dripped down all the musicians' faces. The horn player especially was perspiring profusely as he and the singer lobbed the melody back and forth. The bassist's eyes were closed in passionate engagement when the singer put words aside, making up her own elemental language consisting of clicks and grunts. At around midnight, the horn player's muted whimper put an end to it all. And Deborah felt blissfully limb-heavy as if she had sated herself on the sexuality of the music.

In the days following this first date, sex, which for most people was everywhere, was now everywhere for Deborah. She stopped to look in the window of a lingerie store, conjuring an image of herself in the scanty pink push-up. At lunch with Roger, referring to an incompetent secretary, she heard herself suggesting that the girl's talents must lie in the bedroom. That very evening, her eyes were drawn toward a couple French-kissing on the subway. Each of her next dates with Billy was an adventure. Somehow, he got tickets for a new play, *Phantom of the Opera*, and she was thrilled by her first Broadway performance. He rarely spoke directly about himself, but she learned some details over a raucous dinner at the Bedford-Stuyvesant brownstone of his old friend, an NYPD detective named Dolores Johnson.

"Detective Williams," she asked Billy over apple pie and ice cream, "who did you have the skinny on that got your Black ass off the beat?"

"Merit, skill," he smiled, glancing at Deborah.

"Right, you wrote those parking tickets like a great future sleuth."

"Homicide," he answered, "that's where the money is."

By their fourth date she had discovered he had a modest New York City pension and was a year away from another at News Corp. And he had figured out that plants and landscaping were her true passion. He was a great kisser, in a different zip code from Michael or any of her previous beaux.

For their fifth evening together, she invited Billy over for dinner. He came with a nice bottle of cabernet, a dozen tulips, and lots of interest in her soil, fertilizer, how she made the chicken, her former husband, and her relationship with Lizbeth. These ostensibly interesting topics had nothing to do with the how-to-get-naked-together question that was front of mind for each, and by the time she began to clear the table, it was obvious that the apple pie she had baked was superfluous. She didn't even remember how they moved from the kitchen table to her bedroom. When they finally made love, it went on all night and was like a continuation of the music he had introduced her to. Very natural, very wet, and better than anything she had ever imagined.

Czincosca never expressed much curiosity about her personal existence. He never liked it when she left before six p.m., And though incurious about her after-hours life, he possessed a sixth sense that told him something had changed once she took up with Billy. He began to invent crises just before six to test her fidelity, tests she willfully flunked. And as she gave as little ground as possible, he, thwarted, became testier, more critical. Noticing the change, she began to interpret even his neutral comments as criticisms.

By this point in her career, New York City was getting old. The skinheads had taken over Tompkins Square Park, there was a crack epidemic, homicides were hitting new highs. On the strength of her liaison with Billy, she was less conciliatory than normal. Her tiffs with Czincosca became noticeable to all in the vicinity. The sweetness of her nights stood in sharp contrast to the growing unpleasantness of her days.

As part of their romantic improvisation, she and Billy agreed to drive a "help-wanted" car across the country to Western Canada. Despite one or two doses of unpleasant reality—the motel which had "forgotten" to put out the "no vacancy" sign, a hateful look from a gas station attendant—being an interracial couple was not a problem. Billy collected $650 upon delivery, and they flew back on some mileage she had with Northwest Airlines.

She was more worried about the age difference than the race thing. But for Lizbeth, it was the other way around. "Deborah, what are you smoking?"

She actually had tried weed a couple times with Billy and had found it quite pleasant, but elected not to mention it. "Meaning what, specifically?"

"Meaning the man is an American negro."

"Opposites attract."

"I know what father would say if he were alive."

Billy proposed to her following a raucous dinner of roast beef, spinach, baked potatoes, and homemade muffins at his mother's table in Sag Harbor. He did not have to state the obvious. The evening had gone very well, and as soon as they closed the door to her apartment, he said, "Dee, I know I'm a old hoss, but I'm not looking for you to take care of me in my old age. If I break a leg and can't run any more, well, let me tell you, I'm for the till death do us part bit,' but I've got no truck for the 'in sickness and in health' thing. When it comes down to it, you can count on me to take care of business. We'll have ten or fifteen great years together. Then you'll be a well-fixed widow. We're soulmates forever, even after you get on to husband number three."

The end with Czincosca was anticlimactic. No pyrotechnics. No recriminations. After he got over his initial anger that she had made a decision based on considerations other than his best interests, he threw her a nice farewell party. He managed to deliver a toast poorly imitating her British accent and thanking her for her loyal service.

Roger toasted her at a more private gathering. "And so has come the time for the world of high finance to bid one of the brighter stars to have flashed through its firmament a fond farewell. Didi, née Deborah Cunningham, has once again proven beyond a shadow of a doubt the discretion of the well-raised Brit. Never from her lips would you hear a word about her boss's unreasonable demands nor his innumerable foibles. But we know better: 'Didi, find out if anyone in the bullpen knows how to give me a decent pedicure. Buy Amanda a nice birthday present; keep it under a hundred thou. Make it look like something I would have thought of. And don't burst in on me when I am doing my eyebrows.' Didi, I want to take this occasion to promise you that I will personally look out for the Bitch Queen in your absence, especially in this, his period of Narcissian bereavement. Here's to Didi and Billy and their new life together in the Boonies.

"Visit us from time to time when you need a hit of culture."

In Sag Harbor they raised horses. She landed a job at Marders on Snake Hollow Road, where she went to work each weekday in a beautiful nineteenth-century barn. He played sax in pick-up bands. She was thirty-five when their boy, a beautiful cream-colored amalgam, was born. Only at rare intervals did she think of Czincosca, and when she did, in her father's finest tradition, she wished him the best.

CHAPTER 4

PANG'S PEKING PALACE

It was a hot windless day in June of 1968 when Maria D'Amatonio took a job at Pang's Peking Palace in Chicago's South Side, a predominantly white working-class neighborhood of Italian, Irish, and Jewish families. The opening of a Chinese restaurant was something of a novelty, not just for the type of food but because they were going to "deliver." Maria was nineteen. She had just graduated from Loyola Junior College, and her parents wanted her out of the house. Taking orders in a Chinese restaurant was no help to her self-image, had nothing to do with her plans for a future in Hollywood, but it did get her father off her back.

She had been strolling by on her way to the grocery store and had stopped to inquire about the Help Wanted sign in the window. To her mild surprise, she was hired on the spot. Pang left the sign up because he also needed a delivery boy. She was at the front counter the next day when Jed Czincosca came by on his Schwinn. His job interview was a success as soon as he gave a firm "yes" to Pang's only question: "One hour, thirty cent, you keep tip, OK?"

Maria had few reasons to go in the back where two chefs swore at each other in pidgin English and Chinese while they hurled shrimp, peanuts, and cabbage into sizzling woks. The cooks, dripping sweat, hacked away with cleavers at cuts of chicken and pork. Pang was always yelling at them, perhaps exhorting them to hurry or to be quiet while he worked the abacus. Based on what she could tell from her side of the plastic slats separating the front from the back where Jed waited for his next deliveries, he fit right in. His voice was changing, and as it strained to find a register it could sustain, it seemed to weave a natural space for itself in the tonal cacophony. "Standing by for the Kelly," she might hear him say, or "Need another Mu Shu Pork for the Bernstein."

While she waited for phone orders or walk-ins from her side of the hanging green separators, she always knew where a large order stood. A sine wave of noise reached a crescendo as the last dish neared completion. The Chinese shouts attained a fever pitch, then the sizzling subsided, a satisfied Pang shouted out the result of his arithmetic, and when especially pleased would add, "Throw in a couple almond cookie." Then she would hear the gun stapling the tab to one of the brown bags and the screen door slamming. She could almost make out the sound of Jed's tires on the gravel in back. Up front, it was always quieter, except that the two clunky black phones seemed to ring with uncanny simultaneity even in non-peak hours.

Maria rolled in around ten forty-five each morning with her coffee and doughnuts from the Bertollucci's at the corner. The smell of the Formica counters and linoleum floors mixed with a whiff of yesterday's fried pork and reheated peanut oil welcomed her to her new real world.

Before the action started, it was her responsibility to total invoices and call suppliers. Stirring two packs of sugar into her Styrofoam cup, she would stare unseeingly at the Year of the Rooster calendar, with its near-invisible human figures overwhelmed by a vast Asian landscape, while she negotiated delivery schedules with vendors and thought about her recent breakup with Tim, a handsome, conceited apprentice bricklayer who reminded her too much of her father.

What she wanted was to get out of town. On her next-door neighbor's television set, she had watched a woman her age help Flash Gordon stop Ming the Merciless from destroying the world. This was more what she had in mind: fighting the forces of evil, not ending up like her mother, tied to the stove of a man resigned to a pact he had entered into at a different time for reasons he could no longer remember. Early that summer, as she too easily coasted through the duties of her job, time, like the atmosphere of this normally windy city, seemed to stand still, and she wondered if God was punishing her.

This Jed kid seemed self-confident for his age but with the tentativeness you'd expect from a high school boy. She noticed that his frequent laughter gave way to a serious demeanor when he thought no one was looking and that whenever he found a free moment, he'd pick up a book. In the first week after they began work, she happened upon him concentrating on something in his lap. "Hi," she said, coming up behind him. He jumped to a standing position, which sent his paperback flying through the air.

"Jesus!" he exclaimed as he bent to pick up the book.

"I didn't mean to scare you," she said.

"I wasn't scared; I was startled," he replied. And then added, "I was deep into a chess puzzle."

She wondered whether all Jews were so intense. There had been a few at Horace Mann High, but they had kept to themselves. What she had failed to notice about Jed was that he was maximally, totally, completely infatuated with her.

After a week of noncommittal hellos, during a quiet interval, he came up front just as she had put down the phone. "Hi," he began, "You do a great job taking those orders. That one was complicated, sounds like."

"Moo Shu Pork, egg rolls, and fried rice?" she asked, turning away. His ears were rather large, but not so big as to make him look goofy. Duck's asses were in, but he wore his hair in a crew cut. He had a set of perfect white teeth, and when he smiled, he looked older than he probably was.

"Hi back," she added, turning to some paperwork.

"What accounts for your working here?" he persisted.

She put down her pencil slowly to show him she wasn't dying to have a conversation, but finally offered, "Gets me out of the house. The money is no good but—"

"You know how I'm working mainly for tips, right?" It was a question, but he didn't pause before proceeding. "So, anyway, this is my first real job for anyone but my father. I help him with his businesses. He pays me *bupkis.*" He turned a bright red, touched his fingers to his mouth as if he wanted to put the Yiddish word back in, but then regained his composure and picked up where he'd left off. "But I have knocked on people's doors before. You know, trying to sell them stuff like magazines, or fire extinguishers."

"I've never done anything like that," she said.

"Well, anyway," he continued as if she hadn't spoken, "it's a whole lot different bringing folks something they already want. You are welcome. But the concept of 'tip' is not always front and center for them. Sometimes I have to get a little pushy."

Her parents had told her Jews were pushy, but she'd never had an opportunity to see one in action. "For example?"

"Well, when they try to kiss me off with a 'Thank you so much' I might ask, 'Do you need any change? Because I happen to have some here from my previous tip."

"That works?"

"Nine times out of ten."

At which point Pang charged through from the back carrying two bags "Hot! O'Reilly." "Off I go," he said, relieving Pang of the heavy packages and smiling at Maria.

In the ensuing days, they spoke frequently, although in short bursts. She was amused by the way he blushed a bright red when, despite his best efforts to sound manly, his voice soared unbidden to falsetto. She sensed that he was lonely and maybe in need of a friend. She had to admit that she herself was lonely, but thank God she had come to understand that she would have gone nuts if she had to make a life with Tim. When she finally let Tim touch her most private parts, she had been caught in a riptide of guilt and pleasure. But as a growing fear of the Church, her parents, and pregnancy outweighed her desire to please him, the relationship began to unravel. Toward the end he'd begun to complain about her not "putting out," and when he swore at her and accused her of "doing it with someone else," she'd had enough.

Jed, too, had a sex life, albeit a more solitary one. In fact, well before he met Maria, sex had become Jed's central preoccupation. Already by age 12, he had found that he needed privacy more than once a day. He listened avidly to his older brother, Lenny, and his friends bragging about their exploits, not caring too much whether they were true or not. One of them claimed to be regularly "feeling up" and "finger fucking" his girlfriend. Two others said they'd found a house of ill repute that they had visited on the West Side. But because this whorehouse had only one occupant, a coin toss was required to determine which of them would get "sloppy seconds."

A high proportion of what his father had paid Jed had gone to building a secret Playboy library of which he was the conscientious curator. He had read the dirty parts of *Battle Cry* about a thousand times, to the point that he could recite the key paragraph by heart. "Violently, she tore the gown from her body and tugged at the buckle of his trousers. Their bodies seemed to melt together; she sunk her fingernails into his flesh. 'Oh God… God…God…,' she said in a dull interminable rhythm."

From the moment Jed had first laid eyes on the three-dimensional Maria spiking invoices on a spindle, it was as if Cupid had fired an arrow directly from where he imagined her nipples to be under her white short-sleeved blouse into his groin, forcing him to turn away until his excitement subsided. Her hands moved with rhythmic precision, and the light black hairs on her forearm were the sexiest thing he'd ever seen. He instantaneously gave himself over to fantasizing about what kind of bra she was wearing. In the first half hour of his new job, while Pang was explaining to him in marginally comprehensible English what was expected of him, he was already visualizing her getting dressed that morning, imagining his brand-new acquaintance's breasts thrust forward as, sleepily, she struggled with the hooks of her brassiere.

Jed's second orientation session took place as he was about to leave with his first order. Pang called him over to his desk, which consisted of a slab of three-quarter inch plywood atop two sawhorses. Maria, on her stool in the front, was out of earshot. "You deliver Pang food. You my rep…How you say?"

"Representative?"

"Yes. That one."

"Got it. With the client."

"What you mean, client?"

"Client, uh, customer."

"Yes! Customer! And," he continued, "customer like food hot!"

It took Pang speaking right in his face about the need for speed for Jed to snap to attention. Although he was nodding comprehension, he was simultaneously thinking that to have any possibility of success with the beauty a couple or so years his senior, a good first step would be to find some positive way to get her attention. One hint he remembered from the Playboy Advisor is that girls do not like it if you come on too strong. While he waited for tactical inspiration, he decided that his principal strategy would be to play it cool. After work he practiced dialogue in front of his bathroom mirror that he would "spontaneously" engage in with her the next day. "Are you at all interested in politics?" he asked the imaginary Maria. "Do you have a favorite candidate for president?" he tried again, not happy with his first attempt either as to timbre or phrasing.

"I like John Kennedy," he had her say.

"Me too!" he replied, seizing on the chance to demonstrate that he liked Catholics.

Although in person he lacked the courage to discuss more than the weather or how hard it was to wake up in the morning, with every successful deployment of his rehearsed spontaneity, he detected, he thought, a burgeoning rapport. He was on the lookout for an opportunity to be seen in a favorable light, but he knew from his studies that any attempt to push himself upon her was counter-indicated.

His big chance came when she returned late from a bathroom break toward the end of June. He had come in sweating after a two-package drop-off just as one of the phones was ringing. No one was at the front desk, and Pang was probably out back counting rings. Jed was taking down the final information for an order as she burst into the front. Her beautiful long dark ponytail swung around toward him as she glanced from the clock to the receiver he was replacing.

"Thanks. You're a dear," she said walking toward him to resume her position.

"My pleasure," he answered, meaning it.

"Of course, I would have done the same thing for you."

"Really? You...you would?" He felt the blood rushing to his face; he hoped she had not noticed. And she smiled at him as she briefly placed her hand on his shoulder through his moist t-shirt. The nonchalance he attempted to portray as he returned to his post was, he feared, unconvincing.

That night, alone in the room he used to share with his brother before Lenny left for college, Jed looked out past the fire escape into the apartment across the way, where Mr. Lowenstein, who, as usual, was needing a shave and cracking open a beer. Jed took no more note of this than of Lenny's poster of Karl Marx, who stared with perennial disapproval at his poster of Rod Laver. All he thought about was how great Maria had looked in her pleated skirt.

After undressing he stood naked in front of the full-length mirror, wondering how his body would seem to her if she could see it. She must certainly have noticed his arm muscles, which were toned from tennis, but the muscular pecs hidden under his clothing, earned from many reps of push-ups and chin-ups? They might stand him in good stead if only…maybe he could spill something on himself in her presence and just happen to have a spare t-shirt handy. Legs could use a little work. He ran in place, his penis a metronome flopping from side to side until he breathlessly dropped down to do a fast fifty sit-ups, ending with a couple of confirmatory smacks to his flat stomach, then, pushing aside the vestigial Bugs Bunny curtain, he stepped into the shower.

Finally, two weeks after they had begun to work together, Jed approached Maria as she was hitching her pocketbook onto her shoulder to go home. He managed to ask her, cool as a cucumber, but after countless takes in front of his mirror, "Say, you wanna stop by Bertollucci's for a Coke?" Although in the real world of Pang time, hers was probably a normal pause, it seemed an insufferably long interval before she sprinkled the holy water of her radiant smile on him.

"Why not?"

This is the best cherry Coke I've ever had, he thought as she began to tell him about herself. She had been four years old when her father enlisted and was ten at the time he returned with his honorable discharge and all his plans and demands. Eventually he got a job in construction, but the first years were tough, especially with the appearance in rapid succession of her brothers, Tony, Robert, and Gianni. He screamed, her dad, and was a heavy drinker. He wanted her to marry an Italian who would drink beer and watch Bears games with him, settle down next door, and give him grandchildren. Then she confided, looking at him as if he might laugh at her, "It sounds nuts, I know, but…I was born to be an actress."

"Really?" He raised his eyebrows, tilted his head, and looked into her blue eyes, encouraging her to continue.

"In eighth grade at Our Lady of Peace, I starred in Peter Pan, and I know that the praise I got from teachers, parents, friends doesn't mean much, but the thing is—"

"You were Wendy? Tinker Bell?" he urged.

"Wendy," she said and then, after appearing to go into a trance, began to speak in what, with Jed, could have passed for a British accent: "Boy, why are you crying? You say that you are not crying? Oh, yes you are. Where do you live?" She tilted her head inquiringly and gestured toward the heavens. "The second star to the right? What a funny address." And then, returning to the voice he knew, "The thing is that when I was on stage, saying my lines, I thought, this is me. This is what I am here for."

"You were gone there for a moment."

"Well, that's how an actress inhabits her role."

"Wow! You are so lucky! To have a talent. To know what you want to do."

"I must get to Hollywood," she told him, "Hollywood or bust."

"Do you know anyone there?"

"Elizabeth Taylor."

His eyes widened, "You know her??"

"Sort of. I've seen every one of the sixteen movies she's made so far. Did you see her in *Giant*? And she was amazing in *Cat on a Hot Tin Roof.*"

There is a god, he thought as his mind retrieved considerable information about the starlet. Dodging her question, he went on to name each of Taylor's four husbands, sympathizing with her loss in the premature death of number three, Mike Todd, and taking Taylor's side in the controversy over her stealing Eddie Fisher from Debbie Reynolds.

But while he said the words, he could not avoid thinking there was something a little delusional going on here until Maria interjected, "And Elena Pelluso, one of my girlfriends from Loyola, has a place in Koreatown, not far from the studios, where I can stay while I'm going out on auditions." She seemed pleased with his avid attention. He did not hear the Illinois Central clacking to a stop at the station outside, and the waitress had to ask him twice whether he wanted anything else. He successfully requested the check without any octavic changes.

Right before they stood up to leave, Maria smiled at him, thanked him for the Coke, and ever so lightly patted his bare forearm. His skin had never been touched with appreciation by a woman, and his body betrayed him with an irrepressible shiver. His knees were weak with exhilaration, and, as he leaned against the booth for support, willpower failed to deflate his possibly visible erection. "Goodbye," he managed without squeaking as, bent at the waist, he fled the restaurant.

That night at Jed's apartment building, all the windows were open and every fan had been pressed into service. The heat of the city remained so high that Jed wondered whether a second Chicago fire, this time cowless, might spontaneously combust. He heard the Lowensteins' dog barking each time Mr. Lowenstein gave forth with one of his snores. The Polanskis' radio was emitting a drone of news from two stories below about Richard Nixon winning the Republican nomination. The wind from the slaughterhouses out west was, as usual, carrying the stench right into his room. How could he ever fall asleep? He tried thinking about a chess problem. *If I decline the queen's pawn gambit and instead go for knight to queen's bishop three...* Hopeless.

When he first took the job at Pang's, he had imagined recounting it years later as the humble origin story that made his staggering success all the more impressive; but now his fantasies ran more toward enough tip money for a dinner at the Palmer House with Maria, candles, and wine. She would have to order it unless he obtained a fake ID. He went over in his mind again the Bertollucci's scene, concluding that Maria had enjoyed his company and maybe, just maybe, not divined his amorous inclinations. He knew from the Playboy Advisor that the way you first let a girl know you are attracted to her is all important.

He barely heard the bottles being left by the milkman on the back landing as, with the first lightening of day, he could no longer remain awake. At breakfast that morning, only a couple of hours later, his mother mentioned how hard it had been to wake him up, and he merely grunted, but when his father from behind *The Tribune* made a remark about how he had probably been out late on a hot date, he uncharacteristically snapped back, "If you think you're that funny, why don't you try out for the Milton Berle show?" And throwing down his napkin, he stormed over to the pantry with the Wheaties box, then slammed the door extra loudly.

But his father wouldn't let it go: "You see what too much of that Chinese food can do to you?"

Jed was already manning his post when Maria appeared. She had been thinking about him as she had fallen asleep, at a much more reasonable hour, the previous evening. If she could have such a powerful effect just from brushing against his arm, she had asked herself, what would happen if she attempted to excite him on purpose? If, say, she ran her finger ever so delicately over his little peach fuzz of a mustache, what shade of red might he turn? Too bad he was too young to be boyfriend material. During most of the day they said little to one another. Pang was in a testy mood. He did the books every Tuesday, and apparently last week had not been good. Jed, as the least senior employee, got the brunt of it. During the midday rush, Pang was waiting for him in the front when he returned from a delivery.

"Thirty minutes for Seventy-Six and Luella? Cannot keep customer waiting."

"I got there fast, Mr. Pang; ran into a friend on the way back."

"I rely—"

"I know. I am your representative."

"Yes. Palace representative," he always liked to have the last word.

When Jed returned from another delivery in the late afternoon, she was in the back chatting with Sammy, one of the cooks. Not wanting any more negative attention from Pang, he had arrived dripping wet and out of breath. Her own face, glistening from the heat, glowed, and he noticed the perspiration under the arms of her white shirt, the outline of her brassiere underneath. As Sammy turned to the stove, she walked over to Jed.

"That was nice yesterday," she said, "Maybe I'll buy you one after work someday?"

"How 'bout this evening?" he asked, no rehearsal required.

"Yeah, why not?" she answered.

It was mid-July and 101 degrees in the shade. Pang's fans seemed to roil an air angry not to have been left in its unnaturally still state. After the sweltering half-hour ride to Scampini Construction followed by a four-story walk-up on the way back, Jed felt faint, and as he sat down, he wondered how he would live through the next three hours till quitting time. But then it got busy. The phones were ringing. Two different walk-ins appeared around the same time that a family of four arrived for an early dinner. The neighborhood seemed to have been suddenly seized with a craving for Chinese food. He could hear Maria's voice, at first calm, repeating back to the customer, "Beef Bok Toy, Ho Say Gai, Chicken Chow Mein, Egg Foo Young." Once the orders started coming through, he had no time to think. Suddenly, time, which had been marching in place, broke into a dead run. As soon as the cooks finished one dish, they began on another. Jed had no time between deliveries. Maria was scribbling furiously and running back and forth from the phones to the kitchen. Pang was screaming orders, everyone was perspiring, and the cooks were bumping into one another. No sooner had Jed dropped off three dinners than he was back for three more, the maximum his baskets could hold. By nine o'clock, when they got off, he had made $19.75 in tips, and he was soaked through.

Pang was exultant, "Pang right! Plenty people like Chinese!" His teeth were white like the filament of an incandescent light bulb as he gave Maria a rare smile, a dollar tip, and a couple of almond cookies. "I always say, we gross more than $500 a day, we arrive." Jed noticed his English was getting better.

"Way to go Mr. Pang," he said in his manliest voice as they walked out the door. "Congratulations on a big day!"

They emerged to experience a miracle in progress. There was a noticeable breeze coming from the East, off the lake, and the temperature had dropped to seventy-five degrees. When Jed thought about it, he remembered that even on his second to last delivery, he had felt the temperature falling, but he had been on such a mad tear that it really hadn't registered. Now on the street with Maria, it seemed like he had clicked into a groove, that time was passing normally once again and that he was part of it.

"Where do ya wanna go?" he asked.

"Where do you want to go?"

"East?" he suggested.

As they started walking east on Seventy-Second toward the lake, they could see in the street lights the heat, as if glad to have been released, shimmering up from the pavement. What looked like steam coming off the white shoulders of her blouse made it seem like an apparition had descended to join him for a stroll. But he was burdened with the heavy catalog of all that separated them. Hell, she was old enough to have a driver's license! She was a Catholic and, if Jed's parents were to be believed, she, like all her co-religionists, was probably prejudiced against Jews. In any event, he was still rooted in the very community she was committed to getting out of. He saw no way to avoid returning in the fall to a life of physics, math, and English tests, tennis, dirty jokes, chores, and on top of that, applications to college. He planned to go to Harvard, a good 2,983.2 miles from Hollywood, according to *Collins World Atlas*.

Their eastward progress was stopped by the ten-foot-high chain-link fence protecting the South Shore Country Club. It had little barbs at the top, but on the other side, running down to the lake, were green fairways lit by a gibbous moon in a partly cloudy sky. The fence's crosshatched iron wire seemed to raise the question: "Are you a good climber?" the very words Jed heard himself uttering.

"Why do you ask?" she replied. Before he could respond, she had hitched up her skirt and was over the top, coming down the other side. This left Jed in a position of having to attempt to duplicate her agility while she stood watching with her hands on her hips. He managed ungracefully to muscle his way to the top, avoided impaling himself on the barbs—but not without a slight puncture wound to his left hand—and they scampered off in the direction of the water.

"Are you a good runner?" she panted, loping a bit ahead of him.

"Why do you ask?" he responded as he blazed past her.

She was out of breath and laughing like they'd pulled off the crime of the century when she caught up with him at the shore of Lake Michigan. It seemed they should contain their laughter to avoid detection, but their stifled mirth added to the deliriousness of their successful trespass. As it sank in that they were alone in their own private world, their heavy breathing gave way to a solemn silence. He was trembling, only in part due to the cooler temperature by the lake, when he took a tremulous step closer to her.

She did not step back but said: "Oh, Jed. I really like you, but you know—" her tone was sorrowful.

"Know what Maria?"

"Jed, you're too young for me."

"Could we talk about what that means?" he found the will to ask. And then, discovering a superhuman ability that only a life-defining cusp could bring forth, he reached out and took both her hands. When he looked into her eyes, she did not look away. The moon made a long shimmering path on the lake behind her. "Maria, chronological age is...Couldn't we—"

"Jed, you're too—" she started again, but this time she took a half-step toward him until their lips were an inch apart. This encouragement was all he needed to drop her hands and pull her toward him, his hand on the small of her back, just like he had done so many times before in his mind. And suddenly they were actually kissing! Her tongue was in his mouth, and then his in hers! Their bodies were touching, and when he realized that she must actually be able to feel his erection, he was subsumed in a tsunami of excitement.

Nevertheless, he somewhere discovered enough brain capacity for a full-scale panic. What if his excitement should be so extreme that he suffered a heart attack, right then, right there? No one was around to help unless Maria herself proved to be an undercover doctor. No, he imagined her running back to the fence for assistance as he lay there close to an unimaginably painful death. He saw her wringing her hands as the paramedics, after frantically negotiating the long par five, tried to maneuver his body, now strapped to a stretcher, back over the fence. His parents would blame each other for not sufficiently emphasizing the potentially lethal consequences of socializing with gentile girls.

For her part, Maria was astonished at what she was feeling. She was melting from the top down in the electricity that flowed between them. The kiss was supposed to have been part consolation for the impossibility of a relationship and part gratitude for their friendship. This is crazy, she thought, even as she pushed her pelvis into his. She felt him begin to fumble ineffectually with the hooks of her brassiere. This gave her the opportunity to moan "no" and push him gently away while bestowing the possibility of resumption: "I think we'd better stop for now." And she ran her finger just above his upper lip, feeling him shiver as she had thought he might.

They found their way to the huge granite boulders placed along the lake's shore like teeth awaiting a giant dentist. Little waves, pushed by the gentle wind, lapped soothingly. Maria and Jed snuggled, their arms around each other on a mammoth concave rock that seemed to be waiting for them. Hanging their legs down, they gazed at the moonlit intake crib far out in the lake, a barge-like flat gray structure with little dollhouse-sized lights, silently pumping water to the purification plant a few blocks south. She handed him an almond cookie. Neither had ever before tasted one: Superb!

"Paint me a future-you picture," she spoke first.

"You mean where I'll be, say ten years from now?"

She nodded.

"I like numbers," he began. "I want to do something with numbers."

"Like—"

"Like solve important problems."

"What makes a problem important?"

"What makes a problem important," he stalled, "is, um… someone will pay you to solve it. I want to put this period of working for tips behind me ASAP."

"Anything else to fill in the picture?" she prodded.

"I suppose I would be…married, have kids?" The resumption of their petting confirmed he'd chosen the correct answer.

She felt his soft warm hands on her bare back and, pulling his shirt up, touched him the same way. This time though, thoughts of her father and his rules crept in. She looked at her watch. "Oh my god, Jed. It's past midnight! I have to go."

The first thing to penetrate Jed's consciousness the next morning was his mother's accusatory voice: "You were out till all hours young man. I was worried to death." Her subsequent pull on the shades let in a shaft of sunlight that stabbed his eyes. "Where were you?" The contrast between his blissful state when he had fallen asleep around 3 a.m. and this painful awakening could not have been more extreme.

He hated it when she called him "young man." He hated that he was obliged to account for his whereabouts. And he hated that she just stood there waiting for an answer like it was her room when he had to get up and pee so badly. "I'll tell you about it later, mom," he tried.

She wasn't having any of it. The closer he got to saying it was none of her business, the more pained her expression until, finally, she ordered him to "Take out the damned garbage at least" and left the room. Since she rarely swore, he saw with a mixture of satisfaction and regret that she was unusually upset.

What Jed thought he wanted was to run away to California with Maria: Every night they would share a frugal meal, talk about how the day had gone, and then make passionate love before falling asleep in each other's arms. Working as a waiter in a much higher-class Chinese restaurant than Pang's, he would save enough money—even while supporting Maria—until he could open up a restaurant of his own and then a whole chain: Jed's Oriental Cuisine. He imagined Pang's expression, first astonished, then outraged when Sammy quit to seize the West Coast opportunity Jed would offer him.

For several nights after their first evening together on the golf course, they returned, their petting taking them further and further. On their third trespass, they heard footsteps at a most inopportune time; he was rapturously caressing her bare breast, and she had her hand on the bulge in his trousers. The moon was almost full, but luckily, they were able to slip into the shadow of a large boulder before a stocky man in a guard uniform walked by. Increasingly they felt exposed. On a couple of occasions Maria succeeded in borrowing her father's car and they were able to make out near the aquarium or in the parking lot by Soldier Field. But their desire for one another became so intense it was like a being they'd created that now had a life of its own.

On a Thursday evening toward the end of July, Jed returned home to find his Uncle Irving in the kitchen, having a beer with his father. Jed's mother's brother was fifty-five and obese. He collected stamps, coins, and butterflies. "Hey, Jed, my boy! Just the guy I've been looking for."

"What's up, Uncle Irving?"

"Well, your Unc is about to decamp for the first week of August…Club Med. Rumor has it the Gentle Organizers are gentle indeed."

"Sounds fun. Have a great trip," Jed said, turning to leave the room.

"Not so fast, *boychik*," Uncle Irving said, calling him back. "I need a house sitter. You can help yourself to the food in the fridge. I will pay you four bucks a day. But you have to feed the fish."

Jed was speechless.

"OK, you drive a hard bargain. Make it five bucks. But don't *futz* it up with the fish."

Angels come in many forms, Jed thought.

The night that Jed and Maria each made love for the first time in their lives would never leave his mind. "Can we turn out the lights?" she asked. And when he flicked the switch, when the room was pitch dark, he heard her blouse, her skirt, and her undergarments drop to the floor, and he hastened to catch up with her.

"Oh my god!" he said, as he slipped under the sheet, "I can't believe—"

After the uncle returned, they surpassed each other's ingenuity in discovering new venues, and August passed in a blur. They welcomed the windless heat that descended again on the city. The hotter, the better, because that meant it was still summertime.

The Sunday night before Jed was to return to school and Maria to take a train to Los Angeles, they went Dutch on a room in a cheap but clean motel on the Outer Drive. Now they looked through a picture window at the sun setting over their lake. They shared a bottle of La Granja Tempranillo he had bought for $3.99, "clinking" with the plastic cups retrieved from the bathroom.

"I believe Liz Taylor had Conrad Hilton to help launch her in Hollywood," he said.

"They called him 'Nicky,'" she replied.

"Would you let me be your Nicky?" he asked, dropping his arm from her shoulder to her waist, pulling her closer.

"Oh Jed," she turned, then gave him a full, deep kiss. "I would love to do this with you, but—"

"I could finish high school out there."

"Give me some time to get the lay of the land. You can come west for college."

"Yes! That's exactly what we'll do. Forget Harvard. I'll apply to UCLA. Meanwhile I'll save up enough for a rent deposit on our apartment."

She kissed him tenderly on his eyelids and led him to the bed. But the sadness of their impending separation seeped into their lovemaking, inflicting a kind of post-coital tristesse before they'd even begun. Around midnight they played "I Love," a game they'd invented, one last time.

"I love your hair, all of it, the soft hair on your arms," he told her, embellishing a compliment he'd used before and brushing his hand over the hair between her legs.

"I love what you smell like," she told him, "Natural. No deodorant, no aftershave." And she came closer, inhaling a convincingly deep breath. "And," she added, "I love your smarts."

"I love your guts, your passion," he concluded.

The next morning, they arrived at the Twelfth Street railway station an hour and a half before the Southeast Chief's scheduled departure time, as if by zealous acceptance of their fate they could persuade the gods to reverse the verdict. They paused outside to look up to the sign ten stories up, which read, "Illinois Central, Main Line of Mid-America." The purse she was clutching contained her ticket, $35 in cash, and a ham and cheese on rye. He was holding her American Tourister suitcase, heavy from the shoes and clothing it had taken both of them to cram in. Wordlessly, they entered the beautiful waiting room with its vaulted ceilings and long wooden benches. Light streamed in through the vast open windows.

"Is there anything at all I can do for you after you leave?" he asked. "Your parents know where to reach you?"

"I couldn't take a chance on what my father might do. I left a note telling them not to worry, that I'd call them from LA," she said.

She was wearing a full-skirt dress with one large button near the collar, and for the first time since Jed had known her, lipstick, the same red shade that Jackie Kennedy favored. She would have looked completely mature and self-possessed but for the quiver in her lower lip. He kissed her hand, turned it palm up, and folded her fingers over a wad of bills, his life savings of $300 in fives, tens, and twenties. Now, tears came to her eyes. She looked down at the thick wad and began to cry.

"Jed…I, I can't…I can't let you—"

"This money is nothing compared to what I'll have in a few years," he assured her, closing her fingers over the money a second time. And he hugged her, bringing her close so that she would not see his tears.

"I'll come to LA as soon as I graduate," he said. They kissed one last time, touched each other's faces, and clung to a hope undiminished by the smell of the stockyards wafting from the west.

CHAPTER 5
LET'S FACE IT

In 1950, when I was twenty-six and a year away from getting my BA in business, I decided to kill my father...virtually that is. He was sixty-one at the time, and I feared it could be another three decades before he voluntarily handed me the keys to the family pinball machines business. Jackpot had been perfectly healthy when he had inherited it from my grandfather, and admittedly he hadn't ruined it, but on the other hand, he was doing nothing to increase its profits, nothing to grow it. The American economy was taking off like a liberated POW while the business, under my father's "leadership," was just marking time.

It was a conversation with Vincente Reggio that finally goaded me into action. But rewinding the clock a bit, Vinnie and I had grown up together in Grosse Pointe, a wealthy suburb outside of Detroit. We were both extremely smart, but neither of us had taken school seriously. Both our fathers planned for us to join the family business after college. Vinnie's dad, the founder of their family public relations firm, wanted him to take over as soon as possible. Mine planned to spend many years imparting his wisdom on pinball machines before giving me the top job. I was looking at a long, tedious slog, so, when in twelfth grade, Vinnie suggested we hit the road together, I was receptive.

"But doesn't your dad want you to get your BA ASAP?" I asked him.

"Yeah, same as yours; but what's a couple years in the grander scheme of things? Let's playboy around a bit."

In order to put my stamp on the scheme, I insisted that our first stop be my choice. I was obsessed with Sophia Loren and, by extension, Italian women as a category, so refused to shake hands on the deal until he agreed to put his thing for Jewish girls in uniforms on the back burner. But he finally acquiesced to my Italy before Israel, and, upon graduation, after he made the necessary promises to his father and I to my mother, we flew to Sicily, where we picked grapes and learned how to fuck in Italian.

I never had much difficulty finding a way to let girls know that Vinnie was my side man, and, as the alpha male, I always got my pick of the litter. But I had to live up to my part of the bargain, so finally it came time to migrate to Israel, where we found employment in Degania, a *kibbutz* in the north. Vinnie worked in the kitchen while I did jobs having to do with counting crops. There we basked in the carnal energy of the new state for another year until one Sunday morning Vinnie said: "Ralph, we need to move on." He had just broken up with an Aviva someone, and I myself was between girlfriends.

"Meaning?"

"We need to go home and get back on track."

Through the pulsing of my epic hangover, he sounded like a chaperone about to turn on the lights. I groaned but nodded in resignation, not because he was such a timing genius but because I had been thinking along the same lines.

Long story short, we took the SATs. With our very high scores and our parents' philanthropic potential, we probably could have gotten in anywhere, but Vinnie persuaded me that the less academically demanding our school, the more fun we could have. His father cared only about him earning the sheepskin, not where it came from. Mine had assumed I would choose an Ivy League college, but he wisely limited his expression of disappointment to a rueful aside about someone else's son entering Harvard. And my mother? Even if I'd been accepted into MIT Sloan, it would have been something like, "Well, congratulations, I suppose...if you can't get into Stanford."

Anyway, next thing they knew, Vinnie and I were sharing a room at Babson College. I expected it to be like high school but with no fake IDs or gym class. But once in, I couldn't believe the excitement I experienced in learning basic business principles. Vinnie, whose expectations were as low as mine, was equally blown away. "Fuck, man, this shit is relevant," he exclaimed after our first class in marketing. And the new concepts our professors were teaching, like risk/reward analysis, return on capital, P/E ratios, hit us like an epiphany. We continued to party, but through the alcohol and drug binges, brushes with the law, crabs, and the clap, we took our studies seriously. Vinnie's excitement about how he would grow his business was infectious. But at the same time, I was jealous. I could not call Jackpot mine the way he could Reggio & Son.

I spoke to my mother at five p.m. every Sunday, and my irritation with the path I was on was a frequent topic of conversation. "Vinnie's dad has checked out; I mean it's like Vinnie's already running his business from here!"

"Ralph, I understand your frustration; your father could try the patience of Solomon."

"Was Solomon patient?"

"I don't know, but that's not the point."

"What is the point? What is the point of my joining him in the office? Vinnie's dad just shut down their St. Louis operation because Vinnie told him to."

"I am sure your father would listen to you if you had some good suggestions."

"Mom, it's not about suggestions. He's clueless. How am I supposed to learn from a guy who has nothing to teach me?"

"Jackpot is where our money comes from. If you were in the office, you could keep an eye on him."

"If, could?" I thought. Surely, she is inviting me to consider my alternatives.

Then, one night at Roger's Pub, I had been complaining to Vinnie about how dad could never seem to fire the "executive" in charge of Jackpot's western region. The fucking guy had cost us $729 in tax penalties because he was too busy jerking off to file the local returns on time! "Ralph, you are paying an unacceptable opportunity cost," I thought I heard Vinnie say over the hoots and shouts of the other refugees slumming it at this off-campus bar. I understood from Business Strategy that "opportunity cost" was the foregone benefit of an alternative future. But I wasn't getting his thought.

"Meaning what?" I yelled through the din.

"Your dad doesn't have what it takes to fire one lousy incompetent. Imagine what the business could be if you took over now."

"I know, Vin," I shouted in his ear. "But, say I could think of a way. There is more than an insignificant chance it could kill him. Business is everything to him."

Vinnie shrugged, "Ralph, buddy, I know he's your old man, and I don't mean to be callous here, but if he can't live with natural evolution, that tells you something in and of itself. We all have to go sometime."

Let's face it, I thought, draining the last of my fourth Samuel Adams, *in life you have to take certain risks. His lack of drive and vision, his general incompetence, and his poor negotiating skills...they're simply forcing my hand.*

Vinnie's final argument convinced me. "Is what he is doing best for the business or best for him? You heard it here first, pal: If you are not for yourself, who then will be for you? If not now, when?"

I planned my attack meticulously, focusing my attention on father's lawyer Frederick Winston Powell, who was also his lifelong friend. "Ralph, you have to know that what you are asking is not going to be easy for me," was his response to my initial blandishments.

Thus, as bad a negotiator as my father, he had conceded up front that he was willing to play ball and that we were only down to how much it would cost me. What he should have started with, if he wanted a shot at maximizing his position, was, "Ralph, I really can't do this." That would have put him in a much stronger place, and if I had started to walk, he would have had time to do a climbdown. But, like his good buddy, my old man, he didn't know how to play a hand.

"I appreciate that, Frederick, and I am prepared to make this worth your while. I have big plans for Jackpot Enterprises, and I can see your billings with us growing to some very meaningful numbers." What I could also see at the time, but elected not to mention, was that Powell himself was not long for my world. I don't like to lie, but prevaricating for a purpose never troubled me, and I happened to need him for the limited role of turncoat at that particular moment. After allowing him to whine some more ("He's a good man, your father"), I continued to press. "I know, Frederick. A good man. I couldn't agree more. But business is business. He's telling the same stories over and over."

"Yes, but what you want me to do...How will I live with myself?"

"Think of Thaddeus," I argued, knowing the cost of twenty-four-hour care for his autistic son.

"But...but repeating yourself isn't a crime." This feeble push-back was so obviously Frederick speaking to himself for show, it was clear he was mine.

"I know how difficult this is for you," I said. "But we're not talking criminal law here. This is a normal request in a civil matter."

"Civil matter," he repeated, as the planet earth paperweight he'd been clutching hit his wooden desktop with a satisfying *thunk*.

I planned it all summer, and in the fall of '51, I took an extra day after Thanksgiving break before returning to school so I could be in the office when father learned that Powell had filed my state court affidavit averring he was mentally incompetent. Timing is everything, and I had wanted mother to enjoy the holiday before having to deal with his reaction.

"I can't understand why you would do this to me, Ralphie! This business is my life! I'm a young man," he protested. And he actually began to cry, if you can believe it.

"Dad, everyone ages differently. You aren't paying attention to the details. You're too soft." He was my father after all, and I always tried to be merciful…or at least nice about the necessaries when possible. In theory, he could have squashed me, but the very launching of my attack, supported by Powell's excellent treason, was enough. As my father had told me a million fucking times, you just have to nudge the machine without causing a tilt and then wait for the right instant to press the flipper.

"I will fight you on this," he threatened.

"You really want to slug it out in court, dad? Think about mom, our friends. Let's just settle this between us before it gets out of hand."

"I will fight you," he repeated, more softly this time. Like Powell, he needed a little help from me to find the exit.

"Dad, look, this needn't be messy. You can be Jackpot's non-executive chairman. You'll keep your driver, all your benefits."

And…done deal. Jackpot! I called mom from the airport and explained what I had done.

"I see," she said, accepting my fait accompli. She was a woman who harbored few illusions. "How did he take it?"

"Fine," I said, "what you'd expect."

"…"

Her silence asked me a question I was prepared to answer. "He needn't be in your hair. I will get him a place to work not far from the office. I've already ordered some nice business cards that say 'chairman' on them."

"..."

"Embossed. Raised lettering. Thicker stock than his old ones."

And out of respect for her, I actually did proceed to order the cards and have the business rent him a small office a short drive from Jackpot headquarters. I waited a good year before I moved the main office out of Detroit, but then I was able to explain to mom, "Detroit Metro to La Guardia can't be more than two-and-a-half hours door-to-door."

So, due to my perfect execution and some moral support from Vinnie, the very day I got my BA, I became the one hundred percent shareholder of a pinball machine business generating $10 million per year of free cash flow with headquarters in Rockefeller Center. I kept Powell around for a respectable six more months, then dumped him.

Control of Jackpot proved to be a step in the right direction. My high school sweetheart, Lynda Berish, who, in her own way was as ambitious as I was, had been making nice to dad in what she probably thought was a work of many years. She was left breathless by my coup and had to scramble to prostrate herself before the new lord and master...me.

Ha!

And I seized her fiercely, as a pirate king his booty, wedding her soon after the sun set on my victory. I am a magnanimous winner, and since it had not been necessary to have my father civilly committed, I allowed him to participate in the reception, where he managed an almost coherent but blessedly short toast.

"To Lynda Berish! May you enjoy your new life to the extent poss...., to the extent....Well, what I mean, Lynda, here is to some happiness in your new life."

Pitiful.

Anyone, let's face it, can motivate a worker to surpass himself if you cut him a piece of the equity action, but where I excel is getting my employees to put out for base plus bonus, the latter decided by me in my sole discretion. More revenue plus lower payroll equals increased productivity, and, of course, soaring profits. With a solid plan to grow Jackpot organically at fifteen percent a year, a new wife, and, in a New York minute, a brand-new son, I should have been happy, right?

Wrong!

First of all, my son couldn't even speak a sentence until he was over a year old. And he took forever to learn to walk. But I'll have more to say about this ungrateful numbskull later. Another reason I was dissatisfied was that my business still bore the stamp of my father's incompetence. Among his many failings was that he was more into pinballs—I mean the actual physical machines—than cash flow. I'm not saying that there's no place for quality manufacturing or customer service, but these functions must be put in perspective. Even if you could only generate the same level of cash with fewer plants and fewer people, why the hell wouldn't you? Take it from me: more people, more problems.

As was clear to me even before Babson, when it comes to good old American know-how, our workers, let's face it, are at their most impressive in raising their own compensation levels, not in making stuff. So, I sold all my US factories, hired a rep firm to replace my so-called dedicated sales force, and outsourced every damn function I could. By my thirtieth birthday, I had the number of employees down from 1,500 to 120 and the cash flow up to, rough justice, $22 million a year.

Once I had the business going at a good clip, pinballs themselves became almost irrelevant. The name of the game was growth, and while there was plenty left in pinballs, the pace was boringly predictable. The first expression of my restlessness was my expansion outside the US. Well before "global" became a buzzword, I penetrated Canada and Europe; from there I moved onto Southeast Asia and Latin America. At Vinnie's (kind-of obvious) suggestion, I changed the name from Jackpot Enterprises to Jackpot International and doubled the bottom line in three years instead of the five that all my advisors had insisted we'd need. Thrill dill. I needed a still-bigger arena.

When I look in the mirror, I see a bald, muscular, rich, passionate, creative, bold, intelligent man. I am also a highly effective public speaker. Just check out the video of me accepting the Horatio Alger Award. The kids went wild! Above all, I am a realist. I can't seem to do anything about my slight paunch, but let's face it, that comes with age. Unlike a bunch of jerks I know who try to cover their bald spots with long wisps, I get a crew cut once a month. It's cheaper, and hey, let's face it, they aren't fooling anyone.

My cholesterol level and blood pressure are superb. I love to look at fat people who are clearly not exercising. I keep a few of them around in the company to confirm that my own efforts are not a waste of time. I get *The Journal*, *The Times*, and *FT* specially delivered at 5:45 a.m. so I can read them while I'm on the treadmill. I have never had the slightest interest in cosmetic surgery. When I look in the mirror, which I do once in the morning and once at night, I do so with attention to detail and without flinching.

I take no unnecessary chances. Near all four of my principal residences, I keep an ample supply of my own blood. My drivers know the quickest route to the best hospitals in the vicinity (to which I have given just the amount that could be referred to as "lavish"). Even though I'm always stiff, I have stayed away from that yoga crap, preferring instead aerobics and weights under the watchful eye of a trainer who also happens to be a paramedic.

I should have gotten divorced long ago, but to tell the truth, my wife's too good a negotiator, and since she seems comfortable with the title "Ralph Ripkin's wife," why would I give a shit? She probably figures she'll outlive me and, wrongly, that she'll take over the business like that bitch who inherited *The Washington Post.* In the meantime, I buy her jewelry on her birthdays and anniversaries, pay her $200,000 a month, sleep where I want, and take only minimal crap from her. A cheap price, I figure, to avoid, while I am alive, a battle my executors are certain to win anyway, if she's dumb enough to turn down my will's ample posthumous kiss-off and resort to litigation. She's handy to have along on certain occasions and, let's face it, our sporadic screaming sessions are a catharsis I don't get anywhere else.

Every time I do something she could label "outrageous," she uses it as a lever to pry more out of me. The way she got her monthly draw up to $200,000 from $170,000 was on the strength of her moral indignation. It was 1977 when I "humiliated" her by inviting Pamela, a young Cleary Gottlieb attorney I'd been screwing, to dinner at Le Coq Foutu, this fancy-schmancy midtown French joint. Lynda was waiting up for me in our condo that night.

Somehow, she'd learned I'd been there, and she seemed determined to make a big deal about how it was "our" favorite restaurant. I tried to point out that it had been my favorite restaurant, that she had never heard of it until I brought her there in the first place.

Operating at her highest decibel level, she asserted that this was beside the point. "Everything is a goddamn debate with you! Most sane people can keep their mind on the point of a conversation," she screamed.

"I was merely—"

"You want to obfuscate the main topic by changing the subject to who 'discovered' the joint! You're flaunting your infidelities by taking one of your floozies to…what the hell difference does it make that you found the place?"

When she uses a word like "obfuscate," the subtext is "I'm as smart as you." So, while she hyperventilated, I weighed whether to infuriate her with something like "Oh, 'obfuscate' is it? Aren't we using big words today?" or just take the wind out of her sails and concede the point. When I finished delivering myself of a few thoughts about how the use of big words doesn't equal intelligence, she was speechlessly furious, so I thought to add, "By the way, she's not a floozy; she's a respected mergers and acquisitions lawyer." And while she stood there, her cheeks scarlet, her eyes bugged out but still saying nothing, I couldn't resist adding "And PS, she loves me...for who I really am." At which point, she astonished me. She had never before resorted to throwing anything, so my jaw dropped when she grabbed a little bronze likeness of me and, uncoiling her body Olympic-style, discus-ed it through the living room window. The silence that followed the breaking glass did not last long.

"Screw you, Ralph! Anyone who says they love you is just pretending in order to get your fucking money."

Oof, I felt that one like she'd landed a physical blow, but there was no time to think about it. I was calculating the cost to replace the window and worrying about whether my liability insurance would cover possible injuries at street level.

Normally I could have gotten away with a decent stone and a promise never to humiliate her so, ever ever again, but knowing I was in the middle of the Belandia Hotels deal, my first hostile takeover, she went for the jugular. As she well knew, there was no way I'd allow my focus to shift to her petty bullshit.

The biggest cost was not the per-month bump she nicked me for, but the need to rejigger our living arrangement at Trump Tower. Our immediate neighbor, a prickly Russian garmento whose empire was built on velvet lingerie, had had enough of our screaming sessions. So, we were forced to move. I still hadn't met the developer himself at the time, but Giandomenico Vizzini, a mobster friend of Vinnie's who knew him personally, kindly took care of arranging our move to a much larger apartment on a higher floor, which we had to ourselves. Between the interior decorator and the increased maintenance, I don't even want to think about it.

This particular battle was fought seven years ago, and I still resent the hell out of her for her exquisitely timed cheap shot win. But, hey, the views are better, we are less on top of one another, and, let's face it, by keeping my eye on the ball, I got Belandia done, thereby adding a few more bucks to my net worth. (I figure about $750 mil based on latest twelve months' cash flow.)

A good part of what went wrong with our marriage was, simply put, my son. From the moment he was born, Lynda couldn't get her priorities straight. I suppose I would have needed a little extramarital excitement from time to time anyway, my virility being what it is, but my god, she had minimal apparent ability to entrust the little loser to the care of anyone else—even her own mother. When I needed attention, there was always some problem of his she had to attend to. One trait he certainly picked up from his mother was a lack of appreciation for me. If I made an extra effort to relate to him, he always had something more important to do.

I remember one day when he was six or so. I had made a special point to get home before his bedtime. "Hey, buddy!" I enthused when I entered his room. I could tell by the way his face fell that I was a most unpleasant surprise. "What are we up to?"

"Oh…Hi Father." He was already bathed and in his pj's.

"How was school today, little man? Tell daddy what you learned." I was not expecting much.

"I did not learn anything," he replied.

"Not one thing?" I asked.

"Not really," he insisted.

"Well, what am I paying all this money for to send you to a great private school?"

"I don't know, father," he had mumbled when this drop-dead gorgeous twenty-something nanny walked in with an, "Oh, must you be Mr. Ripkin? I am pleased with the meeting of you, sir."

Sensing my distraction, Ralphie returned to his dolls.

"And I could not be more pleased to meet you, young lady. How long have you been with us?"

"Seven almost weeks, sir," she answered. "But I work here in building two years for the Kostyukovskys." From this I inferred, correctly as it emerged, that Lynda had filched her from one of the Russians on the lower floors. (She called them "oilygarchs" even though many weren't in the energy business.)

In the next month or so, I started coming home earlier and so learned that Katrina was both good with my son and great in the sack. Ralphie was understandably disappointed when Lynda sent her packing. But where was I? As he grew older, I tried inviting him to join me on special outings, but it always seemed forced. When I took the trouble to share with him some of the important lessons I'd learned in life, he squirmed as if these pearls of wisdom were so many ants in his pants.

"Junior?" That's what I called him after he started at Columbia Prep. "Papa wants to share with you a story from the world of business. Does that sound interesting?"

"I guess so, father." He never took a definitive position on anything, as far as I know, in his entire damn life. Putting aside one of the Barbie dolls he was still playing with (at age eight!), he gave me his squeamish attention.

"Well, so, today," I began, "this guy comes by the office and tries to sell me a bill of goods." And the kid, who already looks puzzled even though I have said nothing yet of substance, still has one eye on this doll that he clearly cannot wait to get back to primping.

"Did you buy it, father?" he asks, and I begin to realize that I am on a fool's errand.

"Do you know what a bill of goods is, Ralphie?"

"Not really, father."

"Well, in this context—"

"What is context, father?" *Is he doing this to infuriate me?*

I took a deep breath and soldiered on, "Context means the circumstances surrounding something that give it its meaning."

"So, this person wanted to sell you meaning," he beamed. "Did you acquire some from him, father?"

"No! I did not acquire any meaning from him! He learned a lesson from me!"

"What lesson was that, father?"

"That you can't put one over on Ralph Ripkin!"

"So, you showed him that you are not as stupid as he thought you were. Right?"

At a certain point, what can you say? Speechless, I excused myself, to his evident relief, with a "Goodnight, Junior" and headed to my study where, two double martinis later, I was able to calm down. Whenever I tried to speak to Ralphie about the central importance of toughness, he always seemed frightened. Of course, always as I was getting to the key point of a lesson, Lynda would intervene, so it was clear from the time he was two that he would be a sniveling little mama's boy. A classic was the time Lynda pulled him out of the pool I had thrown him in so he could learn to swim. Now, thanks to her, instead of acquiring a skill, he has a water phobia, which, let's face it, is the least of his problems.

The other problem with our marriage, as Vinnie and I figured out in one of our many heart-to-hearts, is that Lynda never really accepted my commitment to business. Differently put, except for that brief period before I took over Jackpot, she never really loved me. She thinks, wrongly, that I don't care about anything other than making money. In her mind, she has a broader perspective about life than I do because she reads novels and yaks with a bunch of charities about saving the world while so elegantly carrying her wifely burden. She doesn't get it. It's not about money. It's about winning. Winning is what made this country great. Winning, the drive to prevail, is the essence of what is great about the human spirit and, I daresay, our capitalist democracy.

To be frank, perhaps I err when I say she doesn't get it, because every time she wants something from me, she wages a brilliant battle. She defines the stakes, the rules, the venue, the timing. Her record is better than Muhammad Ali's.

I had allowed Lehman Brothers to help me with some of the technical aspects of the Belandia takeover, but let's face it, their main value added had been to introduce me to Le Coq Foutu. I became well known to the maître d' and all the waiters, and as an added attraction, I often ran into a number of my business associates there. Unfortunately, after Belandia, "relationship managers" (basically professional investment banker ass-kissers) figured out that I often dined there and managed to bump into me "by accident" at the hat check.

So, all of a sudden, I had a pile of fancy name cards from "managing directors" of all the major banks. Young guys in thousand-dollar suits bursting with ideas about companies I should acquire. It didn't take me long to figure out that they knew next to nothing about the actual businesses they were peddling, that they didn't really care what I bought as long as I bought something and paid a fee. Their job was to figure out what would please me and make sure they provided it. For the hell of it, I once let it drop that I had read about the pleasures of fly-fishing. The next thing I knew I was in northern Finland with a small group of CEOs pulling salmon out of an Arctic stream.

Though a senior banker named Frankenberg was my main contact at Lehman, the firm sent a younger man named Diamond my way. The other panderers just wanted in, but since Lehman was in already, his job was to increase their "share of wallet," meaning get more of my business, earn more fees. Diamond seemed to live in mortal fear he'd be blamed if I took my business elsewhere. Watching him squirm when I screamed about some Lehman flaw became, I admit, a new form of entertainment. But then one day he asked: "Would you have any interest in raising a few hundred million dollars of permanent capital at around 3 percent without giving up any equity?"

"How are you going to pull off that miracle?" I bit.

"Well," he could hardly contain his euphoria once I'd swallowed the bait, "I need for you to meet this amazing guy who's in charge of our Structured Finance business. Smartest guy on Wall Street."

I had met Goldman's "smartest guy on Wall Street," Morgan Stanley's, First Boston's, and was no more interested in meeting another overeducated, overcompensated prick than I was in meeting a really skilled auto mechanic who wanted work in one of my garages, but cheap money is cheap money, so what the hell.

"This is Jed Czincosca," Diamond said when he brought him by the office. "The guy I told you about."

"It's good to meet you Mr. Ripkin," he said. And then he just sat there, mum, looking at me as if I were applying for membership in his country club.

"I understand you are peddling capital on attractive terms," I said, breaking the silence.

He took his time before replying: "I am not peddling anything, sir."

Diamond jumped in, "What he means, Ralph—"

"My error," I interrupted, speaking exclusively to Czincosca, "I thought you had some genius technique for raising inexpensive capital. I obviously misheard your colleague here." And I started to stand up to show the arrogant dick who was who.

"Guess so," this Czincosca replied. He stood and was about to offer me a farewell handshake when Diamond interceded again.

"Whoa, whoa, whoa. I mean, c'mon fellas. We do have some thoughts for you, Ralph. Jed, please just sit for a second and tell him what structure your team has come up with for Jackpot International."

Czincosca appeared to be considering whether it was worth his time to stick around. I was impressed. My father's old lawyer could have learned a trick or two from this young man. He sat again. "Basically, it's a structured convertible preferred," he said, like he was making a concession not to me but to Diamond.

"Doesn't 'convertible' mean it converts into equity at some point?" I asked. And then, turning to Diamond I spoke in a much harsher tone. "I thought you said 3 percent, no equity give-up."

"It would be 3 percent more or less," Czincosca said. "And the amount of equity the preferred converts into would be *de minimis.*"

"I see. So 'without giving up *any* equity' becomes 'without giving up *much* equity'?"

"Correct," Czincosca said, looking me right in the eye. "Why don't I just describe the deal to you and if you like it, fine. If not…well, I am sure Roger here can find other ways for Lehman to be of service to your amazingly successful company."

And I thought *Wow. That's the most convincing compliment I've had in years. No piling it on. Just a passing kiss.*

When he described this security they'd concocted for me, I was impressed. I probed with a bunch of penetrating questions, which he answered convincingly, and by the end of the conversation I could tell he really admired me. We shook hands on the deal right then and there.

Once that security was successfully placed, I continued to fuel Jackpot with an inflow of cheap capital from Lehman private placements. Thus, the only limit to the growth of my business was my own imagination. I controlled an integrated manufacturing and services business that, fueled by Lehman, had come to include not just pinball machines and hotels, but pari-mutuel betting systems, slot machines, vending machines, and cruise ships generating over $335 million a year in cash flow.

But I was restless.

Actually, "restless" did not do justice to my state of mind. Though I dropped off easily, especially after a session with Doris, the brilliant Jones Day attorney I met during a takeover, I was not getting enough sleep. Doris was a forty-one-year-old whose feelings for me were obviously genuine. She loved me for who I really was, a living rebuttal of Lynda's "anyone who says they love you is just pretending" which, let's face it, is a wound that not only hasn't healed but seems to have worsened. What woke me began with a sweet dream in which I am introducing Doris to my mother. In my sleeping mind, mother warms to her immediately. Usually, I get through a few scenes where the two of them are delighting each other. But the next thing I know, I am sitting upright in the middle of the damn night recalling the actual conversation my mother and I had almost half a century ago when I told her I planned to marry Lynda. Night after night after night, until sometimes I can't tell if I am dreaming or recalling.

"The Berish girl?" she asks, feigning surprise. We are at home in the sunroom, but there is an impressive thunderstorm brewing outside. Large drops begin to pummel the glass roof as I pour her a cup of Earl Grey.

"Yes, Lynda Berish, the young woman I introduced you to a

month ago," I say, speaking loud enough to be heard over what has suddenly become a cyclonic downpour.

"Of course I remember her. Good looking. Dresses well enough. Why her?" She is looking shrewdly at me over her teacup.

The real answer was that Lynda had a great figure, loved oral sex as much as I did, and worshipped me for all the right reasons, but I could hardly win mother over with these attributes. "She is a person of high character, loves animals and babies," I paused long enough to see this is getting me nowhere, "and she comes from a good family." A flash of lightning followed by a loud bang accentuated the word "family." At least I have her attention.

"What do they do, this family?"

"Her dad runs Associated Re, a successful reinsurance operation."

"Never heard of it."

"That's because it's a wholesale business...serves large corporations."

"Still—"

"Mother, what does that matter? You've heard of it now. It's legal. Makes money."

"It's not about money, Ralph, it's about standing."

"It's not as if everything dad did was squeaky clean."

"He was never convicted of anything...or even indicted. Our reputation is as good as anyone's," she harrumphs.

"Anyway, I am sure you'll like her well enough when you get to know her," I said, ending the conversation.

But I was wrong.

I brought Lynda by the house a couple weeks later. She was wearing a tight shirt with what I told her was one undone button too many. Predictably, my mother glanced disapprovingly at her cleavage. We were back in the sunroom again, but this time on a beautiful sunny Saturday morning. My father was present, presumably for the purpose of passing around the bagels and bearing witness to the interrogation.

"So, Lynda, congratulations," mother began.

"On what?" Lynda answered as she wiped a smidge of cream cheese off her lips. "Can I get you anything, Mr. Ripkin?" She had turned toward my father, but mother insisted on her attention.

"On landing my Ralph."

Lynda laughed tentatively, as if my mother was making a joke. "Oh, well thanks," Lynda said. "Of course, we're not married yet." I could read my mother's annoyance. She hated statements of the obvious.

"Mom," I interjected. I could almost see her in the ecclesiastical robes of a twelfth-century inquisitor. All I could come up with was, "You're not supposed to congratulate the bride." And I laughed, I'm afraid, imploringly.

Mother accepted the implicit request…to an extent. "Well in this day and age, we all know that asking the parents' permission is a formality, so congratulations to the two of you," she said with a significant glance at my father, which he correctly interpreted as a command. He snapped to his feet and mother said, "Okay then, it seems as if your father is ready to get to his desk." And she rose, extending a hand in Lynda's direction. "Hope to see you again before too long." *Thank god*, I would think wiping my brow with a towel I now keep by the bed, *at least, mother being dead and all, I don't need to go through this shit all over again with Doris.*

For whatever reason, I have never been as ambitious in my whole life as I am now. Most men, when they turn sixty-five, begin to work on their golf game or some frickin' hobby. I want more victories. I need them, and let's face it—look at the so-called competition—I deserve them. I look back on a life that may be half over, and I worry about what my legacy will be. I can't stop comparing my achievements to those of the men who built General Electric, J.P. Morgan, News Corporation, and the other enduring empires. I am realist enough to admit that to ensure my place in history I am going to need some luck. For much of my life, everyone has wanted something from me. I am so used to being flattered that it takes a real genius to get me to believe it. But let's face it, I let a good number of them make the attempt: deans and presidents of universities, charitable fund-raisers, lawyers, and the ever-present investment bankers. Each category possesses its own techniques and its own fascination.

Other than Doris, who makes a nice living and clearly doesn't love me as Lynda said to "get to your fucking money," the only one I really trusted was Vinnie. Besides Doris, no one understood me like Vinnie did. We discussed my place in the history books several times a week. One of his post-Belandia ideas took a little selling on his part, but after I had thought about it, I had to agree and changed my company's name for only the second time in its history. Let's face it, he was right to point out that a) "Jackpot International" sounds lowbrow, b) it no longer describes what the business does, and c) a company's name should reflect its culture and its personality. The name Ripkin Global Leisure fits all the relevant criteria.

Then, in laying the groundwork for a cover story he was placing about me in *Fortune* magazine, Vinnie persuaded me to add some "color" to a few of my non-business achievements. So, I allowed him to embellish the heretofore unrecognized role I played during the Korean War. And I began doing a few highly visible good deeds, as when I let CARE put some food and blankets on our ships heading to post-hurricane zones.

It was Vinnie, too, who introduced me to Roy Cohn, the power broker who died about four years ago. I thought I knew the political ropes, but through Roy and Vinnie, I took my political operation to a whole new level. At first, I was downright amazed at how little money it took to win the affection of a member of the House of Representatives. A senator or a governor was no big deal either, and pretty soon I knew them all,

Democrats and Republicans, incumbents and challengers. I had to establish a Washington office just to manage the traffic. By now, I am used to dining with kings and presidents.

And presidential aspirants. If I can get the right nincompoop in the White House, I will be more than a historical footnote. Much more. I hate to say it, but a war would likely be a terrific opportunity for greatness! I could bring RGL's full resources to the service of my country. I mean look at the German industrialist, Albert Speer; everyone knows what he did for the Third Reich. Don't get me wrong. I'm not praising Hitler, who we all know was a very bad guy, I'm just saying my know-how and acumen need a larger canvas in order for humanity to recognize my, let's face it, special skill set.

The problems with Vinnie began about a year ago, soon after Doris and I fell in love. The fact that she seemed to dislike him from the outset had nothing to do with it. No, it began when he started being quoted in some of the articles he placed about me. And the next thing I knew, he was mentioning my name on TV as if I was his creation. To my credit, I tried to warn him.

"Vin, I saw you last night on CBS."

"Yeah. Thought it went pretty well."

"I didn't love the part where you talked about our leaving the country for a few years after high school as if it was your idea."

He laughed. Laughed! "It was my idea, pal. Anyway, I'm just trying to raise your profile." He paused for the expected approbation. But not getting it, he continued, "What's wrong? You need someone in that role."

"Not you, Vinnie. That's not what I am paying you for. You're an advisor, an architect, not a spokesman."

But he was too deep into the fun he was having with the Cohn/Trump/Sinatra crowd to register my cautions. The final straw was what I heard him tell Trump at Sammy Davis Jr.'s funeral: "He pretty much does what I tell him; how much do you need?"

The conversation that I could not but have with him took place last week. And it was the saddest one of my life. I invited him to lunch at Le Coq Foutu. Knowing he can get emotional, I decided one super last meal in a public place was a precaution worth paying for. I suppose I was unusually reserved, because no sooner had the tiramisu and cappuccinos arrived when he said:

"OK, Ralph, something's bugging you. What's up?"

"Vin, remember that time, we were around ten, when that huge Irish guy in our class… what was his name?"

"Kevin. Kevin Kelly. Eighth-grade kid. Thought he was tough."

"Right," I said. "He was bullying me, and you kneeled behind him. We didn't need to say anything. Not before. Not after."

"I remember," Vinnie said. "You pushed him over, and we were out of the playground before he hit the ground."

"And we ran all the way to your house looking back once in a while. We raided the fridge. Shared our first-ever beer together."

"Uh huh. Where are you going with this, Ralph?" he asked, beginning to suspect something.

"Vinnie, it's been swell. You've been a great advisor, but Vin, I think I can take it from here."

I ran a tab at the restaurant so there was no need to call for the check. I thought about saying I hope we'll stay friends as I pushed back my chair. But I needed to get out fast because I can be sentimental from time to time, and I didn't want him to see any ambivalence. He was sitting there, his mouth agape as I walked out onto Madison, and I thought to myself, *That was a hard one. But if you're not for yourself, who then will be for you? And if not now, when?*

CHAPTER 6

INTERNAL AUDIT

I had only been at Lehman a couple weeks when my boss, Pensky, the head of Internal Audit, brought me along to the office of a big wheel named Czincosca who ran the Structured Finance department. We arrived on time but had been sitting outside his office tapping our feet at 2:44 p.m. when he finally intercommed his snooty, hoity-toity British-accented, attractive secretary:

"Is my 2:30 here?"

She responded all deferential, like he was some kind of god, "Yes sir, Mr. Czincosca."

From where I sat, I'd been watching him shoot the shit with a guy who laughed ass-kissingly every time he made a joke. All Czincosca had needed to do was get up off his butt and invite us in like a normal human being, but no.

"You can show them in now, Deborah." As we were crossing the threshold, I thought I heard him whisper "... or should we chill 'em another five?" right before the subordinate cracked up again. The secretary, this Deborah, was dressed all business, but you could see, speaking of asses, that hers was world class.

The first time I laid eyes on Jedediah Czincosca, I felt every hair from my tailbone to my neck stand up straight. I knew from his first and only glance in my direction that I had been judged a fat insignificant bean counter. His eyes, as they passed over me, seemed to take note of each bead of the sweat on my forehead, the airplane pillow of fat which encircles the back of my neck, the hair on my knuckles. He was one of these guys who had graduated from the best schools and who probably could have dated any girl he wanted. Custom-tailored everything. Silk tie, all black, embroidered with a highly stylized white and yellow bird. Pearl cufflinks. I wasn't sure whether I had learned from my mother to hate guys like this or whether it was in our DNA. We are decent Italian working-class stock, and I dislike smart-ass fops as much as she does.

Pensky kicked things off with a "Well, Struck Fi had a damn good '88, didn't it? Congratulations."

"Yeah well, you know. Good market conditions." This false modesty made me want to puke. We all knew the markets had sucked.

After stroking him a bit more, Pensky got substantive. "So, I just want to cover a couple routine questions, and then we can let you get back to work."

Czincosca nodded regally: permission granted.

"Could we talk about Wimbledon last June? I see the top two guys from IBM were our guests, but did anyone join you from here? I'm just wondering why the bill was so high for what was essentially a long weekend."

The resentment this evoked was easy to read. Czincosca paused more than a couple beats before answering as if to say, "If you are going to waste my time, I'll waste yours." He drummed his fingers while we all waited. Then, at last, "Happy to answer, of course, but just curious. My group brings in over $100 million a year. Why, pray, are a couple hundred thousand a matter of interest?"

I was just learning the ropes and wasn't sure how Pensky would answer, but that didn't stop me from wanting to jump from my chair and strangle the arrogant prick.

"Routine. You check the little things."

"..."

"Well, Motherwell," and, with a small movement of his head, he indicated the lieutenant, "me, of course, and our wives, the

IBM guys and theirs." He paused, before adding, "That's eight altogether," as if that should explain it all. And when he again didn't see any light bulb go off over Pensky's head, he continued like Pensky was a handicapped student in a first-grade class. "We stayed at the Connaught. Nice hotel. Along with Bill and Betty, Ron and Suzy. We took a private cruise up the Thames to Stratford and back, some tennis lessons from Nick Bollettieri, dinner at Michelin three-stars in the evenings. Round trip for eight on the Concord? Adds up." And then, as if he'd suddenly recalled an incredibly important fact, he hit his head with his palm. "The tickets! Do you have any idea what they're getting for the Men's and Women's Finals these days?"

I wanted Czincosca in the primordial way a mongoose wants a cobra. But I held myself together by tuning out the rest of the conversation, and then I followed Pensky back down to our floor. It took me two years to get primary responsibility for the Structured Finance department audit. By then, Czincosca had created another profit center called the Proprietary Trading Desk, the sole purpose of which was to invest the firm's own capital. This activity too fell under my purview, and, despite having no evidence at the time, my working assumption was he created the Prop Desk to trade on inside information.

I prepared for days in the run-up to my first solo meeting with Czincosca, pouring over trading records. My mother, as well as the nuns and priests who had beaten study habits into me over the years, would have been proud of my rigor. But despite numerous private practice preps, the one thing I couldn't master was Pensky's professional niceties.

"So glad you could stop by," Czincosca began, lying from the start. I was encouraged by this. "May I offer you a cup of coffee? Or is there some form I'd need to fill out first?"

"No, thank you, Mr. Czincosca. But I appreciate the attempt at humor," I replied without smiling.

"What questions can I answer for you today?" he asked, abandoning the soften-him-up strategy.

"Most of them have to do with the Tele-Communications Inc. spin-off."

"Oh, too bad. Motherwell had a conflict. He is point on all the Prop Desk trades. Next time, if you let me know the subject matter in advance, we can be more prepared. But…what's on your mind?"

"Well, Motherwell, if that's who it was, went heavy long on TCI when everyone was running the other way. Then he held the position even as regulatory fear tanked the stock. I'm wondering how he was so confident. It looks as if he knew in advance that TCI was going to announce a spin-off and that the market's fears were unwarranted. And those weren't the only times last year he was uncannily right."

"So? He's a smart guy. That's why I put him in the driver's seat."

"Nobody is that smart."

"Perhaps that's a failure of imagination on your part, Cherubini." The temperature had gotten instantly Arctic.

I stood. "We'll see about that…Czincosca. Let him know I will need some of his time next week." I walked extra slowly toward the door, fantasizing that I would hear his footsteps as he ran to clip me from behind. But he kept his cool, depriving me of a chance to wheel around and deck him.

Our relationship, if you can call it that, deteriorated from there. Each time I spoke with him, he came up with some slippery way of explaining how his group had been able to see infallibly into the future, and I had a growing conviction that I would be doing Lehman a big favor if I could nail this guy for the crook he likely was. Turns out I was a student in Corporate Politics for Dummies while he was teaching the fucking course. Pensky was asked to do the heavy lift.

"I'm sorry about this, Bobby. But I am going to have to let you go," Pensky said, after inviting me into his office one Friday afternoon. His elbow was on his desk, his cheek resting on his hand as he leaned toward me. He seemed relaxed and matter of fact. "These things happen."

"What things?" I asked.

"I guess I'd call it a culture fit problem...Well, you're good on the numbers, but that's only part of the job. People have to feel we are all on the same team. Not just within Internal Audit but also, you know, with the bankers."

I knew Pensky wouldn't do this to me if he didn't have to. It was like Czincosca had clocked him and taken over his body, but pointing that out wouldn't have accomplished anything. He felt bad about it and helped me land a position at the growing hotel chain I've worked at for fifteen years now.

In the hotel business I applied the lesson I learned from my Lehman dismissal: When people like you, it helps you do your job better. From my first day here, I brought forth a general jolliness, which I deployed to convey the right balance between We're-All-On-The-Same-Team and We're-Going-To-Get-To-The-Bottom-Of-This. I began to laugh frequently to put others at ease. And it worked. I have risen to head up the whole Internal Audit department. I'm the Pensky of Belandia!

During the last fifteen years, big changes have taken place. Belandia has enjoyed a huge growth in the number of properties; I've lived through three CFO changes, two major rebranding campaigns, and Jackpot International's takeover of the company. Since Jackpot is a Lehman client, the takeover put me back in touch with my former colleagues...which rekindled my interest in Czincosca and his rotten success. I began a practice of having lunch with friends from the old days, and I was not shy about my suspicions. But I needed better information. A week after stepping on a speculation scheme in Panama, I had a eureka moment. That secretary on thirty-one I used to flirt with, Abigail? She had a mane of long black hair and a horsey face. Chubby like me, but her tits were bigger. I called her for coffee, and we began to meet for a fuck once in a while. By that time, she was working for the Lehman CFO.

I first met Katy in 2004 on a swing through our properties in the Middle East. I'm going to say (even though it's more complicated than that) that I trace the beginning of my problems to her. She was a concierge in our Riyadh property. She hadn't found a life outside the hotel, and I guess I looked like somewhat of a catch, being a hotshot from headquarters and all. I sensed she was bored out of her mind, and when I made my first attempt at flirtation, she responded with an encouragingly neutral ambiguity. I asked her "out" for a drink in the staff lounge on three. It went fast from there.

To say that Katy was better looking than any woman I had ever dated would be an understatement. At five foot seven, she was two inches taller than me, and if you saw us together, "What the fuck?!" would be more likely than, "What a nice couple." I kept pinching myself the whole eight days I was there. With Katy, not only was I unashamed of my pear shape; she convinced me that it (I) was sexy and offered frequent uninhibited proof. Initially, I thought she had no agenda other than physical pleasure and a little positive emotional reinforcement. When she came, she clutched a fold of my stomach fat with one hand and one from my ass with the other, whispering "Bobby" in my credulous ear so convincingly that I knew I had launched her into an ecstatic realm.

But it was much more than her physical beauty and the great sex. She had an honest and open laugh, a vivacious curiosity. She was the daughter of a farm worker, grew up in Iowa in a shack with an outhouse. Her mother cooked with water from a pump. I was sure my own mother would accept her. I was head over heels, and I began to imagine our conjugal life…

the two of us (and baby makes three?) living in a Larchmont Tudor Norman with a small mortgage I could probably secure on excellent terms in this interest rate environment (twenty years at 5 percent per annum with a balloon payment at the end to keep the monthlies manageable?). I'm thinking two-car garage, modest backyard, not more than fifteen minutes from the train station...

My team and I completed our investigation of the suspiciously low Riyadh RevPAR numbers with a solid case against an assistant manager named Fayez Bourdi, reporting to the relevant parties that he and several co-conspirators had been skimming systematically from the mini-bars and jobbing the Pay-Per-View charges. Theirs was a boringly simple scam, so I nailed them before leaving town and was satisfied to learn that in the ensuing weeks, Revenues Per Average Room shot right back up to more typical levels.

Katy and I remained in constant touch. Emails were flying back and forth like orders and confirmations on a trading desk. My long-distance phone bills were going through the roof. For the first time in my life, I felt loved for who I was, deeply accepted, flaws and all, by a woman other than my mother. I broke it off with Abigail at Lehman, telling her that I had fallen in love, but I was sure that my Czincosca suspicions had been adequately conveyed to her boss in the previous months. Katy and I made plans to visit our respective parents. But first we hungrily planned my return to Riyadh.

To travel to the Riyadh Belandia, I needed a decent corporate reason unless I was going to use up vacation credits and, having spent so much time there in the recent past, nothing plausible occurred to me, so best I could do was to schedule a Friday–Sunday stopover on my way to a routine audit in Kuala Lumpur. Before the flight from JFK, I drove to Malden to take my mother out to dinner. By dessert it was clear that I had her support and that she was eager to meet Katy, so when the apple pies à la mode arrived, we turned to the topic of Czincosca.

We'd continued to talk about him, even during my Belandia years. He hadn't come up in a while, but no name was needed when I remarked "You know? I wish even today that I could gut that creep."

There was little chance she'd tell me to let it go, and in fact she didn't. "Me, too. One of your father's few good points? He was big on revenge."

I went straight to Katy's room when I landed, and we made love all weekend. I hid when room service came, probably not fooling anyone. We finally surfaced for air the Sunday of my departure when we went out for dinner at Set Al Sham. The shawarma and kebabs were great, and I waited till after we finished tasting each other's desserts (rosewater rice pudding for her and the umm ali for me). She was wearing a beautiful low-cut yellow dress, but her head and shoulders were covered modestly by a matching shawl.

"Look," I said, as I handed her a simply wrapped little box, "this is for you." When she opened it, she gasped. The ring had a large sapphire in the middle with little diamonds all around. A Jewish friend had introduced me to his pal at Levinson's on Forty-Seventh, where this Moyshe-something sold it to me "wholesale" for $23,000 plus tax. I figured wholesale meant they kept their commission to only four or five thou between them.

"Will you marry me?" I asked. It was the purity of blind love speaking.

"Yes!" she squealed immediately with sheer delight. And being in Riyadh, where a public embrace would have been frowned upon, I took her two hands (in a way so as to hide my hairy knuckles) and gave them each a tender, modest kiss. She put the ring on, and we began talking about parental visits, dates, wedding plans.

"This is happening so fast!" she said, adding, "Which is a good thing! It's perfect! I've never felt this way."

"For me, it was love at first sight," I told her.

"Let's not drag out our engagement," she said, and we agreed on a small ceremony in two months when she would return to the States to meet my mom.

My doubts began to surface before my plane from Riyadh left the airport. It's probably obvious that auditors mustn't take anything at face value. To tell it like it is, I am not only no exception, I am an exceptionally suspicious person. If you inform me that you were out with so-and-so for lunch, it occurs to me that there is a way to check that assertion. It's not that I assume you are lying, just that I wonder if you are telling the truth. My default position is distrust. And then I conjure a whole narrative of what you might have been doing instead of having eaten lunch, which I might take the trouble to verify if my alternative reality seems both plausible and consequential enough.

At least I have no illusions about the extent to which I have incorporated suspiciousness into my way of being. In my daily life, I have learned to mask my doubts about what folks tell me, but there is no doubt that challenging whatever is put forth as true has been, along with my comforting demeanor, a key ingredient of my rise in Belandia's Internal Audit department.

I've wondered where my doubts about others' stories came from. The explanation I arrived at is simple: the from-nowhere paternal infidelity that busted up the Cherubini family when I was twelve. I should have seen the signs. Who throws his underwear in the wash and takes a shower as soon as he walks in the door every night he's out late? In contrast to my dad, I told myself I was an honest, deeply reliable person who would never let my mother down. In contrast to me, many of my classmates cheated on their homework and stole from their parents. This afforded me many chances to observe their alibis and facial expressions when they professed innocence.

When it came to Katy, suffice it to say that, as the too-good-to-be-true reality of my engagement roused my suspicions, I was powerless to resist using the tools available to me to validate her love. I ordered up all her emails from the two years prior to our meeting and all those since. What I found was earth-shattering, and I took the confirmation of my doubts very, very hard. The emails revealed two other liaisons in which she had used endearing language identical to those in her notes to me: We could be so happy together; we are made for each other blah blah blah. If I had only those correspondences to go on, I might have forgiven both her previous romantic disappointments and her inability to invent novel ways of expressing herself.

But then I came upon one to a girlfriend of hers describing me as, first, "The Jolly Ferret" and thereafter simply "The Ferret." In her notes to this Naomi, she had bragged, "The Ferret bought me dinner" and, "I had The Ferret take me to a movie," confessing that she had real hopes for "this one." The night after I had proposed, she wrote "The Ferret bit." And then I found one that said, "The sex has been the hardest part, but repulsive as it is, I think I can make it through the wedding." I couldn't believe she'd been faking it in our lovemaking, and that realization alone destroyed me. The satisfaction of dodging a bullet was scant recompense for the clear-eyed view of myself from the perspective of a beautiful woman who I had wanted to be loved by, one who'd been cynically using my insecurities to entrap me in the coils of conjugality.

From this revelation, I went downhill so fast that if there had been a men's luge for self-destruction, I could have won the gold. Far from losing my appetite, I began to comfort myself with vast quantities of carbohydrates. Salty snacks and sweets of all kinds were my constant companions. Though I calculated that the twenty pounds I gained in the month after breaking it off was only a 7.14 percent delta from my normal two hundred eighty, there was no way to forgive myself for being a fat, unlovable slob. You might say, "Get over it; everyone has romantic disappointments," but for me, whose belief that I could find my way to love and acceptance was already tenuous, this was, in retrospect, the last straw. My previous affairs had given me glimmers of hope, but those eight days in Riyadh had been my full-on Garden of Eden; now having been hurled headlong into an inescapable harsh reality, I was wallowing in my new world of reconfirmed, intensified self-loathing and anger.

But guess what? There was plenty of vitriol left over for my blood feud with Czincosca. I was pretty sure that in addition to cheating on the company, he was having sex with many beautiful women besides his wife, a likelihood which only served to turbocharge my previous efforts. But all my whisperings to former colleagues in Lehman Internal Audit continued to come to naught. One of the most infuriating aspects of the situation was that I couldn't fairly call it a "feud" since my nemesis didn't even know I was throwing punches. The guy seemed untouchable.

Given the breakup with Abigail, I had to find new sources of information and new conduits that would help me sow the seeds of his downfall. I needed to nail him! I kept sending hints to friends at Lehman, but my last tip about the ATT/BellSouth deal announced in March of '06 was a whiff. Even though Czincosca got in big before the announcement, my pals in Audit there, once again, came up dry. Motherfucker!

Meanwhile, back at Belandia, what had been the minor annoyance of a simpleton for a boss became an unbearable insult when Whitney van Dyck, a lateral hire who knew nothing about the hotel business, succeeded the borderline competent Richard ("call me Richard") Plimpton, who retired at the age of forty-nine to spend more time with a family he didn't have.

Whitney ("call me Van"), our three-months-on-the-job-born-to-wealth-Yale-graduate-arrogant-cunt of a chief financial officer let me know that she would appreciate my not "barging-in" on her but rather that Matt, her equally supercilious secretary, would be happy to arrange a meeting any time, as long as I gave them a week's notice. Crises would, of course, be accommodated, but it was understood that pushing the emergency button was a privilege not to be abused. It's undoubtedly true that Whitney's imperious attitude along with her good looks, her intelligence, her self-confidence, and her obvious view that I was a cipher to be put up with as a professional subordinate undeserving of any invitation to her legendary Hamptons cocktail parties, greased the piste of my downward descent.

After I broke up with Katy, I should have sought professional assistance, and I did. Not, however, the talking cure. I mean with psychiatry, you can't just phone it in. I know; I've tried it. There is no substitute for being in the same room as your therapist, an impossibility given my travel schedule. No, the therapy I went for was prostitutes, ever more beautiful, and therefore ever more expensive. As I moved up the prostitutorial food chain, I discovered Platinum World Escorts, a firm with global reach. Ten thousand a night payable in cash, plus a tip of usually another thou.

As my addiction to this sex therapy became more intense, liquidity issues began to emerge. Or, differently put, I was running out of cash. My stock options were worth $700,000 on paper, more or less. But, if you will forgive a bit of off-color humor, unlike with hookers, you can't eat the spread in stock options. Nevertheless, given my reliable work history, B of A was happy to lend me $400,000 at LIBOR plus 8 percent on a recourse basis. My weight remained constant at three hundred give or take as I blew through that sum at the rate of almost $70,000 a month. An eyebrow was raised by my loan officer five months on, but he acceded to my request for another hundie.

Even at my most depraved, I am not without discipline, so I stopped paying for premium porn, cut my Marlboro Lights to two packs a day, eliminated my charitable donations to Fordham, and canceled all my extreme sports magazine subscriptions except for *Kingpin Skateboarding*. Notwithstanding this self-restraint, I was only able to bring my average spend on expert assistance down to $15K per week on average ($17K if you include the hotel rooms, the Perrier-Jouët champagne, and the caviar); so, I wasn't kidding myself. I had become a sexaholic, and without another source of cash, I would soon be Kumaritashvili hitting his final curve.

I called my mother from wherever I was in the world every Sunday at 11 a.m., and she must have heard something disturbing in my voice.

"Bobby, I need to look at you. When can you pay me a visit?"

If she could read me that well on the phone, I knew I needed to get organized before seeing her in person. I told her I was traveling, thus buying a couple weeks. And as far as the Belandia side of things, with my new austerity program, I had two months, easy, to figure something out. During my years in the business, I had gathered quite a database of attempted scams. Of course, the ones I knew about hadn't ultimately succeeded, but they gave me a good sense of what doesn't work, in addition to which I had a number of advantages going for me. First of all, unlike my hapless predecessors, I was at the top of the pyramid, a position which gave me several tools unavailable to them...like a deep knowledge of how cash moved through the chart of accounts.

Second, my liquidity crisis was coming at a propitious time since my once-a-year appearance before the Board Audit Committee would soon remind them of my solid stewardship.

I was scheduled to meet with them on March 10, when the focus of my formal presentation would be my deployment of staff resources in the current year. Then there was to be a discussion of cybersecurity issues. One of the directors, a former Silicon Valley entrepreneur, would, predictably, ask a bunch of show-off questions that I would answer with aplomb, and, in describing my planned audit schedule, I would present myself as a frugal protector of corporate resources, ranking my audits so as to give proper weight to likelihood of breach and magnitude of potential damage. In executive session, they would probably ask how I was getting on with the new CFO. I would have to plant a seed of doubt about her without a full-frontal attack, just to cover my ass if van Dyke took a shot at me in her own confidential moment with the committee.

I needed a plan highly unlikely to be discovered. I poured myself a double of Glenfiddich and thought about the exculpatory disclaimer of Ernst & Young, Belandia's outside auditor in our last 10-K filing. "These consolidated financial statements and financial statement schedules are the responsibility of the Company's management." Yep. The integrity of the numbers underlying the financials was up to us, meaning, mainly, me. By one or maybe two refills later, I concluded that the best way to siphon cash was the old fake invoice ploy but done for amounts that would be rounding errors in some larger context. In a chain growing from a base of fifty-nine hotels, construction projects were recurring, often in new locations, and even if in existing ones, they typically occurred after intervals of at least five years, so while some past suppliers would be involved, there would also be many new ones. Invoices for "fixtures" or "cartage," say, of less than a hundred thousand, I figured, would be unlikely to raise any suspicions. Cairo went off without a hitch. Then Madrid. Warsaw, my biggest score by far, didn't seem to raise any eyebrows. I couldn't feel 100 percent comfortable until we got through the next audit period, but I thought I was good for the foreseeable future.

The professional sex workers notwithstanding, I was delighted to get a call from Abigail. First of all, free is free. Second of all, she was still a promising pathway to helpful information on Czincosca. "Hi Bobby," she began when I picked up, "it's been a long time."

"Yeah," I said. "Still at Lehman? Still working for the CFO?"

"Yeah. But a different one. They needed a 'better communicator.' I'm sure you've noticed. The stock's been falling like a rock."

"Yeah, stock's in the tens; probably means my favorite dick is down to his last few hundred million."

"We should get together. I've got something for you."

"Something—"

"Something that's going to make you happy. I mean, in addition to what makes us both happy."

I couldn't wait, and we agreed to meet at her place, a two-bedroom in the mid-fifties, that very evening. She liked it from behind, which was fine with me, and once we took care of that business, we lay there and smoked cigarettes while she tested my patience. "C'mon baby, gimmie what you've got."

"I just gave you what I got," she said through her neigh-like laugh. I pinched her not too hard. "OK, OK. I was listening in on her calls yesterday, as she likes me to do, when she told your favorite guy that we had a deal with an Asian buyer for the whole company at $25 a share. I can play you the recording."

"$25? Recording?"

"Of course. We record all her calls."

"Go on."

"So, I kept my eyes out for those forms where you have to report your trades."

"16Ds?"

"Yeah."

"And?"

"And sure enough, the next day, namely yesterday, when the stock dropped into the sevens? Your guy swoops in and buys 2500 shares."

"No way. He would never do that small a trade."

"I'm telling you."

"For sure? Czincosca?"

She lit us another cig. And it was then I knew I had him. Hell, they got Capone for tax evasion, not murder. We fucked once more for the road. I could hardly sleep that night. I lay there, my heart pounding as it does when I am about to pounce. The next day, I stormed into my office and slammed the door. I looked at my screen and saw that the Lehman stock price had dropped to half of yesterday's close. I rang Dorothy on the intercom and bellowed, "Get me Sam in Compliance!" Since she didn't respond I added, "Lehman! Lehman Compliance."

"Not available," she came back on, after a beat, to tell me. I looked at my monitor in fascination as the stock continued to plunge. I rang Sam myself this time as well as a few others, but no one picked up. It was like I was yelling about an outstanding parking ticket while they were all falling from the Empire State Building. I was devastated. After all these years, I finally had Czincosca cold, and no one was there to give a shit. I was literally tearing my hair in frustration when my own phone rang. "It's your mother," my secretary told me.

"Hi Bobby, honey."

"Mom, I have him dead to rights, but I can't get anyone to pay—"

"Honey, I have some very bad news."

Bad news? I thought. *What could be worse?*

"There's no great way to say this. Cancer. Lymph nodes. Three months."

I began crying as soon as we hung up, and I couldn't stop. But the phone rang again… insistently. Dorothy must have been away from her desk, so hoping it was Sam, I pulled myself together and picked up. It was, unprecedentedly, Whitney van Dyke herself on the line.

"Come to my office now," she said without preamble. "And bring your Warsaw file."

CHAPTER 7

COLLATERAL DAMAGE

IN 1971, BEFORE THE BREAKUP, IN THE DAYS WHEN AT&T WAS STILL MA BELL and seniority counted for something, Dennis O'Mahony chose Harvard Square. Nobody was better at troubleshooting, and Harvard itself came to rely heavily on his way with a phone. When Dennis arrived, the problem was as good as solved. But truth be told, Dennis arrived no more than necessary. Not that he was lazy. He simply had a deep appreciation for service sector realities: Your boss has no reason to refrain from working your ass off, and the amount of attention the clientele requires expands with the slightest encouragement, so, if you're too available, your time is devalued just as surely as, in the manufacturing sector, an oversupply of widgets drives down their price.

Dennis was good at fixing phones but a true genius at surfing safely through the sea of forms constantly created by AT&T's management. At the end of a day, he would fill out his Time On Site Analysis (or whatever crap name they were giving it) and listen to his supervisor, likely a kid just old enough to shave, give him an eager-beaver talk about Corporate's decision to "get much more granular about repair time." It was all bull, but going along with the latest you-can't-manage-what-you-can't-measure fad seemed a small price to pay for a few extra hours a week of freedom.

Fiona, his childhood sweetheart and wife of five years was similarly underchallenged at work. She was an "account manager" at Celebrity Tours, the small travel agency near their home in Norwood, Massachusetts. In the office window's large poster, under the words "YOU TOO CAN ENJOY THE CRUISE OF A LIFETIME FOR FOURTEEN DAYS AT A MERE $395 PER PERSON, SATISFACTION GUARANTEED," a well-known plumber from their blue-collar community hit golf balls off the stern of *The Fantasy*, a ship with two pools, three restaurants, and hundreds of video games. Fiona had been happy to get work shortly after their wedding, but now she was bored, and time was weighing heavily on her. A child, she didn't care whether it was a boy or a girl, would be the solution, but she and Dennis had been trying, and endless doctor visits had failed to produce the hoped-for result.

Fiona was an observant Catholic. Her religion helped her through the monthly disappointments and the tedium of her workdays. She looked forward to church, where every Sunday the comfort of a society that included her parents, siblings, cousins, aunts, uncles, nephews, nieces, and in-laws awaited her. And there, too, she found the true solace of prayer. For she believed in the saving power of Our Lord Jesus Christ. Dennis's abandonment of the faith in favor of Taoism, an exotic Eastern religion, had produced a breach with both her side of the family and his—one which Dennis must have predicted and in some sense sought.

At Saint Christopher's, she was forced to endure expressions of "concern" from parishioners she suspected of using her husband's truancy to burnish their own self-regard. She was long out of excuses for Dennis. He'd had the flu, work emergencies, trips to sick relatives too many times. She had been reduced to agreeing they should all pray for his soul. Perhaps someday he would return, miraculously saved, to the fold.

In prayer, she struggled not to think about the probability that he, right then, was getting high on marijuana and doing tai chi in the woods behind their bungalow. At least he no longer referred in her presence to the Eucharist as The Hokey Pokey. Although

God knows what jokes he made with his Harvard friends or his other godless buddies when she was out of earshot.

The tedium at Celebrity Tours was tolerable, relieved as it was by her evenings and weekends with Dennis. But, two weeks before her thirty-third birthday, everything changed. They left the doctor's office in a daze with words like "motility" and "polycystic" in their ears. It was now clear that the chances of them producing a child together were remote. Few words were spoken on their ride home. They limited their dinner talk to Bobby Orr and the Bruins, but after they'd cleaned up, prepared the percolator for next morning's coffee, and turned out the lights, Dennis stopped Fiona in the dark hallway that separated the kitchen from the bedroom and brought her close. "I'm so sorry, Fee," he whispered in her ear.

"It's no one's fault," she said. "It must be God's plan." But the injustice of it made it difficult to reconcile her faith with her new reality.

"We'll be alright," he reassured her. "We need to just go with the natural flow."

"I wanted it so much," she lamented for the two of them.

After the unwelcome news, the Celebrity job came to seem especially intolerable. Even beforehand she had been asking herself, *What do I need this aggro for?* Unfortunately, the answer was clear. To live in Norwood, they needed the income, and most of the available alternatives paid less or were much longer commutes.

The Celebrity clientele was OK once they actually got on the darned ship, but holding their hands while they vacillated between one package or another was wearing thin. Just last week, Ann Murphy—who, since her husband had been named Norwood Fire Department supervisor, had begun putting on airs—made her go through the whole rigmarole for a two-week luxury deal on the *Monte Carlo*, only to settle, as Fiona knew she would, on the *Fantasy*'s basic economy cruise. By now she and Dennis had been on every one of the ships so many times that the discount benefit, originally a "perk," had become an obligation. Moreover, her boss's halitosis had gotten dramatically worse. She doubted it was her imagination.

She would have raised the issue of moving to a less expensive locale with Dennis, but he was set in his ways, and she thought that her idea about moving to a cabin on a lake in Maine could be destabilizing to her husband, whose laid-back persona was a thin veneer. So, one Sunday afternoon after they'd made love, she made another suggestion she'd been toying with: "What do you think about our getting a dog?" He opened his eyes to say, "Let me think about it," before falling into a deep slumber. She wasn't sure if he would remember.

Dennis's workdays adhered to a pattern with few variations. After a cup of black coffee, he would sit in his truck, smoke his first joint of the day, and read *The Globe* sports section. He might well have been present at the actual Patriots, Bruins, or Red Sox game and therefore in an excellent position to critique the writers. Their seats were no better than his and their analysis far inferior. Extrapolating from the sports writers' failings, he was certain that reporters for the Business, Metro, and front sections were equally biased, lazy, prone to oversimplification, or suborned by their future employers.

On the Monday morning after Fiona floated her dog idea, having completed a thorough reading of the paper, he continued his project of learning to roll a jay with one hand and thought he almost had it. Then, around noon, after going through the motions—splicing a wire or two, testing a connection—he walked over to Jimmy's Bar & Grill, a windowless sub-street-level joint near the Square where plumbers, carpenters, electricians, construction workers, and day laborers came for a beer. As always, he brought a book.

When students wandered in looking for a connection with "real people," a redhead in dungarees and an AT&T shirt reading a book might attract attention. Dennis never started a conversation, but, if a gownie had enough curiosity to speak to him, he might put his reading aside. Who were these kids who had been selected to lead a privileged life? What did they know that he didn't? Although he was initially fascinated to learn about their boarding schools, European vacations, Picassos, country clubs...the stories soon got old. With the last book of *The Alexandria Quartet* face down in front of him, he was thinking about Fiona's dog idea and polishing off a beer when a young man sidled over. The guy was wearing chinos, a polo shirt, and glasses with thick black frames; since he was also carrying a book bag, he was undoubtedly a student. Older than an undergrad, probably business school, his eyes shone with the ambition typical of his type. "Hi. Jed Czincosca," he began. "What are you reading?

"Durrell," Dennis replied duo-syllabically. He was preoccupied and not particularly in the mood.

"Mind?" the young man asked, turning the book over. "Oh, *Clea*. My favorite. Buy you a beer?"

Things were delicate with Fiona, and Dennis knew that she would appreciate him getting home. He stood up slowly. "Thanks. Gotta scoot. I'm usually here around noon," he said, leaving a generous tip for Billy and walking up the four steps into the sunlight.

A dog? What the hell. Could make sense.

The very next day Dennis was reading *The Way of the Tao* when Jed strode into the bar like he was pleased to be on time for an appointment.

"Taoism," Jed commented, again turning the cover to read

the title as he sat down on the stool next to Dennis. "You're into Lao Tzu?"

"All in."

"You're a Taoist?" Jed asked, looking slightly surprised. "Had you for a Catholic."

"Well, wrong. Catholics try too hard. You seem pretty wound up, which I assume means you're from one of those try-hard religions."

"Jewish. Sort of. And yes, I don't think there's anything wrong with trying hard. If you want something, you have to work for it."

This could be an interesting experiment, Dennis thought, catching Jimmy's eye and holding up two fingers. Given the disappointment at home, beginning a new friendship might not be the worst idea in the world. When the Millers arrived and he started to explain Wu Wei, the concept of doing nothing, going with the flow, Jed interrupted.

"No disrespect, but I took a course on comparative religion, I'm familiar with the concept—"

"You may well be," Dennis said. They could hear Johnny Pesky from the TV at the other end of the dark beery room commenting on another losing Red Sox game. Dennis slanted his glass, watched the beads of condensation roll down. "But are you really capable of letting go?"

"Honestly, Dennis. I'm not even sure I know what 'letting go' means."

"Ever smoked weed?"

"No. I'm on a path to a career where, marijuana being illegal and all…" he trailed off. Dennis put a couple of fives on the bar. "Come with me."

When they arrived at Dennis's truck, Dennis helped Jed to push aside the wires, pliers, socket covers, and technical devices strewn around the passenger side and dashboard. "Hold it in as long as you can," Dennis instructed as soon as Jed had gotten used to the idea that they were going to break the law in an official AT&T vehicle. After several puffs each, they fell into a discursive discussion of Freud, Einstein, and the meaning of life. And then they sat there in the ambient smoke, staring through the windshield at people with book bags buying newspapers and candy bars, petting the vendor's cat at the Harvard Square subway kiosk.

"You see what I mean?" Dennis finally asked, breaking the silence, looking at his guest through the wisp curling upward from the roach.

"You know when Alexander Graham Bell completed the first phone call?" Jed giggled so lazily it sounded like the laughter equivalent of a drawl. "I doubt he was happier than I am now. The ambition, the anxiety? Still there, but they're like fires I'm looking down at from twenty thousand feet." But what he looked at was his watch. "Whoops. Class on regression analysis. Fifteen minutes." Dennis leaned across to open the door. Jed appeared to be almost skipping as he walked down Mt. Auburn Street toward the B-school campus across the river.

That afternoon, Dennis, too, was in a good mood, marred only somewhat by a job that required a complicated two-hour change-out of a switch in the musty unair-conditioned Langdell Library basement. But he continued to mull on his wife's idea. Unlike Fiona, he had a life outside of Norwood, one which had produced a new friend. But Fiona? He worried that Jesus wasn't enough to bear the load of her disappointment. *Something to take care of? Probably do her some good*, and that evening after punching out and thinking about breeds as he drove home, he walked in the door and said to Fiona, "Sure."

"Sure, what?"

"Sure, let's get one. How about a Great Dane? They look scary, but they're as sweet as your peach cobbler."

"I think they only live seven, eight years."

"You like puppies; when he dies, we'll get another one. They're supposed to be easy to housebreak."

The adoption of Lester a couple months after the doctor's conclusive infertility news did not alter Dennis's workdays. But on many lunch breaks, his new student companion showed up at Jimmy's. And another change was his routine at the end of the day. Instead of stopping at the Belfry to down a few with his Norwood buddies, he headed straight home. And what a joy it was to light up and liberate Lester for a romp in the woods. At dinner he and Fiona invariably discussed Lester's diet, his misdeeds, his development, his intelligence level (extraordinary for a Great Dane), his exercise regimen, and in general, the quality of his days. As the dog grew, he was presumed to have valuable opinions and insights.

Fiona never took to Dennis's upwardly mobile young men but put up with the intrusions for his sake. Students came and went. Before Czincosca she never saw any of them more than once. But then, with him, Dennis broke precedent by inviting him to stay for dinner after one of their cannabis walks in the woods. She served a simple meal of ham hocks, cabbage, and baked potatoes. "I am so pleased you invited me, Mrs. O.," Jed began, as if she had. And as if she had granted him permission to mangle her last name.

"You can call me Fiona," she said, hoping he'd leave early enough for her to watch *The Johnny Carson Show*. Jonathan Winters was to be his guest for the evening, and she loved Winters' nee nee na na na na nu nu schtick.

"Well, Fiona, just so you know, I am a huge fan of your husband. And I hope we, too, can become friends."

"I am sure we will," she replied, glancing over at Lester, who was observing her closely, his huge head on his paws. She wished he hadn't seen her telling a white lie.

"And I just want to say that this food is delicious! Was it your mother who taught you to cook like this?" He was simply trying to be nice, but his every word rankled. Perhaps it was his designer haircut?

After she served the peach cobbler with Häagen-Dazs ice-cream, Dennis lit up a joint, and the two men began passing it back and forth. When she excused herself to wash the dishes, their guest's offer to help struck her as unmasculine. By the time Dennis came upstairs to join her and Lester in the bedroom, she was almost asleep. But she sat up to say, "Did you see the way Lester looked at uh, you know—"

"No, I don't. What are you talking about?"

"You know, your friend Jeb."

"Jed, for Christ's sake. How many times have I introduced you to this guy?" She hated it when he said hell or used Christ words.

"OK, Jed then. The way Lester looked at him suspiciously." She turned her eyes toward Lester for confirmatory support. But he clearly didn't want to get involved and chose the moment to reposition himself for a look out the dormer window at the fireflies.

"Jesus, Fee. What is there to be suspicious about?"

"I don't know yet. But I could tell from Lester's reaction that your buddy was only pretending to like dogs."

"Seriously? Well, then he's a hell of an actor! He couldn't stop petting him." And he turned toward the Dane, "Am I right pal?" The sound of Dennis's voice elicited a glance, but Lester was in firefly land.

Fiona seized on Lester's unresponsiveness. "See! He knows you're wrong but doesn't want to hurt your feelings. And, also, what do you need these hoity-toity Harvard boys for? Are we supposed to be grateful another rich kid comes out slumming to Norwood?"

Dennis was furious at her misinterpretation of what Lester really meant, to say nothing of the put-down itself. "Well, Jesus fuckin' Christ, that shows how little you know. Jed is from a working-class Chicago family. He earns his own goddamned tuition money."

"I won't speak with someone who takes the Lord's name in vain," she said, turning away from him and pulling the covers over her head. He grabbed a blanket and left to sleep on the couch.

In the truck, the woods, and sometimes just walking by the river but never again in their home, Dennis gave Jed many opportunities to absorb his take on the issues of the day. Dennis was "for" the US in the Cold War, but, if forced to choose, he would rather the Bruins win the Stanley Cup. John Kennedy was a mafia-loving power-crazed sex maniac who had likely screwed Marilyn Monroe to death. A bunch of self-serving capitalist plutocrats ran Wall Street, this last May's stock market plunge being Exhibit Number One.

Jed didn't want to argue. "I've been around this mulberry bush with my Marxist brother. In the world we have…not the one we might want…once surplus value has been created, it must be rationally allocated. That's where Wall Street comes in."

"If Wall Street was, maybe, more civic minded—" Dennis said laconically.

"For sure—" Jed replied with the same dismissive agreement as he might have to "Nice day."

Yom Kippur of 1975 fell on a Sunday, and at dinner that evening Dennis was in an expansive mode. He and Jed had spent most of the day smoking up, with Lester in tow, in the woods. That evening, although Dennis was well aware of what he chose to think of as Fiona's "reservations" about Jed, he was attempting to soften her view with a few Jed stories. Even by dessert, he had failed to notice she had hardly spoken.

"More coffee?" she asked, thinking of ways to redirect the conversation.

"No thanks. You know, Jed seemed extraordinarily stoned today, and when I mentioned it, he told me he was fasting."

"Well, that's one of the more positive things I've heard about him."

"And I was surprised, too, so I said to him, I said 'I thought you weren't religious.' And you know what he said?"

Fiona pursed her lips; confident she wouldn't have to wait long.

"He said, 'What does religious have to do with it? I'm just hedging my bets.'"

"'Do you always hedge?' I asked him. 'Always,' he said. 'Except when the outcome is 100 percent predictable.'"

"You know what honey?" she interrupted. "I know you like him, but, frankly, I really don't need to hear another—" but she stopped herself. Lester's head was cocked empathically in Dennis's direction. *He looks unusually glum, don't you think?* Lester seemed to suggest. She changed tack: "Is something bugging you, honey?" she asked.

"He's leaving town to seek his fortune." Once again, Lester had hit the nail on the head. "Well, you can stay in touch." She hoped not. "And there are other smart young men you can hang out with."

Fiona needed several hours less sleep than Dennis, but he liked her to be at his side, so she often lay there twisting her hair until he dozed off, only then tiptoeing downstairs to read a book or listen to *CBS Radio Mystery Theater* on the radio. "I couldn't agree more!" she told herself the very first time she heard Carl Sagan explain the high probability of other intelligent life forms in the universe. And the next day during lunch break, she drove her '65 Chevy over to the Norwood Public Library to take out several books on the subject.

That night, she read till three in the morning. She totally bought into von Däniken's thesis that extraterrestrials had visited the earth many times in human history. There was no doubt about it: the crop patterns, the unsolved UFO sightings, the archeological finds. The government cover-ups were so blatant it was amazing they'd been able to pull the wool over everyone's eyes. However, on the one occasion she dropped a hint at breakfast that higher life forms "walk among us," Dennis greeted the thought with derision, and it put her in a bad mood all day. Discussing the topic with him was as big a waste of time as mentioning her fantasy of leaving town. She needed no further input from him to help her think these things through. She was on her own, and as her studies took her ever deeper into the subject of extraterrestrial life, she became unshakably convinced.

Unfortunately, her conviction made her uncomfortable. *How can I reconcile this with my faith? It's probably wise to see Father Dinkins about it.* And when she couldn't stand the stress anymore, that's just what she did.

"Forgive me, Father, for I have sinned."

"Tell me, my child. Have you sinned in thought or in deed?"

"Father, I have come to believe that we are not God's only divine creation."

"The Bible tells us that God made many other creatures when He created the earth."

"I mean intelligent life; like us, only better," she heard Father Dinkins breathing behind the latticed opening, but he did not speak, so she went on, "...and that Jesus himself may have been an extraterrestrial."

This was not one the white-haired clergyman had heard before, and a very long silence ensued. "God works in mysterious ways, my child," he responded at last. "Today's Church has room for novel theories. As long as you believe in the Father, the Son, and the Holy Spirit, you have nothing to atone for. However, as a precaution, I shall ask you to say ten Hail Marys."

"Thank you, Father."

"And tonight in the shower? Sing one Salve Regina." As she opened the confessional door to walk out into the nave, she heard him muttering to himself.

Once she had what she could interpret as the Church's blessing, a huge weight was lifted from Fiona. She was free to seek the truth wherever it lay, and she found reference to extraterrestrial life in many publications. But her obsession attained a whole new level when she was throwing out the trash one evening. Her eye fell upon an advertisement in *The Globe's* classified section: "Seeking Connection with Fellow Believers. They walk among us. PO Box 41932, Sundown Springs, Arizona." The idea of being in touch with others at her level of understanding sent a deep involuntary tremor through her body. Finally, she would have other people she could communicate with.

As Lester grew from a puppy through middle and old age, the excitement of what became her nightly correspondence animated her days. She made sure that she was the one who always picked up the mail, and she hid the letters, along with a few key reference books, in a part of their closet where Dennis never looked. Having learned from "the community" what the best means of making contact were, she told Dennis that the pink light she kept in the window for months was there for good luck. She was sure she'd chosen the correct shade, and it had flickered encouragingly once or twice, but it never worked. Neither did any of the frequencies on the machine she purchased from Adaptive Sound Technologies. She would have left it going during the day on the theory that her nightly signaling time of between 11 p.m. and 1:30 a.m. was the dead zone for ETs, but she could tell it drove the dog nuts. On a cruise they took in '79, she dropped a note in a bottle off the deck. ("You can trust me. Fiona O'Mahony 532 Elm Street, Norwood, Massachusetts, 02062.")

At seven, Lester died of old age. They had seen the day coming, but it didn't make the loss any easier. They buried him in his favorite glen, and before the last soil covered his inert form, she slipped a small laminated piece of paper under his paw commending him to the attention of the higher beings she knew had the power to ease his path. It was months before they could even think about another dog.

In 1984, with their second Lester getting old, Fiona was promoted to office manager when George Safidas seized the occasion of Celebrity's merger with Timeless Voyages to retire. She never sought the position, and now, in addition to the customers' déjà-vu demands, she had forms to fill out for the new corporate parent. Her ET life and her time with Dennis helped her maintain her sanity. But a slow-motion collision was headed their way from Dennis's world, and she was worried about him. Like the death of their first Lester, the fact they'd seen the government breakup of AT&T coming made it no less of a shock when it happened. The very year of the Celebrity takeover, Ma Bell was swept into the competitive mainstream as if telecommunications were just another business. Suddenly, Dennis was no longer working for The Phone Company; he was working for one of its progeny, NYNEX, the neologistic Regional Bell Operating Company. And the veneer of his Taoist placidity began to show cracks. No amount of cannabis or tai chi stopped his raging at the "incredibly fucking stupid" bust-up.

The new NYNEX CEO was an acolyte of General Electric's "Neutron" Jack Welch, famous for vaporizing workers while leaving plant facilities intact, and Dennis was finding even the modest amount of work he was obliged to do ever more of an imposition. Like Fiona, Dennis had new forms to complete. And the incursions on his freedom in the form of corporate brainwashing were intensifying. Seminars on "boundarylessness" and "stretch goals" were trickling down to the worker level, engendering varying degrees of irritation and ridicule among Dennis and those few old timers who harbored no dreams of climbing corporate or union ladders.

In the last three months alone, Dennis had received one memo on how proper dress can yield "meaningful bottom-line impact," one on haircut requirements, and a number on quality assurance in that new Six Sigma language they had all been forced to learn. He had made his bed and had been lying in it for over twenty years. His pension had vested, but having waded through the Plan Alternatives Brochure, he calculated that if he quit right then, he would only receive a thousand a month. They were trapped.

Thank God they each had coping mechanisms. Dennis's was a series of new acolytes who listened to his sermons on living in harmony with the universe...before they left to turn their education into money. Fiona had snipped from *Down East Magazine* and secreted away some photographs of Maine lakes, but it was her life on the new "internet" which kept her sane. By '94 Fiona had become well-known on www.ufo.com, where her handle was "T-Bel." Dennis would have been shocked to learn that she was the leader of a school of thought known as Extra-Cathlo-Terrestrialism. As T-Bel she took on those benighted souls who couldn't see the aliens in their own backyards and who accordingly limited themselves to sending unanswered rocket and radio messages into outer space. Rejecting their ignorance, she had over the years carried on correspondence with a number of the more like-minded.

When they first appeared on her screen as Bo and Peep, T-Bel had found the Heaven's Gate leaders easy to talk to and seemingly in close agreement with her own views. But after the "ChoirMaster" changed his name to "Ti" and Peep changed hers to "Do," she found them increasingly doctrinaire. Fiona's own reputation in the ET community grew, based in part on the attacks directed at her by Ti. She was accused of being a "passivist" at a critical juncture when action was required. According to Ti, T-Bel was patient to a fatal fault, leaving it up to her "little green men" to manifest themselves when the true extraterrestrial would never do so unless one proved one's worthiness by "paying the ultimate price." As a devotee of an "imbecilic" way of thinking, T-Bel had come to represent for the Gaters (as she scornfully called them) a dangerous deviant.

For Dennis, when "Lucent" was carved out of AT&T in '96 as a separate equipment manufacturer with its own angry asshole of a corporate symbol, it was damn near the last straw. His days became too unpleasantly complicated for a fifty-nine-year-old. All kinds of equipment were being connected to the phone system. Customer dissatisfaction had become a quality-of-life issue. It seemed like he was calculating his monthly pension on an almost hourly basis. It came to a little under $2,000 a month. Fiona would certainly want to keep working at Celebrity, but even so, they really wouldn't be able to make ends meet in Norwood. And knowing how little Fiona liked change, Dennis determined to avoid sharing his escapist thoughts with her until he had a plan worked out.

The day Lucent stock began to trade in the public markets, Dennis skipped the company-wide seminar on Improving Your Work Habits and sat on a barstool at Jimmy's reading *Siddhartha*. At about 1 p.m., in his peripheral vision, he saw a couple of kids in polo shirts grab a seat at the end of the bar. As always, he remained prepared, were they to express curiosity, to hold forth on some aspect of Taoist thought…like spontaneity and the Three Treasures.

He still loved watching the eyes of these would-be CEOs widen as he explained how he had detached from all of his desires. Often, they would buy a drink for him. But after checking the "hobnobbed-with-hoi-polloi" box, they invariably repaired to their own world. These particular two tossed down their book bags and immediately launched into a stage-whispered conversation that Dennis couldn't help but hear over reruns of the previous night's Patriots game.

"I can't believe they took Simmons."

"He's not dumb."

"But $125K a year?"

"That's standard now, dude. And that's before bonuses."

"How much is a bonus, do you figure? Ballpark?"

"Could be another fifty easy. And get this. They're handing him a $30K 'moving allowance!'"

"Get the fuck out of here!"

"Yeah, no shit. Lehman is rolling in it."

"Well, here's to your getting an offer from Bear."

At this point, the young men clinked glasses and dropped their conversation into the register reserved for talking about women. Dennis rose from his chair, tucked *Siddhartha* into his windbreaker and, nodding to Jimmy, walked past the snickering students and out the door.

The afternoon sun, always harsh upon emergence, made his eyes water as he stepped onto the sidewalk. Pulling his cap down over his eyes, he ducked into the phone booth across from the Crimson Corner newsstand and placed a call to Information.

Four minutes of hold-music later, a British woman picked up the line, "Jed Czincosca's office, Elena speaking. How may I help you?"

"Hiya, Elena. Dennis O'Mahoney from Boston."

"Hello, Mr. O'Mahoney."

"Hi. Uh, I was hoping to speak to the man himself. Is he in? I'm an old friend of his. From Harvard."

"Just a moment, Mr. O'Mahoney. I'll see whether he's available."

The hold music started again and continued long enough for Dennis to trance out completely by the time Jed picked up. "Dennis?"

"Jed! Good to hear your voice! It's been ages!"

"Is everything all right?"

"Oh sure, sure."

"Fiona's okay?"

"Same as always. And your wife?"

"Amanda and the boys are great."

"Great! Great to hear. Now, Jed, I have a little issue, and I don't want to waste your time, so I'll get straight to it."

"Alright."

Although it was only fifty degrees outside, Dennis felt a drop of perspiration on his forehead. "Normally I wouldn't bother you about something like this, but I'm thinking about making a change, a big change. Now, I've put enough away to cover a rainy day, but I want to be sure we have enough—"

"Are you asking for investment advice?"

"Mmmm. I want to put all our savings in one place where it's working for us, and I don't have to think about it."

While he waited, Dennis heard what sounded like an eraser tapping on a hard surface. "So, I don't generally make recommendations of individual stocks, but I will just say that, personally, my largest position is shares of Lehman Brothers. The financial sector will have its ups and downs, but finance is a growth industry. Lehman is as close to a sure thing, in the long run, as you can get."

"Really?"

"I can't promise you'll get rich quick."

"I'm not interested in that."

"But if you want a safety net for you and Fee with some dividend income and growth, well, that's what I'd suggest."

"Thanks, Jed, that's terrific. That's just what I needed. They're not working you too hard over there?"

"Just hard enough."

"Still smoking that reefer?"

"If that word refers to an illegal substance, I feel compelled to say no at this point. But let's get together again one of these days."

"Let's."

"Stay loose."

"You too."

Dennis hung up the phone just as he felt a vibration at his hip. He was being paged by the office. He sighed and picked up the phone again.

On the morning of March 27, 1997, when Fiona saw *The Boston Globe* headline "39 in Cult Suicide, Trying to Reach Spaceship," she was so shaken she spilled her coffee on the front section and had to sponge it before she could read the article to the end. It was indeed Heaven's Gaters. Her wows, gollies, and gees got no attention from Dennis who was deep into a sports section article about the Celtics 92–105 loss to the Bullets. At the Belfry, everyone was talking about it, but Dennis was preoccupied with the issue of how to sell his nearly complete retirement scheme to Fiona. He added his vote to the unanimous verdict that they were a bunch of kooks and went home early.

At dinner Fiona didn't raise the topic. She needed to talk to someone she could trust. But she was not sure she dared let her guard down to Dennis. After Dennis fell asleep, Fiona remained awake for hours communicating with her followers. So, by the second morning of sensational reporting, she knew the details before reading the paper. *The Globe* revealed that most of the followers of Ti and Do were middle aged or older, that most of them had packed five dollars in quarters, toothbrushes, and other items potentially useful in the planned rendezvous…and that the Heaven's Gate men had been castrated. She pushed the first page in his direction and asked, "Have you been hearing about this?"

"Uh huh," he said, but when he read the castration part he was moved to comment. "Now that's commitment."

"What is, hon?"

"Voluntary castration."

"Could you pass the pepper? I don't think they made it."

"Made what?"

"The link-up. You know. With the ship…if there was one."

"What ship? What do you mean if there was one?" Dennis was staring at Fiona, his mouth and eyes wide open.

"You know. The spaceship, and anyway it's a sin to kill yourself, even for very good reason."

"Fee, what the hell are you talking about?"

"I am talking about thirty-nine people who do not get how these things really work."

"Hah! You can sure say that again!" At this point Dennis believed that he and Fiona were agreeing that castrating yourself, grabbing five buck's worth of quarters, and taking your own life as a way to link up with some creatures from outer space was insane. He hadn't figured out that his wife of thirty years harbored a well-researched, unshakable conviction that higher beings were all around, routinely visiting the Earth to intervene in human affairs, and that the "right" approach to connecting with them was to understand "their ways," not to take God's law into your own hands. Fiona didn't say anything of this, but she folded and unfolded her napkin enough times that Dennis was finally compelled to ask, "Something wrong, Fee?"

"Oh no, no, no," she said, aligning the angles of her silverware. "I just feel sorry for them. Those nuts have bought themselves a one-way ticket to hell." And with that, she popped up, kissed Dennis on the cheek, patted their fourth Lester, and headed toward the carport. "I knew they were idiots soon after I met them. Bye, hon."

"What do you mean 'met them'?" he called out after her. But she was off. Clearly didn't want to talk about it. When the door closed, Dennis called in sick, rolled a couple of joints, and invited Lester to a long walk.

Dennis had known Fiona since he was twelve and she was ten. He still remembered the first time he had seen her. Sister Mary and Sister Theresa were turning a double Dutch rope for the fourth-grade girls who waited in line to charge in and chant about strawberry shortcake. Fiona had those mischievous eyes that flashed in the sun as her pigtails bounced and her pug nose crinkled with concentration. In that first moment he knew, though he couldn't have put it in words, that her effervescence would be the perfect counterpoise to his somber detachment. He was able to initiate the start of their friendship almost immediately but had to wait several years before she would think of him as a boyfriend. His courtship continued after she graduated from high school, and they waited several years before she allowed him to slip the ring on her finger. At first, they had done everything together: cooking, movies, crossword puzzles, long walks, sporting events, cruises. But now, though they ate together and made love weekly, he was worried about whether things were on a sound footing between them.

When Dennis and Lester Four entered the woods behind their house, Lester was moved by the humming energy of late spring to rediscover his younger self. He bounded gamely a short distance ahead and barked at something, then trotted arthritically back. As Dennis lit up, he figured this Lester to be about eighty-four dog years old. He had become like his master, a creature merely going through the motions, now no longer chasing after what he didn't really want to catch. In a clearing, Dennis stopped to do his tai chi. Ever more slowly, with a control that gave way to a letting go, he turned and turned until his own pulse and that of the forest were singing together. He forgot he was sweating, didn't notice Lester's boredom.

Once finished, he was hungry, as he had foreseen he would be. But knowing he would think better on an empty stomach, he had packed nothing except the two blunts, the second of which he proceeded to light as he continued his walk. He had known Fiona was different from the moment he first laid eyes on her.

But what the hell did she mean "met them"? *Where could she have ever crossed paths with these lunatics? She must have been referring to the internet. But "met them" implies more than just looking at some website. She must be into it pretty good if she has met, even virtually, those Heaven's Gate nuts. What the hell is going on with her?*

He was barbecuing a couple of T-bones from Star Market when she came in that evening.

There was a bottle of Chianti on the table, rutabaga to go with the fresh bread from Skippy's, and a Caesar salad. When it came time for dessert, he passed her a piece of his homemade strawberry shortcake (her favorite) and began, "Um, Fee, just thought I'd ask, but you seem to know a lot about that Heaven's Gate crowd."

"Yeah, been in touch with them for years. Always thought they were a bit unhinged."

"Years? A bit?" Dennis struggled to stay calm. "And what were you in touch with them about?"

"Extraterrestrial life. I didn't need for them to commit mass suicide to know they were nuts."

Dennis smiled with relief. "Yeah. Nuts without nuts," he chuckled. "And all so's to meet some little green men. I mean, extraterrestrials, give me a break."

She glared at him as if he'd suggested a second crucifixion of Jesus.

"What? What'd I say?" he blurted.

The ice was breaking, and he was in freezing water over his head. As she explained her thinking on intergalactic travel, the origins of the pyramids, and how to decode crop writing, he felt like he was grabbing edges and not getting any closer to shore. Sometimes you just have to listen, he admonished himself. At first, as she spoke, he thought, *I am married to the Unabomber. Every sentence has its own internal logic, but really? We're surrounded by creatures from outer space who walk the earth? You think you know someone…*

"Fee, I gotta tell you," he heard himself saying, "I'm here for you baby, but I think you may need some help."

She sat for a moment, staring, her jaw muscles working like she was chewing on leather. But then she jumped up, grabbed Lester's leash, fastened it brusquely to his collar, and, neglecting to put on a hat or scarf, began to pull him out the door. Lester was obviously nervous, looking back at Dennis over his shoulder while Fiona whispered something to him that Dennis couldn't hear. Dennis had ample time to put the kitchen back to rights during their unusually long walk. For two days he and Fiona spoke only through Lester who, by the end of day one, had something to say about their goings on in the form of a steaming deposit in their bedroom.

This is clearly not a great time to raise the topic of a big move, Dennis thought to himself. *It would be very unfair to suggest that she should give up the support she obviously needs from this community.* At breakfast on day three, Fiona turned to Lester: "Tell Mr. Know-It-All that just because a person can't prove something does not mean that she is crazy." Lester seemed to have paid such intelligent attention to her words that when he turned his black head to Dennis, whimpering as if to say, "She has a point," he half expected the dog to speak these very words.

"You are right, of course," he admitted without the benefit of canine assistance. "Just because you can't see something doesn't mean it isn't there."

Fee searched Dennis's eyes for any flicker of facetiousness. "Without proof either way, why should we assume we're alone?" She challenged him.

"Good point," said Dennis.

"It's actually a pretty arrogant assumption, if you think about it."

"Absolutely."

Sensing sincerity, Fiona softened. "You know there's a satellite that's been orbiting the earth for three hundred thousand years?"

"No kidding?"

"Nobody knows how it got there, but it's been detected by NASA multiple times."

"Who knows?" Dennis reflected as she went on. "Science has its limits."

So, when she finished explaining about the Black Knight and the 1963 cover-up involving astronaut Gordon Cooper, he went for it: "Lester's not getting any younger."

She tilted her head in a way he interpreted as encouraging.

"I think he needs more of an indoor/outdoor thing," he said.

"What do you mean?"

"Well, I was thinking, I mean, I know your work at Celebrity is important to you, and your family all lives here, but we would only be a short plane ride away, and I'm sure they have your kind of church out there."

"What? Where?"

"And the air is very clear, so you can see the stars, all of them, at night. Beyond the solar system. Distant galaxies. I will get a telescope. We could send messages. We'll get high, watch the entire *Nova* series together. I'm talking the desert, maybe a hundred miles outside of Phoenix. Cacti, coyotes. I'll pack a six-shooter."

She moved her chair closer to him, put her hand on his. He was only almost old. There would be plenty of time to get him straightened out. "Could we afford that?"

"Don't worry; it's cheap out West, and I've put our savings where they're safe."

Fiona pretended to think a moment. "How about Maine? The air is clear there too. We could raise pigs."

Yes! he thought drumming his fingers on the table like he would have if he'd needed time to consider the idea. "That could work for me," he said, giving Lester a wink as if they'd just put one over on her.

CHAPTER 8

THE INFORMANT

DURING THE 1933 SCHOOL CHRISTMAS BREAK, FRANKLIN WASHINGTON brought his eight-year-old son Johnny down to Wall Street. The boy had left Harlem twice before: once for a church picnic at Roosevelt Island and once on a class visit to the Natural History Museum. It was time for him to see more of the outside world. Frank was sure his clients would accept the lad's presence, if only because of the holiday spirit. Maybe having his son with him would lead to bigger tips, and if Johnny developed an interest in shining shoes, they could someday work together. The building superintendents trusted Frank. Johnny would see how casually they waved him in, permitting him to work the floors without interference.

He explained to his son beneath the boy's poster of Jack Johnson, the world's first African-American heavyweight champion: "I'm takin' you ta Wall Street 'cause that's where the money is. And the white man? You don't scare him, he ain't gon' hurt you. See, you "Mista" him. And you don't look right at him. Now, tomorrow? You watch me and don't say nothin' 'less I give you the nod. Sleep good. We be leavin' six-thirty sharp." Johnny looked down at his father's shoes and noticed they needed a shine.

The morning that Frank and Johnny headed down to Wall Street, FDR was in the White House, and hope was in the air. The suicides that had followed 1929's Black Tuesday had dwindled to a trickle. Everywhere in the Financial District you felt the barely contained optimism of an incipient bull market. You saw it in the trader's foot tapping for the light to change, heard it in the lilt of a secretary's voice as she talked to her boss, smelled it in the sweaty uniform of the elevator operator as he rotated his rheostat controller. Johnny watched the operator with great interest, his heart rising to his throat as his first-ever elevator lifted them skyward. He had never seen so many white people in one place. They were spinning dials on a sea of telephones, tearing paper tongues out of machines, striding purposefully around as if under the direction of an invisible taskmaster. He observed how his father sat down to work at a customer's feet with a "how-you-doin'-today-boss?" He watched him fuss over a shoe, taking longer than a perfect shine required, and he received his dad's explanation, "Da point ain't speed, boy. Client need ta feel he got his money's worth." Johnny observed how Frank snapped the rag and primped the shoelaces, how he ended with a ceremonial tap on the toe. And how he accepted tips, smiling without looking the customer in the eye, a grateful two finger salute to his forehead, and a "Thanks, boss."

Their last customer was a heavyset young banker with amazingly straight black hair. His pores were large enough to be visible from where Johnny stood. He had his own little office.

"Dis heah my boy Johnny, Mista Sawyer," his father said with a respectful inclination of the head to a man fifteen years his junior. "I'm learnin' him da buisness." Johnny said nothing; kept his eyes on his father. Without looking up from a document, Sawyer grunted, apparently an invitation to begin. Johnny stood behind his sitting father as Frank began his work. Sawyer continued studying through glasses with thick black frames, not saying a word or glancing in their direction. When the ritual was completed, he picked up two nickels from his desk and deposited them in Frank's hand. Johnny waited to see when, as with the others, the tip would be forthcoming. But Sawyer was again buried in his pages. That is, until just before Frank was about to stand. At that moment, Sawyer raised his head for a moment, catching Johnny staring at him, and when they locked eyes, it was too late for the boy to look away.

"That kid's yours?" he inquired in a Southern drawl. Frank scrambled to his son's side, and Johnny feared it was time to pay the price of violating his father's no-look rule.

"Well, here you go, boy," said Sawyer. "Take this nickel and buy yourself a chicken wing." And turning his back to sharpen a pencil, he added, over his shoulder to Frank, "Bring your little pickaninny in any time you like."

Because they were behind him, Sawyer didn't see Frank's clenched teeth as he put a hand on Johnny's neck and eased him out of the room. With his father's hand still planted firmly on him, Johnny turned and looked up from the nickel into his father's eyes. Then, stepping far enough away for his dad's hand to fall back to his side, Johnny offered him the Sawyer coin. "I'll buy you some a dem candy buttons on paper," Frank said, assuming the burden of the offering. His tone was normal, but his jaw muscles were working, a detail Johnny remembered two years later when the race riot of '35 broke out.

Back in Harlem, the whites Johnny crossed paths with were the Jewish shopkeepers and landlords...guys like Melvin Cohen, who came to collect his thirty dollars on the first Tuesday of every month. One of those Tuesdays not long before Johnny's tenth birthday, his mother ran out to buy some eggs for a cake, leaving him alone with two tens, a five, and five ones in an envelope. "If Cohen come when I'm out, jus' give it to him," she said. Johnny must have looked worried because she added, "He ain't gon' bite you."

No sooner had she left when he heard footsteps on the landing. Johnny opened the door before Cohen knocked. His first time alone with a white man. "Well, look who's here!" Cohen remarked.

Stepping over the threshold, he rubbed Johnny's hair as if it were a rabbit's foot. Johnny flinched but handed him the envelope. He opened it and counted the contents, humming to himself.

"What's dat song, Mista Melvin?" Johnny asked to his own and Cohen's surprise. He braced himself. *I Mista-ed him, pop.*

Cohen smiled a big smile, and Johnny concluded he must have asked a good question. Cohen put his hand on the boy's shoulder. "'Hatikvah'...Israeli national anthem. Would you like to learn the words? They're Hebrew."

Figuring that Hebrew was a secret language known only to white folks, Johnny saw his chance, "Yes please, Mista." And to Cohen's amazement after he'd sung it once straight through, ending with "Your turn," Johnny sang it back to him perfectly.

And that is how it emerged that Johnny was an extraordinarily good mimic. Cohen, who knew all his tenants' schedules, began to show up when the boy was alone in the apartment. Johnny seemed particularly taken with old Yiddish stories and came to look forward to seeing Cohen around five o'clock in the afternoon. By the time he got to high school, Johnny was near fluent in Yiddish and could read Hebrew. "Make sure he don' go snoopin' round when he in here, and clean his water glass good when he gone," was all his mother had to say about it.

Cohen was proud to show off his young friend at Goldstein's Deli, where many expressed their delight by putting pennies in Johnny's hands. Johnny was a natural performer. And he started down the path of imitating one and all, so by the time he was eleven, he reckoned he knew four languages: Harlem English, Brooklyn English, Hebrew, and Yiddish.

One of the few things Johnny could do to rile his father was to question his insistence that Johnny graduate from high school, but toward the middle of tenth grade, that's just what he did.

"What's da point, pop? I don't need no diploma to shine shoes."

"If I done tole you once, I tole you a thousan' times. If you want respec', you needs a education."

"How anyone gonna know if you got a high school diploma? Don' nobody wear da damn things on they shirts."

He was just being a fifteen-year-old, but his father slapped him across the room. "You finish school, you do what you want. Till then? I know what best fo you."

PS 184 was a tough school with many of the boys landing in state juvenile detention centers before graduation. The trees near the entrances were barkless from the knives they carried. Fights broke out frequently near the girls' lockers. On any given day, many kids would be out on suspension or just playing hooky. Nevertheless, Johnny himself managed to get through the entire four years without having to use the pearl-handled Schrade switchblade stiletto he'd bought as insurance against a possible failure of his diplomatic skills. Unless you count as "use" the time his senior year when he pulled it on one of those pimps who loitered around the school.

The older man had flashed a bank roll at Tiffany, the beautiful sixteen-year-old he had a crush on. Johnny had moved in close enough to hear the man say, "See this here wad of fifties? I'ma take good care of you, sweetheart." And when this jackal grabbed her wrist, Johnny sprang toward them instinctively. Once the would-be predator saw the eight-inch blade that appeared from thin air and heard a whisper from Johnny, he took off like a German rocket.

"What'd you say to him?" Tiffany looked at him gratefully with her soft brown eyes.

"Not much," he smiled, trying to hide his trembling until the adrenaline subsided.

"C'mon, what you say."

"So, what I said? What I said was somethin' long the lines of 'I sees you 'round here again, you sleazy muthafukka, I'm talkin' ever, the Red Cross ain't gon' have nuf blood to save yo' sorry ass."

"He seemed convinced."

Lucky he didn't pull a gun on me, Johnny thought. He was still shaking, but he maintained a brave front. "I'd like to think it was my phraseology, but it mighta had something to do with the fact that after concluding my remarks, I took a bite outta that right ear of his," Johnny told her.

And then, to add weight to the embellishment, he mimed spitting an earlobe onto the pavement.

They laughed like teenaged whooping cranes and headed off to share a root beer float...their first date.

By the summer of '43, with his high school diploma finally in hand, Johnny was dying to get out of his parents' apartment. He and Tiffany needed a place of their own. And a rift had been growing between him and his father on the subject of the white man, one which went critical over the two-day-long August riot ignited by a white police officer shooting an African American soldier. "We can't allow dese lootas ta drag down da community," Frank opined.

"That looting, Dad? That *is* the community. And that community talkin' 'bout jobs, 'bout how the army treat our folks."

"Talkin' is talkin'. Lootin' is lootin'. The white man, he ain't about ta change. Them Negroes done set us back fifty yeeahs!"

"And what you think they should do stead of lootin'? Get down on they knees for every white man with ten cent?"

The look on Frank's face filled Johnny with instant regret. The stroke which Frank suffered the month following this exchange made it impossible for Frank to continue working. Johnny had no choice but to take over downtown. No routes, it was soon clear, were as lucrative as Lehman Brothers, and he began to put in fifty-hour weeks in their landmark building. There, a team of first-year associates tasked with assessing the threat of racial strife to American Airlines' profit margins had determined it to be negligible.

"Give the Neegrah an inch, he'll take a mile," Johnny heard Sawyer say to a colleague named Hathaway.

"Riots in Detroit too; maybe it's housing conditions," Hathaway ventured.

"They like to live like that; that's why they come north in the first place," Sawyer explained. Johnny sent the top of his shoe polish can clattering to the floor, a reminder there was another human in the room.

"What's the matter, boy, you drunk?" asked Sawyer. Hathaway laughed.

"Don't drink, sir," was all Johnny could muster as a reply.

Soon Johnny fell into a routine of entering the Lehman building at 8 a.m. sharp. He wore dark khakis, a dark t-shirt, and black footwear, sneakers in the summer, boots in winter. Like his father, he was polite and as unnoticed as the liveried waiters who were the circulatory system serving partners and clients; he was an invisible capillary to their veins and arteries. Unlike Johnny, however, who didn't have a natural base to return to, these waiters had their sitting area near the walk-in kitchen freezer. But Johnny needed to keep moving, wandering the halls, waiting to be waived in for a shine. Until the day the only Black waiter, Randolph Lincoln, took pity on him. "C'mon," Lincoln said, shouldering open the kitchen's swinging door. And whoosh! The steam. The warmth. The noise. The aromas! With his feet almost certainly still firmly on the floor, Johnny was nevertheless taking in the scene from somewhere near the ceiling. *Oh my God,* he was thinking, if indeed he was thinking at all, when a challenge from the sous-chef, Lorenzo Scarlatti, slapped him back to reality.

"Hey, bambino, scuzza. Whaddaya need-a?"

"He needs a place to sit," Lincoln pushed back.

"This-a cucina, not-a the sitting-a room-a," the sous-chef replied.

"C'mon Scarlatti," Lincoln said. "The kid's not gonna make any trouble. What's the big deal?"

Scarlatti must have been having a bad morning. His face turned a bright red. "The big-a deal? The big-a deal," he said in a voice, made more menacing by the fact that he was holding a carving knife, "is he doesn't-a belong-a." And turning his attention exclusively to Johnny, he screamed, "Now get-a the fuck out." And still holding the knife, he took a step toward him. Lincoln had pushed himself in front of Johnny and picked up a rolling pin when Roland Escoffier, Lehman's latest star chef, spoke up from behind the stove: "Zee boy, he may seet."

In the ensuing weeks under the protection of Escoffier, Johnny did his best to dodge the hazing which rained down on him. The Irish didn't have any more use for a Black in their world than the Italians did. Lincoln shared Frank's view of the white man, and in order to keep his place in the oasis, Johnny followed his advice to "stay cool," grudgingly enduring the watermelon jokes, the questions about his "huge dick," and stories of the ghosts they thought all Black people were afraid of. Eventually, thanks to Johnny's willingness to run an errand and give a strategically timed free shine, even Scarlatti wasn't actively gunning for him.

He began to sneak tastes of leftover dishes and was thrilled with the sensations he experienced. He began to watch the chef's every move. To be able to create something that gave such pleasure and that people would actually pay for...*I can learn this*, he told himself, already imagining a world where the smell of coq au vin and fresh-baked bread made the odor of Kiwi shoe polish a thing of the past.

Back in real life, most of the partners were decent tippers, and it wasn't long before Johnny was clearing fifteen dollars a week. Though the going rate for a shine was fifteen cents, they usually rounded it up to a quarter. Soon Johnny developed a concluding ritual different from his father's. With his left hand he pulled his shirt pocket forward making it easy to flick a flying coin in with his right hardly touching it. His signature two-fingered victory sign and high-voltage smile completed the transaction. Few bankers wanted a conversation with their shine. Most gave Johnny about as much acknowledgment as they would a ceiling fan, speaking louder into the phone to be heard over his work. Racist cracks about Black sports or music luminaries were not uncommon ("You Negroes sure have rhythm!"), but Johnny held his tongue. Only late at night would he deliver stinging retorts to a glass of J&B.

When anyone paid more than a quarter, it would normally be a senior partner, but there was one associate who routinely handed him a half dollar. At twenty-six, Allen Frankenberg was only five years older than Johnny. Unlike the others, Frankenberg didn't work during a shine but instead paid attention to Johnny. Occasionally he asked a question about where Johnny got his polish or what would constitute a good day's haul. One day as Johnny was installing himself at Frankenberg's feet, the banker spoke: "Seventeen dollars more or less. That's what I figure you clear a week."

Johnny looked up, surprised, his hand involuntarily dropping to cover his wallet. "That's close, Mr. Frankenberg. Your observational powers are impressive," Johnny said, lowering his head to begin the shine.

"How does this happen?" Frankenberg asked.

"How does what happen, Mr. F—"

"How does it happen that you're so well-spoken?"

Johnny blushed, continued his work. He heard his dad warning him: *Dis white boy ain't no exception. Do not trust his ass.*

Frankenberg said nothing; Johnny stopped. "I would like to tell you that I went to some great schools," he said, keeping his eyes on a shoe. *Look here pop. I gots ta do what I gots ta do.*

He was grateful when Frankenberg ended the ensuing silence, "My folks speak English with a German accent."

"Uh huh," Johnny stalled, getting a nice rhythm going with the brush.

"I lost my accent in kindergarten, you?"

"Well, Mister—"

"Call me Allen, please."

This invitation made Johnny even more uncomfortable; in all his time going around with his father, he had not seen such a breach in the dike that separated them from the clientele. He was afraid to put his finger in, afraid not to. *OK. Pop, let me just hear what he gon' say.* He looked up again at Frankenberg, and they held each other's gaze for a moment. Johnny ignored an image of his father gesticulating wildly, put down his brush, and when Frankenberg stood, he did likewise. "Well…Allen. It's just...It's no big deal. It's just that I am a pretty good…I'm pretty good with languages."

"C'mon Johnny. Let's get real," said Frankenberg. "You don't have to put on that poor, humble Negro act with me. You're an impressive young man. You must have ambitions."

Johnny was building up the nerve to say something about cooking when Frankenberg preempted him. "You try not to attract attention, but when you do, you put people at ease, they go back to whatever they were doing. And you? You see it, hear it all."

Johnny remained silent looking uncomfortably at Frankenberg's starched shirt collar. Outside Frankenberg's office, they could hear phones ring, footsteps passing briskly by. "I'm not sure what you—"

Allen walked by him and closed the door. He turned, and lowered his voice, "There are certain kinds of information you may come across that could make it possible for you to do much better than seventeen a week."

"I don't want to get into any trouble."

"We'll figure it out together. Just keep your eyes open. I wouldn't ask you to do anything inappropriate." When they shook hands, Johnny wasn't sure what they had agreed to, but he felt Allen's soft skin on his calloused palm pulling him over the threshold to an easier world.

What they figured out together was that many of Frankenberg's colleagues were cheating on their wives, abusing their expense accounts, and doing one thing or another they would prefer to remain confidential. Johnny's "reports" proved invaluable in the internecine Lehman battles. In August of '48, Johnny told Allen that a partner who had been giving Allen an especially bad time had been using company cars to ferry his wife, kid, and schnauzer out to the Hamptons while, in the city, he charged strip clubs to his expense account. After that partner hastily left The Firm, Allen gave Johnny his first "bonus." Allen couldn't stand Sawyer, and the following year, the fact that Sawyer was having sex in the copying room with Bobby Lehman's secretary cost Sawyer a mandatory leave without pay. Johnny's bonus that Christmas was more than his annual take from shining shoes.

One of the first things Frankenberg did upon becoming a partner in '51 was to get Johnny hired by The Firm. His position as one of the service staff paid sixteen dollars a week, an amount which, given taxes, yielded less than what he'd made when he started at Lehman, but it came with healthcare benefits. And that was before tips. Out of his first Lehman paycheck, Johnny donated five dollars to the National Association for the Advancement of Colored People.

Each Christmas without fail, Allen gave him an ever-higher amount, which he had taken to calling "a token of our special friendship." And with every passing year, as the movement for racial justice gained strength, Johnny donated increased amounts to evermore radical organizations. By '53, he and Tiffany had saved enough money to pay rent on the four-story walk-up they would live in for the rest of their lives together. And over his subsequent years of Manhattan commuting, Johnny's five-block walk from the train became a routine. Emerging from the Lex, he switched into his Harlem mode. An entertainer comfortably connecting with his audience, he worked his way through the crowd. Some harmless flirting: "Hey, baby, you lookin' mighty fine tonight!"

"Johnny, you talks like a man of action, but my eyes ain't discernin' no movement in this here direction."

"We gots to give it time for our love to grow, baby. Dis heah thang we got goin' too important to rush."

He slipped the drunks some change when they put in the effort to get vertical:

"How'd the market do today, Johnny?"

"Was good for some, not for others."

"How was it for me?"

"You made ten cent. Don't be spendin' it on booze now. That Thunderbird gon' kill you," Johnny said.

"Count on it, my man. Dis goin' to my college tuition."

But one of the winos, a dropout from PS 184, invariably stationed himself a block from Johnny's building as if it was his job to end Johnny's day on a down note. One night his shot was: "Hey, Mista Big. How it feel to be a house nigga?"

Usually Johnny just walked past, but this time, he stopped, "How it feel ta sit yo' ass on da ceement all day?"

"Best up heah than downtown suckin' white cock."

"I shine day shoes, don't suck day cocks," he said, but his comeback sounded lame even to him.

That night, after the boys were put to bed, Johnny was at the stove as Tiff began the nightly rehash. "You know that Umberto? SEIU steward?"

"Gay guy? Anesthesiology?" Johnny was sautéing some haricots verts.

"Yeah, well, on break, he's a total hoot, like he's been sniffin' his own nitrous oxide. But when he gets all union-y, he's as serious as a quadruple bypass."

"Uh huh."

"So today he tells me the docs want to lose Jorge Garcia,

that scrub in special surgery. He's had his three warnings...tardiness, absence, insubordination kind of thing, but Umberto? He's not buyin' it. Says it's trumped-up bullshit and that we need to support the guy, so he's called a meeting. Are you with me?"

"Uh huh." Johnny, who had served the green beans with bronzed sea bass and tomatoes on a bed of tarragon, took his seat. Tiffany continued, choosing to ignore the fact he was tearing a paper towel into little strips.

"Well, I don't really know this Garcia. But when I see him, he always looks wasted. Anyway, I suppose I have to learn the facts, but I wonder if there might be a little special something goin' on *entre estos dos chicos* if you get my drift."

"Well, definitely sounds like *una posibilidad*," Johnny said. He looked down at his right hand, which had been riding on his leg as it twitched under the table.

"Yeah. I'll keep you posted. Call me crazy, but you seem preoccupied. Something happen in the land of mammon?"

He'd been thinking about how to raise the topic for days, but now, delay was no longer practicable. He cleared his throat. "Actually, this might be a good time to tell you about a recent conversation I had with Allen..." He saw instantly that his by-the-way-now-that-you-mention-it tone had produced the exact opposite effect than intended; he had said nothing of substance, and already she looked suspicious. Whatever. He had no choice but to continue. He took a sip of water. "So, the two of us were alone in his office and he says: 'Johnny, my friend, the information you have given me over the years has been invaluable, and I'm thinking maybe the money I send your way from time to time is an inadequate expression of my appreciation.' And when I try to brush it off, he goes 'In part, thanks to you, I am a major player here. You've got a wife who works but two kids to support. You're smart, your insights and judgments are impeccable, and you know more than a lot of the young men we hire.'

"'Uh huh' I give him, meaning let's get to the point.

"'Well, I just had a deal come in that some of my partners and

I are thinking about.' Then after another 'uh huh' from me, he, you know, adjusts his tie, sits up straight, 'It's a for-profit prison based in Tupelo, Mississippi. Major buying opportunity due to a couple of recent suicides. Most of the inmates are, um, African Americans.' Tiffany stopped chewing. Johnny wiped his mouth but pressed on, quoting Allen, 'And if we invest in the equity? There would be a chance to make some serious money.'"

Johnny looked at Tiffany for a sign of approval but, seeing none, continued anyway. "So, as soon as he finishes, he's relieved, like he's gotten something off his chest, but I'm still waiting for the punch line. Finally, I figure I better help him out, so I ask: 'What am I supposed to do to earn that money, Allen?'

"'Well, you know about Black people,' he says. 'So, I would like you to fly down there with Diamond and give me your personal recommendation on whether to proceed. Then, if we do, we put you on the board, we give you some kind of title like 'Senior Advisor,' so, in addition to whatever stock plan we set up for directors, we pay you some shares for your ongoing advice. I'm thinking your ownership position could be worth a half million bucks, depending on the IPO valuation of course.'"

Tiffany couldn't contain herself any longer, "So let me get this straight; the basic business is incarcerating Black men?" She stood and began clearing the table.

"Yes," Johnny admitted, "but the living conditions are supposed to be OK, and, um, there is a born-again element. Management brings Jesus into the lives of the prisoners, and when they've served their time," Johnny continued, shouting over the garbage disposal, "they are less likely to commit crimes. According to Allen, if that's true, there could be a whole chain of these things."

When the disposal had whirred to a stop, Tiffany spoke, "A chain. A chain of prisons."

"I'm just thinking about it," Johnny said. "Although tomorrow—"

Tiffany turned from the sink, and seeing her angry glare he stopped, shifted direction, "C'mon Tiff. The prison business already exists. This would take me to a whole new level. We could move to a nicer neighborhood. Maybe even save up enough for the restaurant. And consider how much more we could give to the Congress of Racial Equality." Before he reached the word "Equality," she had turned off the lights, leaving him seated alone in the dark empty room.

When she emerged from their bathroom the next morning, Johnny had a tie on and was tying a newly shined shoe. She was standing near the dresser when she said, "So, you are chump enough to think that what Allen wants is your judgment, your opinion? Tell me you're not deaf, blind, *and* dumb."

"Give me the benefit of the doubt," he pleaded. "Let's take it a step at a time. Today I do a day trip with Diamond, and we'll come to some preliminary conclusions."

"A day trip to Tupelo? How? Through Atlanta?"

"Actually," he grinned sheepishly, "we're round trip from Teterboro. Private jet."

She could barely contain her disgust. "Let me know how it all comes out, flyboy," and she left for work. Waiting out on the tarmac that morning, he found the note in his jacket pocket: "I will not pay our bills with blood money." That night when Johnny returned home, there were none of the familiar cooking smells. The kitchen tablecloth they had purchased together a sunny Saturday ago for ten dollars looked stark in the absence of place settings. The boys had been fed and were in their room. Johnny, considering giving Allen a green light, had been wondering whether Tiffany's opposition could be overcome.

As soon as Tiffany entered and stood across the empty table from him, he began his prepared remarks: "I talked directly to a number of the prisoners. They are very well treated."

"Oh, 'directly' is it? You mean you didn't ask one of your minions to do it and send you an executive summary?"

This was not the strong start he had envisioned on the flight home. "Tiff, I—"

"Let me make myself clear, Mr. Teterboro," she interrupted,

her voice an octave above normal. "No amount of money you give to CORE can make up for what you are thinking to do. You know I'm talkin' truth."

She was so on-fire pissed off, smoke might soon be coming out of her nostrils. "Just listen to me for a minute," he begged.

"Johnny, this is not an on the one hand, on the other hand discussion." He heard the click, saw the glint before he knew what he was looking at. He hadn't thought about the Schrade stiletto in years, so was caught off guard when she stretched all the way across the table and cut the cloth down the middle. "There's no gray here baby. It's black and white." And, ripping the tablecloth in two, Tiffany threw both pieces in the trash. The hemispheres that the knife left in their table commemorated the agreement they reached without much further discussion.

By '61, the year Johnny put his career as a venture capitalist to bed, Allen was referring to his annual check as Johnny's "partnership share." JFK was in the White House, and Johnny calculated that he'd spent half his life shining shoes at Lehman Brothers. At thirty-six years old, he had been on The Street longer than many of the bankers. After the Greensboro sit-ins and the liftoff of the Civil Rights Movement, the inability of his Lehman employers to understand the basis of Black anger was becoming intolerably frustrating. A comment about the movement such as, "Why can't they just assimilate like all the other immigrants?" could drive Johnny to the point where he couldn't stop himself from subjecting the offending banker to a covert "disciplinary action." Allen himself was never late to a client meeting because of a mysterious flat tire nor made to suffer an inexplicable week of constipation. Hathaway, Sawyer, and a handful of others were another story.

The winds of change were blowing the fog away. Black people were more seen, and Johnny himself felt noticed; bankers began to speak with him about topics other than the weather. The racist jokes that partners had unselfconsciously delivered in his presence gave way to their direct "what-do-you-people-want?" type questions. The liberals, of course, were at pains to show how sympathetic they were to racial equality. "Johnny, just so you know, I sent a nice little check to the NAACP yesterday." Johnny, who thought he'd heard it all, was nevertheless shocked when Diamond, then a newly minted vice president, stopped him after the murder of Martin Luther King to let him know that the assassination was "a big deal, right up there with the death of Robert Lehman."

"Tell you what, baby," Tiffany said when he told her the story. "Let's us send a check in Diamond's honor to the Student Nonviolent Coordinating Committee. Did you see that speech Stokely gave in Oakland last night? Ooooweee!"

"Let's!" he agreed enthusiastically. But he stayed up late, nursing a scotch, reliving the scene, and thinking about what he might have done differently.

By the late seventies, with one boy working for a Black media entrepreneur and the other studying to be a civil rights attorney, Johnny had to admit that Lehman had been good for him. What he thought of as his "information retrieval business" for Allen, well, he could do it in his sleep. Likewise shining shoes. Strangely, though the job had become so automatic, he found it ever more difficult to show up for work. By February of '74, he'd used up half his sick days for the year.

And what had started as a little after-dinner drink had evolved into a pattern worth worrying about. He was staying up too late, and those times when he got really well-oiled, he'd begun to speak to himself in the accent of his pre-Cohen childhood. Like the night of April 8 when Hammerin' Hank Aaron became the all-time MLB home run leader. Johnny turned off the TV and after his second double scotch looked again at his March Citibank statement. He had saved $37,024.91 in cash, not near enough to start a restaurant.

What a Black man sposa do in this heah country a ours if he don't sing or play sports?...life a crime? Tha church? Kill gooks? As always on weekdays, he arose with a hangover and made it to the office on time.

The real world, the world outside of Lehman, seemed to be taking a breather. The Vietnam War was over, a president had resigned, Ma Bell was on the path to dismemberment, Roberta Flack was being killed softly, and the Beatles were ready to let it be. Mandela remained incarcerated on Robben Island, while Johnny, although admittedly with less noble justification, was also trapped. Trapped at a Lehman Brothers where, with no eponymous leader, there was struggle and contention. The elevated level of backstabbing should have been interesting, but Allen was making noise about retirement, and Johnny was ever more preoccupied with one question: *How can I save enough to open that restaurant?*

It seemed at first when Jed Czincosca appeared on the scene that he was irrelevant to such considerations, and, accordingly, Johnny paid him no special attention. Until he saw the young man in Allen's office. Allen gestured toward the young man.

"I would like to introduce you to a new banker."

"We've met," Johnny said.

"Jed, it's important to have friends you can trust," Allen said, looking at the young man over his glasses. He spoke with the full gravitas of his senior position, and Jed nodded acceptingly like Abraham receiving God's travel instructions.

"I am heading to an uptown meeting," Allen said as he closed the office door behind him leaving the twenty-four- and fifty-two-year-olds standing awkwardly opposite each other. The ship's clock, which Allen's secretary religiously kept wound, struck seven bells.

Jed broke the ensuing silence. "Allen has given me a sense of how…helpful you've been to him. Um, I'm sure Allen figures that when he retires, well, it will be good for you and me to have begun a mutually beneficial relationship. What do you say?"

"I don't know what you mean," Johnny lied. *How could Allen have told this puppy of our special relationship?*

Johnny's expression must have told Jed it was damage repair time because he rushed to say. "Look, if you don't want to discuss it, that's groovy with me. I mean I thought you could use a little extra money. You know…for some restaurant thing or something?"

Wow! Shouldn't Allen have let Johnny himself decide who to share his most personal secrets with? For an instant, Johnny toggled to his father, who was hovering over Jed's left shoulder. His dad's triumphant expression said it all. "Uh, huh," Johnny stalled, trying to think what if anything he needed to say.

But, as before, Jed simply pressed on. "Look. I wouldn't be asking a lot. However, unlike Allen, I'm not interested in petty gossip like who's *schtupping* which secretary. What interests me is information that could move a stock price."

Johnny's heart was beating like he'd run up a flight of stairs.

"I'm not prepared to do anything illegal," he cautioned in an echo of his earliest conversation with Allen.

Jed looked hurt for a moment, and then said with a straight face, "It doesn't take any preparation." He waited a beat then laughed, "Just kidding. I know the laws. We'll keep it kosher."

Johnny felt simultaneously angry and fearful, as if he was a second-string catcher traded to a team in an unknown city. But he liked Jed's firm man-to-man handshake and the way he looked him in the eye.

So, he learned to listen differently than he had during the early Allen years. Once Jed became a partner in 1983, he sharpened his guidance to Johnny. As Jed put it, "I'm keen to know who's working on what deals, and which partners need to sell Lehman stock. I'll take it from there." When Johnny overheard that Diamond was working to divest part of the Liggett Group to Pernod Ricard during a hostile takeover attempt by City Investing, he could tell by the warmth of Jed's "Thank you!" where that information ranked on his usefulness scale. Johnny had no opinion on what Jed would do with the information. *Not my problem*, he reassured himself. But he'd begun to hear rumors about the SEC's interest in "insider trading," and he was beginning to worry. He mentioned the issue to Jed, who seemed unconcerned. "What we are doing is perfectly legal. Trust me." *We?* Johnny thought. Shortly after he had elicited Jed's reassurance, Johnny's now deceased father started to reappear in daydreams and soon most nights: *It's like in dem war movies, son. Nigga gone take da bullet while da white boy? He scamppa away, live happily evah afta.*

Johnny wasn't sleeping at all well. He was dying to say, *I hear you, Pop. I'm outta there.* But it looked like many more years before he could save enough money.

Frankenberg's retirement following the sale of Lehman to American Express in '84 left Johnny with only a single source of supplemental income, one he was increasingly uncomfortable serving. Although the buyout put lots of money in all the partner's pockets, including Jed's, it also seemed to have ruined some plan Johnny's young patron had had for even greater wealth. It wasn't that he wished Jed any ill, but still. How, Johnny wondered, could he be the one to scamper away before they started bringing in the bodies. He had almost concluded that he should stop feeding Jed information, but then he came upon something that was too valuable to resist.

A certain partner had been hired by a corporate raider who'd been secretly planning a hostile takeover of the Walt Disney Company. Unfortunately, Johnny's "bonus" would not be paid until December. He needed a way to turn the news into cash before it was public, and then get the hell out of Lehman Brothers.

"Jed," he said on the Thursday after he'd come up with a plan. "I've got something for you."

"Great. Let's hear it." (Pretty much what he'd expected.)

"Umm, I've come across some info about a raid. The target is large, lots of trading volume."

"Terrific! That's just the kind of thing we can work with."

"Jed, listen. I can't simply give you this information and hope for the best. Not to change the subject, but I'm only a few dollars away from being able to start my own business."

Jed frowned, "Wow!"

"Wow, what?" Johnny asked disingenuously.

"Wow as in, 'Wow, you're not changing the subject. This is a stickup operation."

Johnny was prepared, "Jed, please don't think of it that way. I'm just trying to do right for you and my family at the same time. I can't wait until the end of the year."

"And why's that?"

Johnny looked at Jed's manicured fingernails. This was not the moment to insinuate that his boss might be engaging in criminal behavior. "If I had, say, $150,000, I could be out of here and in business in time for the Christmas season," he said, naming the amount he believed Jed kept in his office safe.

Jed pursed his lips. "Tell you what, give me the skinny, and I'll do the right thing." Upon which he reached for a patent leather overnight bag. "I'm heading out to Long Island tonight to beat the traffic, so just tell me what you know. We can discuss timing and amounts on Monday." And he stood there expectantly.

It's now or never, Johnny thought. "Funny," he said. "I think that pretty blond third year associate—what's her name? Gail something down in M&A? is also leaving about now for a long weekend on Long Island. Of course, it is a long island, and coincidences do occur."

Jed stiffened. Johnny could see him swallow. "Sit down," Jed said, doing so himself. And twenty minutes later Johnny left his office elated, carrying the requisite funds in a large envelope filled with hundred-dollar bills.

After a few practice weeks in late December, the official opening of Black Ivy, Harlem's first "haute soul" restaurant, took place on the first national celebration of Martin Luther King Jr., January 20, 1986. Advertising would have been a waste of money by then; the lines were around the block. Despite the added expense, Johnny had insisted that only linen tablecloths would do. He had paid special attention to the lighting and banned all smoking from the premises, a stance which represented a serious risk in those days, but one necessary to keep the focus on the food itself. By late October, when the Mets beat the Red Sox in the seventh game of the World Series, Johnny had his liquor license, and diners needed a reservation several days in advance to get a table.

In the twelve years of its existence while Johnny was alive, there was hardly a night when he himself was not cooking. He loved it! One of his most popular dishes was Ribs à la Frankenberg. When Jed came by soon after the opening for the first of the free meals he'd extracted as a final concession, he complained, "What about me? Why no 'Something à la Czincosca?'"

Johnny laughed, "You really want to advertise our relationship? Let's give it a beat…but I'm thinking Chitlins Jedediah."

On his deathbed, through the prednisone and morphine, Johnny's thoughts flitted to Lehman and The Street. It was in the Lehman kitchen he'd formed friendships with the best chefs in the world, the ones whose names the bankers dropped to clients over lunch: Gagnaire, Ducasse, Fournier. The nurses at Mount Sinai did not know why he was chuckling as he recalled cooking with these greats at his home. But suddenly he began to choke with laughter because his thoughts had turned to one of his most gratifying disciplinary actions. He had launched the attack after overhearing a Hathaway comment about Bluford, the first Black astronaut ("Seems a rather costly way to get rid of them"). After the nurse administered a sedative, his family, which gathered around his bedside, observed a mysterious contented smile. He was reliving the day after the Bluford comment, when he barely had time to get out of the way as his final tap to a resplendent loafer coincided with Hathaway's sudden attack of diarrhea.

His family had the comfort of knowing that Johnny died happy because he literally laughed away his last breath. He had taken himself back to the moment when he stood outside Hathaway's office enjoying the coincidence of a badly clogged toilet in Hathaway's private bathroom and his malodorous meeting with one of Lehman's most important clients. Too late, Hathaway had screamed for an air freshener and had run around the office spraying everywhere. The last words Johnny heard were spoken by the CEO of AT&T: "Jesus, Bill, your office...it smells like someone took a shit in a pine forest."

Johnny died from the same cancer and on the same Sunday as Stokely Carmichael, the civil rights firebrand who, before he moved to Africa, counted Tiffany and him among his largest donors. On the Saturday of Johnny's funeral, the Abyssinian Baptist Church was filled with his friends of all races, ages, and walks of life. Stokely Carmichael, aka Kwame Ture, who had coined the term "Black power," was the subject of a long obit in the *New York Times*.

CHAPTER 9

THE FALL

On this cursed day, September 15, 2008, I have lost the power of speech. Horrible as it is that Lehman Brothers, the firm I dedicated thirty-one years of my professional life to, has declared bankruptcy, it's even more horrific that I, Jedediah Robert Czincosca, will need all the luck and skill I can muster to avoid the same personal fate. For now, I feel no desire whatsoever... no ambition, no appetite for anything, including sleep. I sit here vestigially at my desk in our Park Avenue duplex, which will soon be on the chopping block, self-medicating with smoke and drink, trying to persuade myself that there is still something worth doing. Standing to relieve myself of the urine I generate feels monumentally demanding, and to answer the phone, or even grunt in response to Amanda's ministrations, pointless.

But what I need to do now...what I need to do now...here is what I need to do. I am a smart person. I am sure that if... if I think about this disaster analytically, how something this bad could happen to me will certainly become clear. My friend Chuck Greenhall, a sixty-year-old triathlete, doesn't miss a day of exercise, is in fantastic shape. He dyes his hair black to negate his male pattern baldness, thinks his always-on tan hides his wrinkles. He tells me he weighs himself twice a day, once after he wakes up, but before defecating, and once in the evening just prior to retiring. Since he knows from experience his nightly weight loss, there is little point to the morning weigh-in, but it gives him reconfirmation of his extraordinary fitness. I have seen him proudly pat his flat stomach, in the men's locker room. He never walks by a mirror without an admiring glance at his own well-toned pecs. For a guy my age, he looks fantastic.

I'm not as obsessive about my financial shape as Chuck is about his physique. My MO for years has been to restrict my net worth calculations to once a month. But when Lehman stock hit an all-time high of $86.18 back in February of '07, I didn't need a calculator to figure my 4,641,448 shares (including option equivalents) were worth around $400 million. Because it was not yet then the end of the month, I was not supposed to add in the art (north of $100 million), and the houses (Manhattan duplex at least $17 mil based on comps, the place in Quogue, twelve-ish), the various private investments offered exclusively to Lehman executives (maybe another eight?), petty cash of a couple million in banks with ATMs all over the city, and a couple hundred thousand in my home safes. Nor should I have gone on to subtract the liabilities (virtually none except for some outstanding credit card debt of less than fifty thousand and a few million of accrued taxes I planned to defer indefinitely).

Anyway, when I finally green-lighted myself to do the "official" calculation early that March, the LEH stock had made an unusually steep drop from that pinnacle price. In fact, it was a screaming buy, so I called Liam Pennoyer, my Bank of America high-net-worth-individual handler who, after years of making love to me via private art tour tickets, wine tastings, and the insights of Morgan's crystal ball market wizards, was delighted to hear that he could help with something I actually gave a shit about. He confirmed on the phone that B of A would loan me the $25 million I was looking for. "I can see why you'd like to pick up a few shares in here. Come over, get the paperwork out of the way." When I dropped by his office the next day, he offered great terms—prime plus 25 bips.

"We may as well set it up as a facility so that you can draw on it as needed. Let's make it an even hundred million. Of course, we'll need your personal guaranty." This last oh-by-the-way didn't worry me because even if I were to draw down the entire $100 million, I would utilize it to buy undervalued stock, a value for value exchange, so there would be no meaningful risk for either me or B of A.

"It's great to be in such capable hands," I said.

"We know you and your outstanding reputation." He patted me on the back as I exited the dark paneled conference room with panoramic views of the city, where coffee and cookies had greeted us about a half hour earlier.

"And of course, we have a big cushion underneath us," he added with a chuckle, referring, I thought justifiably, to the Lehman securities I already owned, which were worth about $360 million at the time. "Hope I didn't drag this out too long," he said winking at me, and then, just before the elevator doors closed, "Jed, if there is anything, I mean anything I can do for you, please know that I am here 24/7." After the elevator descended the forty-four floors to the lobby and I returned to my office, I looked at my watch: fifty minutes round trip.

Adding in the shares I would use that $25 million to buy, my new share total would be approaching five million. The great thing about my stock position was that you had to go all the way back to the third quarter of 2004—three years ago for Christ's sake—to see the stock trading below $40 a share, and at that ridiculously low number, my holdings would still be worth twice the entire borrowing facility! I wished my father was alive so he could see how well I had learned my lesson from watching him shackle himself to risky businesses; with Lehman stock, there was so much trading volume, I could lighten up any time I wanted to. And best of all, the stock price had unlimited runway on the upside.

At dinner, about ten days after that first $25 million stock purchase under the facility, I chose not to mention that the stock had taken a momentary dip and was trading at ten bucks less than what I paid for it. "By the way, honey, I forgot to tell you I'm set up to borrow $100 million any time I want. How cool is that, huh?"

"What do you need debt for? I don't like borrowing."

"It's called leverage. It's a good tool if you know how to use it," the implication being that I, Jedediah Czincosca, did. She seemed prepared to drop the subject. No voices were raised, no more criticisms offered. We sat there for another moment in tolerable silence. *All quiet on the Western Front*, I thought as I gave her a kiss on the forehead and repaired peacefully to my study. But the gods were laughing.

I am the one who created the Structured Finance group and the Proprietary Trading Desk, but that didn't stop the powers that be from sending Motherwell, whom I had mentored and who was my chief operating officer, to explain the situation to me. "Got a sec?" he asked one afternoon as he flopped down on my couch, placing the pillow Amanda had embroidered with "The Harder I Work, The Luckier I Get" under his neck and stretching his lanky frame until his feet rested on the furthest cushion. I continued to look at the day's trading results on the double screens of my company-issued Dell desktop. But he'd never just walked in and assumed, without invitation, such an eloquently casual position, and, probably because of this implied presumption, I felt a warning shot of adrenaline coursing through me. He thought better of his body language and sat up. "I'm not sure there's any great way to say this, Jed," his voice was wavering in a way that captured my complete attention even as I continued to stare, now unseeingly, at the screen. "You've been so good to me over the years."

I took a deep breath, which I hoped Motherwell didn't detect. Could this be the moment that I was dreading, almost expecting? As I swiveled slowly to turn in his direction, I reassured myself that he could not read my mind and that whatever he might say next, I would have some wiggle room. Contemporaneously, I worried. *You've been paying less attention to details. You know how things work on The Street.* I was fascinated with what he would say next but desperately wanted not to hear his words. I needed time to gather my thoughts, slow things down. Keeping my poise, I arose from behind my desk and installed myself in the chair a mere four feet away from him, smiling insouciantly.

He soldiered on, "I would never do anything to hurt you."

"Hey, we lost a few bucks today on the Russian desk. Not your fault," I feinted, delaying the predictable.

"Jed. It's not that," he said, glancing at the window as if he wished he could fly through it. "It's that I have an offer to run my own show at Merrill Lynch."

Ooof! I certainly hadn't seen that one coming. I knitted my eyebrows, waiting. My mouth was dry; I couldn't swallow.

"I don't want to leave, and I'm not saying you stifle me in any way. It's just that—" *Clever,* I thought, *very clever. Now it's up to me to 'do what's best for The Firm.'*

"When will you tell Willy about your decision to resign?" I asked, still stalling. I knew that the chances of him having gone this far without the full knowledge and support of Willy "The Gorilla" Gould, Lehman's famously aggressive CEO, were low in the extreme. Motherwell was one of the Firm's biggest producers. Gould would no way allow him to leave for Merrill.

"I...I, um...look I—" He had all the cards but was playing his hand like a pussy.

"I hope you got your deal in writing. Neal and Fagany are wily pricks. Can't be trusted." I was still in my mentor mode but my mascara was melting. This was becoming excruciating, and not just for him. I found the necessary words, "Tell you what, Joe, stick around."

Motherwell exhaled, looking at me like a grateful child.

"I get the message. The Firm can't afford to lose you and

there's no room for two queen bees in the hive. I am happy to hand you the keys," I conceded, not saying when.

Each of us knew that I would take that question up directly with Gould. Even though, as the Firm had grown, my relative contribution had diminished, I still had enough stroke to schedule a talk with the Great Man about the details of my soon-to-be new situation. But Motherwell and I also knew that he could easily run my profit centers without the benefit of my considerable experience, thank you very much, so my objective had to be to negotiate the best unwind possible. This would mean an orderly transition period. I would retain my seat on all the key committees for at least a couple years, obtain a written guarantee of some to-be-negotiated but high single-digit millions of annual compensation, and maybe pick up a few perks like lifetime health insurance. I would be no more difficult than the situation required in order to obtain these results.

Gould kept me waiting in his private conference room for the fifteen minutes required to communicate the incredible demands on his time. His main chauffeur and two members of his security detail had been visible outside his office when I had been shown in by one of his assistant secretaries, a sign that soon after addressing the Czincosca situation, he would descend in his non-stop-from-the-thirty-first-floor elevator to the gated internal driveway out the building's back door, where one of the Cadillac Escalades he favored would whisk him away. He was squeezing me into his busy schedule.

"Willy is running a little late," a cheery young woman I hadn't seen before bubbled when she'd escorted me to a comfortable Eames chair with a good view of photographs featuring Gould cutting ribbons, ringing stock exchange bells, and relaxing with various leaders of the free and unfree world. That every US president from Ronald Reagan to George W. Bush was represented reminded me how long he himself had been in power. "May I offer you something to drink?" She sounded like a recording. After about ten minutes she returned to say, "Willy apologizes.

This urgent matter he's working on is taking longer than he expected." I had no reason to doubt Willy knew he was keeping me waiting but every reason to disbelieve he had sent this low-level perky emissary in with an apology. He never apologized for anything.

"Sit down, Jed," he said when I was finally shown into his actual office. And then, without small talk, "I understand you had a productive conversation with Motherwell." Gould was dark-complected, with a prominent nose and full eyebrows scrunched together, glowering as if he intuited I was about to say something obnoxious. He still retained a full head of hair, largely black, save for a touch of gray at the tip of the sideburns, but a large forehead was gaining territory. I had known him for many years and could not remember having seen him laugh. In his presence, I felt a kind of coiled menace that made me want to protect my throat. I never liked Gould, but I was certain until the end that he knew what he was doing. Even though I was Lehman's third-largest individual shareholder, he owned more than three times as many shares as I did. I resonated to his style, which like mine was aggressive opportunism. If nothing else, the guy had balls.

"Yep. What's the deal?" I replied, showing that, like him, I had no time for bullshit.

"Well, you will no longer be a group head effective Monday noon. Might as well make your resignation from the Executive Committee at the same time. We'll give you a nice office on four.

Wow! Bang! So fast? So soon? Suddenly it was hard to breathe. "I will take Sally with me?" I stalled.

"Work that out with Personnel."

I was about to protest that no way would I share an assistant with the other Formers on Dinosaur Row when he showed me the palm of his hand and, looking down to scribble some comments on what appeared to be a prospectus, added, "We'll vest all your options. Your monthly draw continues for the foreseeable future. You'll have the same shot at a bonus as always."

"Willy, here's a better plan: Let's wait until after the annual meeting," I wanted to say, but I knew it was futile and couldn't get the words out.

He put a document in his briefcase, stood up, walked past me, then, turning, extended his hand, and as mine rose to shake his, he yelled over his shoulder, "OK, Andrew," the cue for his driver to enter and relieve him of the briefcase. My audience was ending. The options he was referring to were worth about $20 million at the time. I had expected them to vest over the next three years in all circumstances unless I was terminated, so, the immediate vesting he bestowed upon me wasn't even a goodbye kiss. Hardly even a fucking peck on the fucking cheek. "Thanks for all you've done over the years," he muttered as he walked out, looking at one of his Blackberrys.

So, I found myself left standing just inside the door of Gould's office, reaching under my jacket to check how thoroughly I had sweated through my perfectly laundered JRC monogrammed shirt when that same junior admin reappeared to gesture, she probably thought hospitably, toward the waiting elevator with her annoyingly toned twenty-something arm. By then I was sculpting a story to cover my humiliation. *I have decided that I need more time to manage my investments and will be establishing a family office to do just that.* Sounded borderline OK. But I was pissed with myself, enraged actually, that I hadn't initiated the change. I mean, Wall Street? Wall Street has no room for old. I knew that, goddamn it. Could have gotten a much better deal if I had planned this and taken the goddamn initiative.

Wall Street lives so intensely in the present that the worst thing you can say about a guy, what they'd say about me when the word got around Monday, is "He's history." I needed to get home immediately to think this through over a bottle of Stoli and a few puffs of that primo weed I save for special emergencies. I had entered the elevator, in shock, my eyes somewhere in the near distance. It wasn't until after the doors closed that

I realized what's-her-name had pushed the down button for me, as if I was too addled to understand my time was over or lacked the hand/eye coordination to push it all by myself.

Once the deal was papered, pretty much exactly along the lines Gould had laid out, I explained the situation to Amanda, "I have decided to turn over control of my profit centers to Motherwell."

Amanda paused mid-chew, "What did you want to do that for?

"It was time. I am moving down to four."

"What's on four?"

I did not like the way this conversation was going. "Some other senior partners. I'll have more time to keep an eye on the stock."

"You've got to be kidding." She was never too great at censoring her bullshit detector.

"What do you mean, 'kidding'? Kidding what?"

"I mean it is inconceivable that you need any more time than you already spend obsessing about the stock. You excused yourself from dinner last week at Le Coq Foutu three times to check the Hong Kong markets! I go to the bathroom at 2 a.m., and there you are waiting to catch the London open. If you've got time for anything, you've got time to follow that stock."

I put my head in my hands like I do when one of my attacks of depression is coming on. "I don't feel well," I said, ending the conversation. I pushed back my chair, walked toward my study with one hand still on my head, and closed the door feebly from the inside.

Although setting up the B of A facility in early 2007 was the beginning of my downfall, I must admit that from the first day I walked through the Lehman doors in '77, I had been obsessed with owning as many shares as I could get my hands on. When

I saw the returns on capital Lehman was getting, it was clear there was no more reliable way to wealth than owning as much of The Firm as possible. I was a mere junior partner when The Firm was sold to American Express nine years after my arrival, and I hated giving up the Lehman stock I'd then accumulated for Am Ex Convertible Debt. I griped about the deal, but I had no choice. I salted away whatever after-tax cash the convertibles turned into and as soon as Lehman was spun out of AmEx in June of '94, I returned to acquiring as many Lehman shares as possible. In addition to all the stock and options I received in compensation, I never missed an opportunity to buy on weakness in the public markets. The Asian Financial Crisis, a soft earnings report, yes!

Some of the best deals I did were with other senior bankers. Like when Brighton, who knew how bullish I was on Lehman, came to tell me the story of his wife, who suffered from some rare metabolic disorder. Seems like she could only be treated by a Shire Pharmaceutical drug that went for $375,000 per year. As he told me of his pressing need for cash, he actually began to cry.

"Gould will kill me if I sell," he sobbed. "He'll see it as a vote of no confidence."

"I'm so sorry, Bob," I was saying. "I wish there was something I could do," when the light bulb went on. "Wait a minute. I have an idea. The stock is at ten bucks give or take. What if you sell me a structured derivative…the right to actually buy your stock any time I want in the future, at a fair discount, say, $7 per share. I could give you $6 a share of it right now and the final buck when I exercise, which you could trust me not to do anytime soon. I will even let you keep 5 percent of the upside. Wouldn't be anybody's business but ours."

My neck was wet when he stopped hugging me. Great thing about it was that the word got around, and I was able to use this template many times over. Weddings, nursing care, second or third homes, I was more interested in the urgency of the need than the use of the proceeds.

Nobody knew more about The Firm than I did. Accordingly, I was always careful to schedule my private closings right after earnings were publicly reported so that some candyass couldn't claim I'd traded on inside information. That I was an exceptionally astute investor was confirmed by the fact that during the ten years since I joined the Executive Committee, the stock had risen to multiples of its initial $3 a share IPO price. If you simply concentrate on one investment that you understand better than anyone in the world, you don't have to keep thinking up new ideas. It's like owning a piece of the earth that keeps enlarging organically.

Sitting on four, I had little to do except think about Lehman and its prospects. The area was a dead zone. No phones ringing, few footsteps, and after five? Forget it. A morgue would have been noisier. It was so quiet I found annoying the buzz of the fluorescent lights I hadn't even noticed in my office upstairs. At least my hearing still worked. My neighbors were a couple of pterodactyls who had done enough for The Firm over the years to deserve a little real estate. Hard to believe, but they were still reading *The Wall Street Journal* at 10 a.m., and from what I overheard, they seemed to have an infinite amount of time for talking to travel agents and caretakers of their estates.

Henry Blyth had notched seven years on Dinosaur Row before I'd arrived. He had perfected the art of sleeping over research reports, hunched at an angle that could have fooled no one. That he was a world-class farter was evident even from my office two doors down. He welcomed me to my new world by asking me to lunch soon after my arrival.

"Great New England clam chowder, eh?" he self-satisfiedly slurped after I'd seen no way to dodge the invite. He had ordered a car to take us from our offices at Forty-Ninth and Seventh to the 21 Club, a two-minute walk away.

"Not bad," I replied, hoping I wouldn't run into anyone. Blyth had been a legendary commercial paper trader, but everyone knew he was history. For me, in this context, he was a symptom, a symptom that I had contracted irrelevance.

"So, how's retirement treating you?" he asked with a twinkle in his eye, just as Atkins, the Morgan Stanley Structured Finance chief, walked by our table. I had seen him coming too late to lean down and hide my face behind my napkin.

"Jed!" he exclaimed, waving his companion ahead with a sotto voce aside. "Old friend. Give me a sec. Meet you at the coat check." Then turning his full attention to me with the fleetest of glances in Blyth's direction, "You dog! On the links too often to give me a call?"

"I don't play golf," was the best I could do by way of riposte.

"Well, if you can find time in your busy schedule," he said, his look resting longer than necessary on Blyth's poorly tied, chowder-stained cravat, "let's do lunch…I mean, at some point."

"Let's," I said, eschewing the opportunity to introduce my fellow diner. I was grateful not to see his expression as he walked away.

From my new window, I could still look down at the people milling about on Seventh Avenue. Some of them, as before, looked up to see the sign scrolling around the building with its ever-changing versions of the same message: Lehman is a powerful money-making machine. But from this lower floor, they seemed bigger, realer. At some point I started closing the blinds.

Petey's wife, Susan, sometimes called to put my granddaughter Allison on the phone. "How awe you, gwampy?"

"Fine, sweetie. You're nice to call your grandpa." She was three years old, and her uninformed optimism lifted my spirits.

"What awe you doing now, gwampy?" Since the answer was basically "nothing," I would have taken this as an accusation from anyone else.

"I am thinking about ways to make money," I answered. Had the advantage of being sort of true.

"How?"

"How what, sweetie?"

"How does money get maked?"

"That is such a smart question!" I said. "I will tell you soon. Could you put your mother back on?" I made a smooching sound, but I was already thinking about all the money Lehman was making in real estate and how I could get my hands on some more Lehman shares, legally of course, before the rest of the world figured it out.

Almost a year after I borrowed the first $25 mil, late December of '07, the Lehman stock was trading in the low sixties, way below the average price of $77.50 I'd paid with the first tranche of the B of A money. One of my moles on thirty-one had told me that Gould would buy in a ton more stock at some point, if only to signal his confidence in The Firm, show his cojones. And I was thinking I needed to get in front of that.

It was around then I returned from lunch to find a cleaning lady in my office. She was stretching to dust the highest slats of the blinds, so I could not but notice, before she heard me and turned around, that she had a fine figure. The carpets were thick, and she gasped when she finally saw me standing a few yards from her. She was wearing a blue uniform which said, "ABM Cleaning–Leave the Dirty Work to Us," and underneath, "Maria Gonzales."

"Oh, Mr. Cheencowska!" she gasped, "I will come back later." I was delighted that she knew my name until I remembered it was on the door.

"That's perfectly all right, Ms. Gonzales. You finish your work. I will just go about my business," I said.

"No, no mister," she said, sending me a fleeting smile and

grasping the handle of the vacuum cleaner as if to leave. She looked to be in her early forties.

"I insist," I said. She blushed and returned to her work. I decided this was a good time to pick up a few more Lehman shares. "Liam," I said, speaking distinctly as soon as I got through to him. "Please send $20 million to my personal account as soon as possible." She had been kneeling to return a plug to its socket when her head shot up in my direction. Very gratifying.

Tuesday of the following week, right after the earnings were reported, I swooped in and acquired 312,000 more shares at an average of around sixty-four dollars a share. Great execution from my man Kelly on the desk! His intelligence would not challenge the measurement capacity of the Stanford-Binet scale, but he knew how to work a buy order.

I can't pinpoint the moment when Amanda started getting intrusive about what I was doing with the Bank of America. She never used to bug me about what I was up to as long as I made sure there was enough petty cash around, but now, it was: "Jed, how much do we owe B of A?"

"*We* don't owe them anything. *I* owe them $45 million."

"This makes me uncomfortable."

"Comfort isn't everything."

"I hope you know what you're doing."

"Please pass the salad," I replied.

By the end of February '08, the Lehman stock had cracked to $51 on rumors that The Firm was overexposed to the real estate markets. Where the fuck was Gould with the $1.6 billion he was supposed to spend buying in stock? Anyway, whatever, my $275 million worth of Lehman stock was worth over six times my B of A debt. This did not prevent Amanda from frequently getting on my case. I found her inquiries extraordinarily aggravating, and we had been on each other's nerves for weeks when she walked into my study the night before I had agreed to leave with her for ten days in Cabo San Lucas. Carelessly, I had forgotten to close the door.

"Hey," she said brightly. She was always in a good mood the night before leaving for vacation. I looked up.

"Hey," I replied brusquely.

"Whoa, someone's not in a great mood."

I waited a beat without smiling, then decided to avoid a tiff. This was the month her father had died. She was perennially on edge this time of year. Why not be nice?

"Always hard to get out of town." Still not what she wanted to hear.

"It's the stock, isn't it? Why don't you just sell, pay off the damned debt, and be done with it? Pick another hobby."

Hobby?! Now I was pissed. She was calling my stewardship of our finances a hobby.

"It's like I am married to a self-destructive screen addict," she continued. "You think because you watch the stock incessantly everything is going to be alright? There are market screens in Cabo."

Relentless! Despite the number of times I had told her to back off. I realized then that just because you love someone, this does not mean hurting them can't give you pleasure. "Now it's clear," I baited.

"What?" she bit.

"Why your father threw you out of the house!" *Ha!* I chortled to myself as she turned beet red. My satisfaction was short-lived, however, because now she was as furious as I'd ever seen her.

"How…how dare you!" She was so livid she could barely get the words out. "You…you want to play the father card? Let's talk about yours…a reckless, serially self-destructive entrepreneur-dreamer who couldn't keep his shit together in the end."

"Look, I didn't mean to annoy you," I said, immediately putting her brutal dig out of my mind (until today).

"Annoy?" She was incredulous. "Annoy is for mildly offensive." She was apoplectic.

I knew I had gone too far, so resigned myself to her venting a bit before I finally sucked it up and attempted the climbdown.

"Look, Amanda. I am sorry. I was insensitive, ungenerous, and in general a dick. I'm sorry."

"So noted," she said after a long pause, and then, as she strode toward the door, "Open or closed?"

When we returned from Cabo after eleven days of bickering, mainly about my "neurotic" need to "constantly" be in the Business Center, the stock was trading solidly in the fifties, so, naturally, I was feeling the urge to average down and buy some more. Kelly was telling me that Gould was lightening up on a bunch of illiquid mortgages and that worries about the Lehman balance sheet were so much bullshit...or as he put it "overexaggerated."

I returned to my office one afternoon in March to find the cleaning lady. She bent to turn off her machine as I entered, and I noticed again her alluring curves. This time, though, I was smacked by the authentic pungent odor of her body as I brushed by. She smelled like honest work. "Hello, mister," she said deferentially as she stood and turned her attention to dusting. This time she did not ask whether it would be OK for her to continue. Two days earlier I had called down $25 million more from Pennoyer, bringing my total debt to B of A up to $70 million. So, the liquidity was waiting when I called Kelly. I kept Maria in my peripheral vision: "Hey pal, I want to buy about $25 million worth of stock at no more than $46 a share. Take your time over the next three days. Let me know when it's done." Maria Gonzales looked at me as Jane looked at Tarzan, and I thought that she was the sexiest woman I had ever encountered. For some reason, I decided right then and there to grow a mustache.

I became used to seeing her at the same time after lunch, around two. I observed that her shirt covered a built-in elastic belt holding up her ABM Cleaning pants. "Tell me, Ms. Gonzales, would it suit your schedule to come later in the day, say four-thirty, five, five-thirty?" I heard myself ask one afternoon. She nodded assent, and the next day she came at five. After five or six days of overlapping with her in the late afternoons, I was thinking of her incessantly. By April, I had a plan.

"Ms. Gonzales," I said one afternoon. "Would you please come here a moment?" I opened the middle drawer of my desk, and when she arrived, I said, "I had $2,000 in hundred-dollar bills in this drawer yesterday." She was standing history-makingly close to me. "Do you have any idea where that money might have gone?" Her sharp intake of breath was covered by my quickly adding, "I am sure it wasn't you. Just want to enlist your help in keeping an eye on things." As I said this, I counted twenty hundred-dollar bills into the drawer. "Those are for you, in gratitude for your past work and your future vigilance." She looked up at me with her mouth open, which was just the reaction I had been hoping for. I pulled her to me and gave her a deep kiss. For a moment, she did not push me away, but when she did, she ran out, leaving the money and all of her stuff.

As the weeks and months went on, she sporadically allowed me to kiss her, and I remember the first time she let me undo one by one the four hooks of her brassiere. My hand was trembling as if it were my first time with my first Maria, the one I still saw from time to time when I was on the West Coast. The money I deposited in the drawer for my more recent eponymous East Coast friend had grown to over $34,000, but she would not permit me to reach into her ABM Cleaning pants. I knew then and know now nothing about her personal situation. Was she married, a mother? Did she live in Brooklyn, Queens, the Bronx? I thought she, worst case, didn't hate our embraces.

By the time I bought my last slug of Lehman stock—based on solid input, not just from Kelly, but from senior friends in mortgage backeds, structured finance, commercial real estate, and compliance—with the last money available under my credit line, it was August, and the stock was down to $20. I was still above water with a lifetime average purchase price of $11.25 a share, but my 7.3 million shares marked to market were worth only $146 million. And now it wasn't just Amanda who was on my case about the debt to Bank of America, it was B of A itself, first in the form of Pennoyer, and then, one Tigran ("Tiger") Bedrossian, a total asshole who couldn't wait to let me know he was from the "Work-Out Department" and that I would be dealing exclusively with him from now on: "I need for you to sell one of your houses," was his introductory hello.

"I would prefer to find another solution."

"Prefer? This isn't about fucking prefer, my friend. But if you want to go prefer, would you prefer that I a) come and take all the pictures off your walls or b) dump the stock, close out your Lehman position, and send you the change, if any?"

As August dragged on and the stock slid to the mid-teens, I sold everything I could without Amanda noticing, other than the Lehman shares, of course. But she noticed anyway and was on my case like embroidery on a uniform.

"Dump it, Jed. Sell the stock. Forget about 'upside.'"

Secure in my superior knowledge, I resisted. What did she know about finance in general or Lehman Brothers in particular?

"The reality is that once this irrational panic is over, the stock will be worth multiples of today's price."

"Reality? How about this: When an overwhelming number of investors disagree with your reality, then their reality wins. It's what's called a market, no?" I hated that she had reason on her side, and we had a knock-down drag-out dinner argument the evening of September 8. The stock had closed at $14.15, and all the shares I owned were worth barely over the $100 million I owed. "Jed, what is the point? Sell! Sell the goddamn shares. A hundred eleven million shares traded yesterday, three hundred eighty-three million today. You won't have any problem finding a buyer!"

Who knew she was watching the stock that closely? I chewed my *duck à l'orange* and poured myself a little more Chateau Griffon chardonnay, saying nothing.

"You are irresponsible!" she finally screamed, throwing her napkin on the table and storming out of the room. She had no idea what Lehman Brothers balance sheet assets were worth. I didn't either, but at least I could rely on the good information my former colleagues were feeding me. I admit to being worried, but this was a bad time to sell.

I was in my study going over the uncomfortable corner I was in when the phone rang. It was Robby calling, almost certainly at Amanda's request. "Hi, dad. Just called to say hi."

"Well, how nice. How are Alice and Sally?"

"Listen, dad—"

"Robby," I interrupted, "can we just stipulate that you asked me to exercise proper caution regarding the family finances and that I seemed very receptive?"

"You mean we don't need to have the actual conversation?" Petey would not have needed me to spell it out for him.

"That's right, son."

"Oh, they're fine."

"Huh?"

"The girls are in good shape."

During the course of the next day, I watched in horror as the stock plunged to $7.79. Before the close, I took $20,000 out of the Maria drawer and bought her 2,500 shares. Due to commissions, the trade came to over $20K, but I ate the difference. And when she came by at five, I motioned her over to my desk to explain the financial maneuver I had generously executed on her behalf. She dragged her island with her vacuum cleaner, dusters, and cleaning fluids over to me and listened to my explanation.

"So, soon you will have a valuable stock certificate for Lehman shares," I concluded.

"You are very kind Mister Cheencowska," she said in a tone that I found encouraging.

Perhaps today was my day. I pulled her close and this time, after I kissed her and unfastened her bra, she allowed me to turn her around, but once again, she stopped me when I tried to reach into her lower garments. And then, out of the blue, she began to cry. The more I tried to comfort her, the louder she got. The odds of anyone being around to hear her were low, but you can never be too sure. I flicked the on switch to her vacuum cleaner and exited over the roar of her machine.

The next day, a Wednesday, the stock halved again to close at $4.25, and it was then I finally realized I was ruined. Thursday, Friday, through the end of the day today, Monday, the 15th, over one trillion shares traded. I capitulated to the panic and dumped what I could, but counting commissions, I got out at an average price lower than today's close of twenty-one cents per share. So, after all these years, my entire pile of Lehman shares is worth only a million and change.

The bank has been selling our art collection, theoretically worth more than a hundred million dollars at some point in the past, but guess what? That was then, and this is now. It's a fire sale! Everyone is trying to change solids into liquids at the same time, but it turns out that when under pressure, solids are flammable. And it all goes up to Money Heaven. I learned that an estivating Pennoyer emerged from his summer cave to snarf up two of my Picassos and one Magritte. Amanda, God bless her, is not bashing me with the I-told-you-so's. The closest she came to reproaching me was a rueful glance in my presence at the empty space where her favorite Thiebaud had hung. Much less chastisement than I deserved. In fact, I am amazed at Amanda's upbeat demeanor. I would say she's coming to grips with our fall to a lower stratum with surprising ease.

I am sorry for the loss of Maria Gonzales, both in the sense of her stock market setback in the Lehman shares and my loss of her. She will presumably fetch what remains of the money in the drawer. Amanda, meanwhile, alarmed at my shallow, strained breathing, gray skin, and profuse perspiration, has been feeding me Xanax. "It says here that thoughts of hurting yourself are a possible side effect," she warned as she handed me my first pill.

"Can you get the desire to hurt yourself from just being near the bottle?" I asked. She seemed pleased that I had spoken, but not with what I had said when she added:

"Also rage and hostility."

"Ha! I like that one. Let me practice: 'Gould, you ignorant son-of-a-bitch. You couldn't even get the fucking Koreans to buy some shares? You had months to figure this out!'"

"That's it honey," she said encouragingly as if I was like a computer that needed a few tweaks before it could sound human.

"WILLY!" I tried again. I liked the sound of it, but all I could think about was the many opportunities I myself had had to avoid catastrophe. *Fool! Idiot! Ignoramus!* I will have the rest of my life to figure out how a smart, talented, hard-working guy like me could be that dumb. Right now, though, I know I have a job to do, namely, sell everything I can get some schmuck to pay me over zero for. And I intend to get right on it, as soon as I can find a generic substitute for Xanax and wean myself down to a couple of milligrams a day in whatever hayseed backwater podunk Amanda is taking us to.

CHAPTER 10

THE WIFE

UNTIL PUBERTY, I WAS A WELL-BEHAVED, NORMAL, PRIVILEGED KID. BUT then, as my body began to cycle through those changes all women know, my infatuation with alcohol put a strain on family relations. This tense period culminated the morning after my junior prom, when my mother found me passed out in a pile of vomit on her favorite Persian rug. Along with the booze came its fraternal twin, disrespect for authority. Dad, a man of habit and order, found it especially stressful not to know where I was by his bedtime. He's the one who taught me the word "abide," as in "I can no longer abide your behavior." But I felt notwithstanding that I had a good relationship with him. In fact, thought of myself as a daddy's girl...that is, until my first real boyfriend came along.

Mom, dad, and I lived on Brattle Street in a beautiful Cambridge, Massachusetts, several-times-renovated, pre-Revolutionary War house with a large backyard, all paid for by royalties on dad's early versions of lithium-ion batteries. By the time I was a teenager, dad had become Professor Peter Watson, a tenured member of the MIT faculty. Money loved my father, and it continually found its way to him, not only through his inventions, but via equity in companies formed by his MIT students.

I was a jock and a tomboy. My friends called me Man. Despite my behavioral issues, I consistently received the highest grades at Putney. I took for granted that I was sexually attractive. The boys seemed to share an obsession with some variation on the theme of kissing me and feeling my breasts. For my part, I was curious about the hardness I felt through their pants. In one instance a boy from the senior class showed me how to help him "get off," an expression totally new to me at the time. It was all thrilling, but the idea of sexual intercourse frightened me... until Matt and I hooked up.

At first, dad seemed to approve of him. I imagined them playing tennis together or discussing the *Pentagon Papers* over breakfast at the Cape. "Nice kid, Mandy," he said when I entered his study following Matt's first visit.

I beamed, "I'm glad you liked him, dad. He is very smart, and he has a wicked sense of humor." Humor, preferably the dry kind, was high on my father's list of positive attributes.

"We'll see about that. But let's get to the important stuff: What does he know about Elizabeth Taylor?" We both chuckled. In addition to love of food and its preparation, I had come to adopt dad's passion for the actress. I look back on those hours we spent cooking together and talking about Liz as among the happiest in my life. "I said he was nice, sweetie, but remember no *Secret Ceremony*." Weaving her film titles into conversation—with extra credit for the year of release—was our little game.

"Don't worry, dad, you're not yet in danger of becoming *Father of the Bride* ('50). In fact, in my solar system, I haven't completely decided whether he has *A Place in the Sun* ('63). But I thought I'd go over to his house to do homework and figure out the answer to that question.

He smiled, "OK, but *Lassie Come Home* ('43) at a reasonable hour."

The first strike against Matt from my father's point of view was that he had a tattoo. I had warned Matt to keep it covered, but when he unthinkingly took off his sweater one evening, there it was. The second strike was that it said, "GIVE PEACE A CHANCE." Dad, who liked a strong foreign policy, saw Matt's decision to print this "hippie folderol" on his body as unforgivably poor judgment and was suddenly quite disinclined to like the young man. Then, somehow, he learned we were smoking dope and having sex together.

Is there a strike four?

Mandy, honey, and sweetie were gone forever, and I was permanently demoted to Amanda. Moreover, his opposition to my staying at Matt's became a ground-zero obsession. His resistance to the relationship was quite a contrast, understandable I suppose, to the permission he routinely gave when I asked to spend the night at the home of my best friend, Sandra Fellowes. She resembled mother but she was shorter and on the girlie end of the spectrum. Sandra wasn't crazy about Matt either, but I think she was just jealous.

In the final stage of the Matt Wars, dad pirouetted from not talking to me at all to intense harassment. Lest you think I finally moved out for no good reason, here is my best recollection, from forty years ago, of the last conversation we ever had:

"So, Amanda, what time will you be home this evening?"

I froze in the foyer. "Actually, I won't be back till tomorrow night. I'm taking my books to Matt's."

"That is not acceptable," my father wasn't looking at me. He delivered this verdict to the television.

"What isn't acceptable?" I said to the TV. "You would prefer I not bring my books?" (We both knew this conversation was headed off a cliff, but even as I pre-mourned the inevitable, I was powerless to refrain from dragging him to the edge.

Dad spun around in his chair, "You know damned well what I mean. This boy is a bad influence!"

"He is neither a boy nor an influence. He is a man and my lover." (Gratuitous, yes, and admittedly, I would have been sorry if the throbbing vein in his forehead had burst, but for Christ's sake, I was almost seventeen years old.)

Pretending to ignore the provocation, dad soldiered on, "You are not to spend the night at the Bernsteins'!" I should have mentioned that he looked down on Matt's father, Isaac Bernstein, who, even though almost forty-five, was a mere assistant professor. Also, sociology was a pseudo-science, Harvard overrated.

"Is that a prediction? If so, there's a high probability that you're wrong."

"Don't get smart with me!" he erupted.

"Dad, calm down, I'm an adult. At my age, Cleopatra was queen of Egypt."

The reference seemed to displease him greatly, if the spittle spewing forth with his next words were any indication. "What the hell does Cleopatra have to do with this?! People died in their thirties back then. It was a goddamned different bloody era!" He rarely swore. We were tumbling over the precipice.

"Not to be pedantic dad, but sixteen years is sixteen years. The earth revolves around the sun three hundred sixty-five times. Add a day for each leap year. Multiply by sixteen. What does 'era' have to do with it? The main difference between me and Cleopatra, dad, is that she did not have a father around to infantilize her seven days a week!" I perorated. (OK, screamed.)

At which point my mother entered with her attempt at peacemaking. "Now, now, Peter, Mandy. Honey, what did you say to make your father so upset?" You had to admire her good intentions.

"I said that Cleopatra was queen of Egypt when she was my age." (Not a great summary from father's point of view.)

"Was she?" mother attempted. "Then maybe you should have played her in the movie! Mandy does look like Liz Taylor, don't you think Peter?"

"Get out," father said in a dramatically faux-calm voice. "Go be queen of the Bernsteins. I won't live with this anymore."

"Sixty-three," I said, getting in the last word. "*Cleopatra* ('63)."

So, with my head held high, I moved to a warm and loving Jewish home several blocks away and began my adult life. The Bernsteins treated me like a daughter until, a year later, I left for Smith College and Matt for Wesleyan. But during that year? It was the Hatfields versus the McCoys. Isaac knew that my father (he referred to him as Herr Professor Watson) saw him as an academic poseur with questionable morals while he saw my dad as a rigid Puritan with anti-Semitic tendencies.

Not much direct contact was called for, but when they serendipitously encountered one another, as in one incident that Sandra witnessed at the Star Market, sparks flew. According to Sandra, it went something like this:

"Good afternoon, Professor Watson." This in neutral but polite tones while Isaac was squeezing a cantaloupe.

My father looked at him coldly.

"Not ripe, the way Amanda and Matt like them," Isaac said, continuing to squeeze. According to Sandra, my dad looked away at that point, gritting his teeth in an effort at self-control. And then Isaac had to add, "Perhaps you didn't hear me when I said hello."

My father hurled the radishes he'd picked up back into the bin. He took a breath, straightened up to his full height, four inches taller than Matt's dad, "You didn't say hello; you said, 'good afternoon.' And frankly, imprecision will be the latest addition to the list of things I dislike about you, Professor Bernstein. That is what they call you, 'professor,' isn't it?"

"Fuck you, Watson!" Isaac said.

"Crudeness will now be added to the list," he said as he turned and walked away, leaving Isaac, his mouth open, still holding the melon.

That year, if dad was the United States of America, mother was Switzerland to my Libya, handling all diplomatic relations between me and my father, such as they were. Her efforts notwithstanding, no rapprochement was achieved. I remember vividly the time I asked mother to tell dad I was thinking I would apply to Smith.

"What was his reaction?" I inquired when she and I met for Cokes one evening around seven at the Club 47.

"You don't really want to know."

"Tell me."

"He said, 'I don't care where she goes.' But he teared up. I could tell he didn't mean it."

"Tell him I don't care that he doesn't care," I said, turning away to dab my eyes. I hadn't totally minded being the focus of a blood feud, but I had felt (and shared) my dad's pain. Childhood images of his expressions—when he knotted his bow tie or puzzled over an equation—were seared into my memory. And when he died during my junior year at Smith without us having reconciled, my rationalizations suddenly rang hollow. The distress I had caused him, which I'd previously managed to think of as the foreordained collateral damage of my need for freedom, came to seem unjustifiable, especially since long distance had already taken its predictable toll, ending my affair with Matt Bernstein.

Knowing how righteously stubborn dad was, I would have been surprised if he hadn't cut my inheritance way back. Nor was it hard to predict he would put everything in trust for mom during her lifetime. But I was shocked when I learned that upon her death everything would go to their favorite charities, leaving me nothing.

At Smith, I majored in nutritional science, a field that existed then mainly in my own mind.

Professor Crenshaw, the head of the chemistry department, had helped me to put the right courses together when I told her about my fascination with food and nourishment. Under her guidance, I studied nutrient absorption, the science of taste, the psychology of hunger, the anthropology of food preparation, and the contextual aspects of appetite. But the best job I could land upon graduation in '74 was in Northampton itself at Sam's Diner, waiting tables for two-ten an hour plus tips. After six months of drudgery, I found a propitious moment. Sam was scraping grease from the grill and closing the register. "Boss, I need to take off next weekend."

He stared at me noncommittally.

"My close high school friend, Trish O'Malley, is getting married."

"OK," he agreed with surprising alacrity. "Just come in an hour earlier the rest of the week." But at closing time on Friday, the other shoe dropped. "No need to come back after the wedding. Business is slow," he lied, hiring his niece the next day.

I needed sponsors, or at least comrades in arms. I was feeling guilty, poor, and rootless. I knew I had a bright future if I could only get organized. Every day since graduation though, I needed to sit motionless, feeling sorry for myself, staring out the window of the cheap apartment I was sharing with a couple other Smith grads who, like me, couldn't think up a good reason to leave town. And now along with the outfits I'd assembled from the St. Vincent De Paul thrift store, I had to pack some version of a story to bring to Trish's wedding, where I would be expected to live up to my vivacious image. I practiced smiling in front of the cracked mirror in our shared bathroom and then hopped a bus to Boston.

With Jed, my husband of now thirty-three years, it was not, for me, love at first sight—far from it. Trish, a world-class manipulator, had seated me next to him, calculating that I'd find him good-looking and funny. I did, but at the same time, he struck me as conceited, a trait that, as she had also annoyingly foreseen, fascinated me.

Notwithstanding feeling somewhat programmed, I agreed to meet him the next day at the corner of Keenan and Mt. Auburn near Harvard Square. This rendezvous turned into a picnic by the Charles, our lengthy and delightful first date. At the Commodore Hotel, where the O'Malleys had installed us bridesmaids, I had trotted out for my high school friends the story about what I was up to (getting a master's in food science, teaching nutrition to underprivileged youth) rather convincingly, I believed. So, I was confident that I was ready to give an adequate accounting to this potentially interesting stranger.

Jed seemed relaxed, mature. When we got to the river, he

pulled a sheet out of his backpack and unfurled it along with some preliminary banter about the great egg salad sandwiches he'd bought from Elsie's, what a beautiful day it was, what a pretty blouse I was wearing. I asked him where he got his nice shirt.

"Barney's," he blushed. "You won't believe this, but it's made to measure."

How sweet! He was as proud as if he'd invented custom-made clothing. My dad had a closet full. A beautiful woman who looked somewhat like Sandra walked by, but he didn't take his eyes off me as I turned my attention back to him. "No wonder it fits you well," I flirted.

And then, party over, he got right down to business, "What keeps you in Northampton?"

"Oh, lots of great friends and," continuing the bullshit, "a couple of professors who are helping to guide me academically."

"Really?" I couldn't tell if it was a rhetorical intervention, or he saw right through me. "You're planning to go to graduate school?"

His smile was a truth serum. My assiduously prepared sketch of a plausible tale dissolved into a reality I had determined not to share, "Well, yes, and no. Yes, I am planning to, but no, I'm not sure I can go through with it."

"Were your parents academics?" Gallantly he was changing the subject, taking the pressure off. His hand brushed my knee. His voice was mellifluous, reassuring.

"My mother is a highly educated housewife; my father was a tenured professor at MIT."

"What was he like, your father?" he innocently inquired.

"He was... he was like—" And the next thing I knew I was fighting to keep my tear ducts from overflowing, spilling my guts out to this handsome unknown who came close and put his arm around me as I told, in more detail than perhaps he'd bargained for, the story of my familial breach. I was embarrassed when I got hold of myself and grateful when he hastened to share some of his own personal details.

In that first confessional exchange, I might have seen the entire DNA of our future relationship. I was the pampered product of a cultured and educated WASP establishment family, sometimes blue about my indeterminate future but basically upbeat. He was from a Midwest Jewish family, but not a well-educated one like the Bernsteins; and he seemed troubled by something I could not put my finger on.

"I was taught from an early age that you have to make a living."

"What does that mean, 'make a living'?"

He looked at me with such frank incredulity that I felt I had said something offensive. "What does what mean? Make a living? What does 'make a living' mean?" And then he began to laugh, first a little bit, and then a lot. I was annoyed. And to his credit, he noticed. "I'm sorry. I am laughing, not at you, but at the—" And he began laughing again. This time I gave him the benefit of the doubt. He had a nice laugh, "—at the disparity in our backgrounds. The chasm."

"Chasm? Backgrounds? What we have here is just a different understanding of how the world works. If you do something worthwhile, contributory, money comes your way, and you live. That's called making a life, not making a living."

Now he was annoyed, "It's not that money just 'comes your way.' You have to earn it! And in any event, I am damned well going to go way beyond making a living."

"What does that mean?" I asked with a growing feeling of discomfort.

"I need to be very wealthy." He was sitting ramrod straight.

"Need?"

"Yes, extremely rich." He moved on to tell about his plan to get a job on Wall Street. As he went on with what seemed less confidence, I wondered: *Was his initial projection of self-assurance just a party trick?*

I decided to change the subject. "Are you an only child?"

"I have an older brother," he said, "an academic." Now he clenched his fists. His knuckles were white. It seemed I'd made things worse. But then, as if reminding himself to return to a role he knew how to play, he sat back and leaned nonchalantly on his elbow. "Lenny relentlessly made fun of me and put me down. He was a genius at teasing me covertly. When he finally got me to hit him, his performance was Oscar-worthy, and I was always the one punished."

"So, you and Lenny were never close?" As soon as I said "Lenny" I saw him tense up again. It was like the name was his property and I, a presumptuous interloper.

"On the contrary, we were and are extremely close," he was pulling up clumps of grass.

"Are you a very forgiving person, then?" I asked soothing, conciliatory. "I mean it sounds as if he was cruel to you."

"Cruel, yes, but he taught me a great deal."

"Like—"

"Like how to project innocence," he laughed disarmingly. I contributed a forced chuckle. And while he was showing me how forthcoming he could be, he confessed to having a little "health" problem.

"I get a tad depressed occasionally, and then I have to be alone for a few hours."

"Well, that doesn't sound so bad."

"Some of my friends don't appreciate it. And it's very unpleasant for me," he said.

"I understand," I said softly. "We all have our ups and downs."

I had never known anyone so wound up. I wasn't sure this guy was for me, but I found his intensity, a kind totally different from that of my father, weirdly mesmerizing. Mom was always overwhelmed by dad's wound-upness, but until the split, I managed it well. So why shouldn't I be capable of handling Jed's fervor? Perhaps his brand was just what I needed. After we had begun dating (and he had astounded me with the depth of his own Elizabeth Taylor knowledge), I brought him by to meet my mother.

"He is a very nice boy, and I am so glad you introduced him. I like him, but one does wonder," she began.

"Wonder what, mother?" I snapped, preparing to put her assessment in my mental folder with her past critiques of my male friends.

"What I mean is that he's a lovely boy, but he is quite the go-getter. One wonders what he would not do to win," she Cassandra-ed and left it at that.

Forewarned is forearmed, but by this time, I was smitten, and I tried not to seem overjoyed when he invited me to live with him in New York City. He was renting a one-bedroom four-story walk-up with some light from a ventilation shaft, but no roaches.

Jed was a buff former tennis star, smart, practical, and if anything, even more intense than I had imagined. The sex and just about everything else between us was good. I loved his nearly hairless willowy body. It was typical then for us to make love twice a night, and I took as much pleasure in the intimacy as he seemed to. I wondered whether my boffing a guy with a Harvard MBA would have been more acceptable to my dad than "that Bernstein punk"; I felt like a real estate agent who had lowered her client's expectations with a bunch of shitty properties, only to have him die before she could produce the winner.

In those earliest halcyon days, a daily dose of sex, exercise, and marijuana, in varying permutations, was all it took to calm Jed down. He continued to be considerate of me, having figured out that when I was blue, he only had to stay out of my way for a while, and my internal gyroscope would put me to rights. I felt great about the balance of distance and attention he gave me, ceding the kitchen when I needed some space and, when I returned to my usual self, listening attentively to my ideas about the Watergate scandal or David Bowie's new hit.

However, as it turned out, my moods were not the problem. They occur within a range you would consider normal. But Jed?

Even before we left the Boston area for good, he slipped into a slough of despond for a day and a half from which he seemed incapable of emerging. He had become a different person, never smiling, speaking only, when he had to, monosyllabically. *Still*, I thought, *what are a couple of stormy days when the skies are mostly sunny?*

But it didn't totally sink in how chronic and black these funks could become until almost a year after he joined Lehman. At first, I was the one who was overwhelmed by the pace, the sheer intensity of the city. I was the one who didn't know what to wear, what to say in the new Condé Nast corporate culture where I'd wrangled a job as a junior *Bon Appétit* copy editor. But at Lehman, Jed had immediately fit right in. His peers were all strivers, salmon swimming upstream, and Jed spoke fluent Fish from day one. He loved what he called his "steep learning curve." I hated what I was learning, which had more to do with xeroxing than cuisine. I felt trapped in the pettiness and futility of office politics. I was mainly in New York to live with him. Everything that went with that was the price I paid for the privilege. Which made it particularly difficult when he experienced his first full-on New York incident. I came home from work one Friday to hear him sobbing in the bathroom. I knocked on the door, gently at first, and then, as I heard the sound of breaking glass, with increasing urgency.

"Jed, let me in."

"Go away."

"Jed, I can help. I love you."

Silence.

"And I took a lot of psychology courses."

He began to laugh. Initially this was encouraging, but then he became hysterical and started breaking things again. One particularly loud crash followed by breaking glass sounded like my Pond's facial cream hitting the mirror. He was screeching with laughter, gasping, gulping for air.

"Jed, shall I call a doctor? Let me in, please honey." I was scared, desperate.

"Leave me the fuck alone," he screamed when his breathing returned to normal. I had never heard such a combination of anger and gloom. He was unwilling or unable to talk to me.

I didn't remember reading anything about this in psych classes, so on Saturday I went to the library and spent much of that weekend studying depression. But I couldn't concentrate. I was frightened to the point of failing to repress the question. Have I made a horrific mistake? And how much I hated living in New York, the beggars everywhere, the sirens, the honking, the garbage smells! I tried to call forth Jed's positive attributes, but I was mainly furious that I had to leave the apartment to find a bathroom. By Sunday morning, only an aversion to quitting was keeping me from leaving for good. I gave it one last shot that evening.

"Talk to me, baby. Tell me what you're thinking," I said through the door.

"Dark," was all he responded.

"Did something really bad happen?" I asked after a decent interval.

"Bad," he said.

But shortly thereafter he emerged, pale and bleary-eyed, with a sheepish grin. Like a flight attendant after three hours on the runway, he thanked me for my patience. At last, he could tell me about an inference a partner had made that he was misusing inside information. And when he asked how I had spent the weekend, he seemed grateful for my recommendation that he see a shrink. What scared the hell out of me, though, was this: If a mere accusation could send him into such a dive, what would become of him, of us, if he had a real, serious career setback? I came to realize that I had on my hands a complicated, neurotic personality with an ineluctable pull toward despondency. By the time he proposed, we both understood that an essential component of my job as wife was to serve as keystone in the workarounds allowing him to function.

When at last he found a psychiatrist, I invited myself to a celebratory cocktail party. The RSVP came back instantly, the hostess was the only guest, and the vodka was plentiful. Alas, what with the stresses and strains of making a new life in a new world, I required fewer and fewer excuses to celebrate. I concealed the evidence of my nightly indulgences and tried to be finished with liquor by the time Jed appeared for dinner. Then a puff or two of his joint would tide me over until a few glasses of wine made me the perfect audience for his war stories. Only with my first pregnancy did I, in a demonstration of sheer willpower I am proud of to this day, put the bottle aside for a few years.

I thought that having a child together would be an adventure that would bring us closer. But after I became pregnant with Peter, our first, Jed seemed to take my occasional despondency as a choice, a volitional decision against his interests. When Petey was finally born in 1978, my focus on our son, named in posthumous homage to my father, strained a relationship that was already far from soaring. As our marriage lost altitude, both the frequency and content of Jed's "attacks" gave me cause for concern. He was obsessed with accumulating as much Lehman stock as possible. Shortly after Petey's birth, Jed borrowed "a significant sum" to buy shares from a retiring Kuhn Loeb partner. This man "needed liquidity" just three months before his firm's acquisition by Lehman. The subsequent "attack" began one night not too long after Petey had been put to bed. Jed weaved into the bedroom holding a near empty Stoli bottle and threw himself face first into a pillow.

"What is it, honey?" I asked soothingly.

"McGinty," was what I thought I heard through the pillow.

"McGinty?"

"Yes, goddamn it, McGinty," he articulated, turning to me impatiently.

"Uh," I said while I weighed the possibility of smacking him. His eyes, scrunched with annoyance, relaxed as he must have realized it wasn't my fault I had no idea what he was talking about.

"Sawyer," he explained. "He's insinuating I found out from

Frankenberg and then ripped off his friend McGinty by buying McGinty's shares at way below the deal price."

"Did you?" I asked, surprising myself with the question. It was a couple hours since I'd drunk or smoked anything, but the room seemed to spin a bit notwithstanding.

"How the hell was I supposed to know that McGinty and Sawyer were tight?" That was all I got out of him as he exited the room, his crooked right arm holding his bottle by the neck.

Mother passed away the year after Petey's birth; she was gone before 1980 when her second grandchild, Robert, was born, and Jed was on the partnership track at Lehman. But she continued to give me the benefit of her occasional nocturnal counsel. "Watch out, Mandy dear. He sails close to the wind," she warned in my dreams with monotonous predictability. And I wondered whether her position in the spirit world gave her access to superior information or whether she was just a voice for my own repressed fears.

"He'll mellow out."

"Ha!" She masked her disagreement by covering her mouth as if the sound were a cough (a trick she had perfected in life) but then shut me down: "I certainly hope so, darling."

Jed and I needed a change. After we had enough income to go out to dinner once in a while and purchase the occasional bottle of cabernet, my thoughts about money had mainly to do with real estate. I was ecstatic when Jed's bonuses enabled us to move soon after Petey's birth—thirty years ago this week—from the rental on Fifty-Second to a three-bedroom co-op on Park and Seventy-Eighth. Being superstitious, I considered it good luck that the year and the cross street matched. And I seized on motherhood as the perfect excuse to drive a stake through the neck of my white-collar existence. I called my supervisor, Betty, to let her know I would not be returning to Condé Nast. "We do have a good maternity policy here," she obligatorily intoned. And then without waiting for a response, "Would you mind if I have that Montblanc pen you left on your desk?"

The move, a mere two years later, following Robby's arrival—into the four-bedroom "with live-in maids" that Jed could use as his study—was a project I handled with enthusiasm fueled by hope, despite the fact that our first upgrade had produced no positive impact on our marriage. The place was on Eightieth, two blocks up the avenue, also an obvious good luck sign. When a renovation of the master bath revealed a colony of mice, I had the city's most expensive exterminators in and out in a flash. I heard Jed could be tough on his Lehman subordinates, but when the installation of my eight-burner Garland was 1/32 of an inch off, I was tougher on the contractor than the exterminator had been on the mice. I made the guy take it out and start over. The wood on the inlaid chopping block had to be redone, and the green I had chosen for the ceiling required several redos. Jed suffered my perfectionism with decreasing patience, but his obsession with work gave me the leeway I needed. Only four years later, I found us the propitiously located Eighty-Fourth and Park seven-bedroom duplex that Jed and I are clattering around in now for a week more until we move out of the city for good.

And indeed, 1984 was an eventful year. Jed, who'd recently made partner, was very unhappy with Lehman's decision to sell to American Express. ("I not only have to give up my Lehman stock but also to pay taxes on the fucking proceeds!") That year, too, Jed's mentor Frankenberg retired, and he hired an unnecessarily good-looking assistant named Deborah Cunningham. Like me, she was tall and curvaceous. Her stomach was as flat as mine before I had the kids.

Deborah projected a brisk competence, and I didn't totally mind her snooty British accent, nor was I jealous of the fact that Jed spent, as he would say "an order of magnitude" more time with her than he did with me. No, what I couldn't stand was what I inferred from the conversations I perforce had with her from time to time: She thought I was a spoiled bitch who had fucked my way to comfort while she actually had to work for a living. I mean, she never said it, but you could tell from our earliest phone conversations.

"Why Mrs. Czincosca, how pleasant to hear from you."

"Please call me Amanda, and by the way, I go by Watson. Mrs. Czincosca was Jed's mother, and she's dead."

"What can I do for you, Ms. Wats—I mean—Amanda?" (Was it my imagination or was she mocking me? I guess you had to be there.)

"Jed says you might be willing to book our flights for spring break."

"Of course, Ms.—Amanda. Just give me the details."

"Well, there will be five of us leaving for San Juan the morning of March 20, returning the 31st in time for dinner."

"Five, Amanda?"

Yes, bitch. The number between four and six. "We have invited a young woman named Ann O'Muilleoir to join us."

"Oh, of course. My error, Amanda. You are bringing an au pair." (Meaning, "Is there anything you yourself actually do?") And now, through clenched teeth, I was asking myself whether using my name in every sentence was outright ridicule or still somewhere in the outer solar system of politeness. "Shall I help you with the hotel accommodations, or is that one of those things you like to handle yourself?"

Maybe I was just annoyed that I was even having this conversation instead of Jed, but I was sure she wanted to say, "one of those *few* things."

"Yes, please. We will be staying at the Ritz Carlton."

"Of course. Will that be all, Amanda?"

"Thank you, Deborah. It was a pleasure to speak with you; I look forward to seeing you again in person one of these days," I dissembled, managing to sign off before being Amanda-ed once more.

It took me a few years, but I finally got her gone.

Like many of the competent women who completed a tour of duty on Jed's desk, Deborah probably had no idea what was involved in being dragged to a corporate event. When I arrived at one of those god-awful galas, I usually tried to find one woman, late twenties, early thirties, close to about 5'5" with dark hair and an athletic figure, who I could follow with my eyes, using her as a *point d'ancrage* as I applied myself to the art of not drinking too much.

Every now and then, Jed would extricate himself from a handshake and sidle up to me, offering some unsavory anecdote about a fellow guest. "You know Ralph Ripkin? The client over there with the red suspenders? He and his wife have a line in their pre-nup: For every nanny he screws, he has to raise her allowance by $60K a month." The subtext of his stories was, *Thank God, we're not those people.* They always sent me back to the bar for another watered-down G&T.

As Jed rose in the firmament of finance, I was his principal witness and, I guess, main beneficiary. I watched and supported him through thick and, as they say, thin. Except that, until this year of the bankruptcy, there was no thin. Over the years, I met a good number of the other Lehman Brothers (and a few sisters considered brotherly enough to have been accepted into the fraternity), and they all seemed to share Jed's relentless ambition. They also shared his love of competition. They reframed every situation into a win/lose contest for the smartest, quickest, cleverest. And richest, which was, for them, the ultimate litmus test. My competitive streak was limited to tennis, although it did annoy me that so many younger people had been able to forge successful careers in nutrition, my field if I'd not been too early. Jed, unlike me, but of a cloth with his "brothers," was competitive about everything, channeling most of his energy into making money, or, as he put it, "creating value."

In contrast to my father's apparently effortless success in the money-making department, Jed's approach seemed to require a huge time commitment and lots of emotional energy. He worked his ass off. And I have always thought of him as "honest" in the sense that he prefers to tell the truth because it makes his life less complicated. When he prevaricates, a few beads of sweat appear on his upper lip. "Perhaps you should grow a mustache," I suggested one evening after he made up some BS about why he needed to miss Robby's chess tournament for a trip to the West Coast. I was pretty damn sure he was enjoying a fling with a Maria-something who, mistaking me for the help, had called from the LA area code and asked me to take a message.

My partner and I had finished a couple sets of singles the night after Jed left for Los Angeles. We'd taken our leave, and she was walking down the path into the low August sun when I spoke to a young pro at the Quogue tennis club, who'd been peeking at me all summer with sex in his eye.

"How about we play a few quick games?" I knew he'd been captain of his New Jersey high school team.

"I don't know, Ms. Watson," he demurred. "Isn't it getting kind of late?"

"C'mon, Max." I then proceeded to dominate him in a set that would have ended six-love if I hadn't thrown one game before crushing him. He couldn't believe the runner-up prize he received in the clubhouse.

And, when Jed headed west again in December, I gave myself an especially nice early Christmas present—one Peyton Chandler, the boys' math teacher. Peyton was harder to abandon than the ball boy, and I sporadically found occasions to return to that particular peccadillo. Once, with Jed on a business trip, I spent a couple days with Peyton, and I thought, *A teacher does something real!* Most of Peyton's friends were educators, and they all seemed to draw a sense of self-worth that came from their work.

When Jed returned, I wanted to talk about my own prospects. "Do you ever think you would have been happier if you'd married someone who had a real career?" I asked him one morning from the other side of his *Wall Street Journal*.

"Huh?" he replied without lowering the paper, and he pushed the carafe towards me as if I'd asked for more coffee.

I decided to change tack. "You know? I'm worried the boards and volunteer work aren't enough for me."

"Fine," he said absentmindedly as if agreeing to something I hadn't asked for. My silence apparently caught his attention, and he lowered a corner.

"So, I've decided to go for a degree at the Culinary Institute of America."

"Whatever makes you happy," he said, returning to the paper.

I had been attending classes for around two months when the topic came up again over soufflé and lemon butter asparagus.

"Delicious. Dora is getting better."

"I made those dishes."

He seemed surprised. "When did you learn to do that?" he asked.

"Last week." I was pleased. At least he'd said "when" and not "where."

My mother, who had continued her habit of visiting my dreams, kept the fault lines of my marriage front and center. Often, right after one of his attacks, she would jump into my night mind with a few of her not-too-subtle hints. Occasionally, she would appear even before an attack. As she had during the late eighties when various bankers were convicted of insider trading. "I am sure he'll be alright—," she affirmed one Wednesday at 3 a.m. while shaking her head no.

"Stop!" I dream-screamed.

In fact, he had seemed especially nervous earlier that very evening when he excused himself from dinner "to prep for my

SEC deposition tomorrow." I had been biting my nails, figuratively speaking, but when he returned from the Thursday deposition, I affected only mild curiosity. "Oh, that?" he told me. "Routine. They're just doing their job." When Lehman returned to the public markets with its spin-off from American Express, Jed recommitted himself to the objective of acquiring as many Lehman shares as possible. The options and restricted stock he was granted were nowhere near enough. He was certain that increasing his ownership of The Firm was the best way to build wealth.

"I am averaging up," he told me, "Using the liquidity we have plus what I can borrow to buy stock."

As he loved to remind me, I knew little about finance, but I did ask, "Is that prudent?"

"Yes!" he said with conviction. "There is no better way to build wealth than to put your eggs in one closely watched basket."

"But what if the stock goes down?" I asked.

"It will," he said. "And when it does, that's a buying opportunity. Over the long run, it's a no-lose proposition."

In the end, though, he was wrong about that. The day of the bankruptcy, thousands of people were thrown out of work. Everyone in our co-op suddenly looked at me like I had leprosy. I canceled all our memberships and subscriptions, tried to recover a deposit I'd made on camp for the grandchildren. Two weeks later, somebody came to haul away all our furniture. I didn't even ask them who they were.

And you know what? I'm relieved. Relieved that disaster took the form of financial ruin. Mother returns occasionally to do an understated happy dance about how right she was, but failing to get much of a rise out of me, she appears less frequently. And so now, in my fifties, I go for the second time from riches to rags. It's a good thing one of us knows how to handle such a reversal. Because Jed? Jed is in shock. He simply could not have imagined that his rock, The Firm he put most of his waking hours into and every buck he could get his hands on, would one day go KAPLOOIE.

He wanders around the house in a daze. Sometimes he talks to our soon-to-be-former accountant, trying to salvage what he can. Sometimes he talks to Robby and Petey or our grandkids. He took one call from his brother Lenny, which left him quite agitated. "Fuckin' Lenny is giving ME fuckin' financial advice," he moaned after hanging up. But mainly he is affectless. He shuffles from room to room in his slippers, ceding all decisions about our non-financial life to me.

Will I miss certain luxuries? Perhaps. But I'm sure I can play tennis on public courts. Maybe I can pick up a few cooking jobs. And damn it, I love the idea of starting over. I have found a rental in a town where we can make a new life, where I can guide Jed through a reinvention of himself. I won't have to make small talk at client dinners with vapid "decision makers," yell at seatmates at impossibly loud corporate gatherings, or pick up early-morning calls from wealthy egomaniacs. I'll grow things. Make things. And the best news of all is what Peyton just told me: She and her three cats will live right down the block.

CHAPTER 11
THE COPE

I AM TOLD THAT ON THE ANNIVERSARY OF A LOVED ONE'S DEATH, SOME, without knowing why, feel down. For me, there's never been any mystery about my sadness in the days around September 15. But on this Friday in 2017, the ninth anniversary of Lehman's bankruptcy, I am not especially depressed. Of course, it doesn't help that there are those who hold that the world would be better off if all bankers were in prison. Not long after the crash, there was even this one nutcase stalking me with ridiculous placards in front of our co-op, and on our last day in the city he screamed: "Shame! Shame! Why don't you just fucking kill yourself?"

I know how to kill corporations. CEOs used to hire us "to consider our strategic alternatives" when they really meant "to sell our company for the highest price," thus ending its existence. For humans, an analogous decision involves more complex considerations, though the shame of the quitter must be present for failing CEO and man on the ledge alike. Once you kill yourself, you're not around to face the embarrassment of everyone knowing you couldn't take it anymore, but still, if you cared even a little about your posthumous reputation...

The problem with most methods is that they leave traces; even arsenic is now detectable. And acquiring most poisons involves traceable interaction with other human beings. Although I suppose if one knew what one was doing one could get enough cyanide from some common pesticides. It's quick, I hear.

My mind drifts back to my father's *farkakte* idea for a business, which enabled one spouse to commission confidentially the death of the family pet, and this reminds me of the guy who hires a hitman to rub himself out. But I couldn't stand the suspense of waiting for that end any more than I could live through the seconds falling from the observation deck of the Empire State building to the pavement on Thirty-Third Street (less traffic than Fifth Avenue). I read somewhere that a poorly cooked fugu, that Japanese puffer fish delicacy, kills twenty or more of them a year. It's said to be fast and painless.

Of course, if "something happened" to me, Amanda would have to handle the details, but after forty-some-odd years managing our lives, that task would hardly challenge her.

Hyperorganized as she is, I wonder if she hasn't already prepared the mourners' seating arrangements and the order of speakers. She went to bed hours ago, so I am free to sit here in my over-upholstered thrift-store bargain and listen to the house complain about the humidity rolling in from the waters off Fire Island. The house is around the same vintage as I am, but, absent some unforeseeable occurrence, I have a good shot at outlasting it.

Lighting up the remains of the joint I've been nursing, I experience that reliable euphoria that, thanks to the miracle of twenty-first century agronomy, is cheaper and faster than when I was coming up. It's also legaller. I have this old roach holder in the shape of a turn-of-the-century door key. When you press down upon it, it opens along a secret fault line, and then it becomes a clasp as you release it. I'm using it to relight what's left of the smoke I started an hour ago, and now I'm ready for the self-examination that brings me to this moment of clarity.

There's no point dwelling on the high points of my thirty-one years on The Street. I mean, what can be learned from revisiting the victories that cumulatively led me to my downfall? (Although that IBM deal that raised my net worth to a hundred million bucks, my first "Unit" as they say, does stand out.) No, I'll begin at the beginning: the day after the Lehman bankruptcy, when numbness gave way to fury. The day when the extent of the damage caused by the leverage and hidden correlations among my investments became finally, irrevocably, unavoidably clear.

I didn't need access to the Lehman website, which was out of order, to know the score. The math didn't lie. No matter how many times I multiplied my number of shares by the twenty-one cents to which the stock had impossibly fallen, I came up with the same $1,533,000 dollar result. Not even close to enough to cover my indebtedness. Multiplier, multiplicand, product. I sat there paralyzed, in a daze, mentally listing the prime numbers embedded in that product, writing it in Roman numerals, trying to rhyme it with something.

I was broke, and I had not a soul to blame but myself. And blame myself, I did. Every waking hour then was consumed with self-directed anger. I was more blitzed than sober most of that period. I bumped into walls, cut myself, stubbed my toes, sprained my wrist, lost thirty pounds. There were times when, like a weightlifter in a failed bench press, I could no longer sustain the burden of my inadequacies, and every day I would discover theretofore unspelunked depths of self-loathing. Nightly, I fell asleep calling myself names.

My main asset, after my creditors took everything else, had become a prepaid life insurance policy for $20 million, a ludicrously insignificant amount before the fall but suddenly more than twenty times my worldly wealth. Thinking nothing of the no suicide condition at the time I purchased the policy, my plan had been to shield what was, in those days, a small sum, from confiscatory estate taxes. My then lawyer traded MetLife a low up-front premium for no time limit on their ability to contest the death payment. Thus, I knew that unless Amanda won the lottery and predeceased me, or I had a strike-it-rich-again brainstorm, that one lousy asset would likely constitute the preponderance of my estate.

I've maintained a vivid memory of Amanda's attempt to comfort me the morning after Lehman's vaporization. We were sitting on the unmade bed in the master bedroom before the imminent arrival of Bank of America's movers. I feel right now her hand gently brushing my arm, and I cringe as I did then.

"Money isn't everything, honey. You still have your health," she said in a gratingly soothing tone. She persisted in her futile attempts, stroking what remained of my hair. "We gave our kids a great education; they are happily married, gainfully employed—" As she worked her way down her list, I interrupted her before she could get to "We still have each other."

"I am sure you're right, sweetheart. What's, oh, around $400 million down the tubes?" I remember how great it felt to say that. I didn't try to contain the sarcasm; I had to punish her for seeing me so belittled. So, I'd hardly paused for breath, "And of course the house in Quogue will be sold." Our boys had grown up in that place. We'd been looking forward to spending time with the grandkids there, but she didn't react, and I pressed ahead. "Darling, I hope you understand, we will need to give up our membership in the Westhampton Country Club." After hitting her with the country club thing, I laughed maniacally to myself. She must have known I was just warming up.

"That's too bad darling, but I understand," she murmured.

I charged ahead, not pausing to explore what she understood. "They won't want you on the board of the World Wildlife Fund or the New York Public Library. I'm resigning from MoMA. We will have to sell the art."

Numbness. No reaction.

Tonight, as I roll a joint using only my right hand, a technique I perfected years ago, I easily call forth images of the paintings which for that last instant remained on our walls:

"The Rothko, the Thiebaud, that little Matisse, the Manets—"

"STOP!" she exploded.

But gratified at last to have evoked an appropriate response, I continued in that same vein for a purgative five minutes. "The Lexus and your little BMW convertible, the weekly facials, Christmas in St. Barths…"

When at last I ran out of gas, she took one last shot at applying salve to the wound. "Well, Jed, it certainly is a setback, but we do have a lot to be thankful for."

Who could have failed to agree—which made her good-sportedness even more annoying. So I kissed her on the forehead and escaped to the next room, where the bank's movers had already begun. Because if I'd stayed another second, I would have screamed: "A setback? A setback? Financial ruin is a frickin' setback?"

When I came to The Street in the seventies, we were the best and the brightest, allocating oxygen to the creatures of the economy; we decided which enterprises got to breathe. Suddenly we were "banksters," leeches on society. Not only was I wiped out, but I was forced to live with the new reality that bankers were to be blamed for everything. No one thanked us for having facilitated home ownership among the disadvantaged. No one praised us for the good years. On the contrary, no matter what the infraction, we were the ones responsible. For example, Bernie Madoff's massive fraud, exposed a few months after Treasury Secretary Paulson euthanized Lehman? That was our fault too!

Do you have any idea what it's like to go from a seven-bedroom doorman duplex on the Upper East Side of Manhattan to a rental in Patchogue? Some artist friends, whose benefactors we had been, lived in the area, and in the fog of defeat, I had gone along with Amanda's choice. A working-class community of free-standing single homes, tiny yards with barbecue grills, Kingsfords bought at Walmart or Garlands on eBay. Nary a Wall Street type in sight, or at least, thank god, not of the senior variety.

In contrast to the alacrity with which our Park Avenue superintendent pounced on our most trivial requests, when something was broken at our Patchogue place, the elusive "Sal" forced us to grovel. And, when he deigned to appear, he made sure to underline that he did not work for me but rather for Mrs. Meyer, my landlord. He was unabashed in his dedication to punishing the one Master of the Universe he could get his hands on. It was difficult not to imagine the pleasure he took in torturing me, especially at three in the morning, when I got up to urinate in a stinking toilet that had been clogged for a goddamn week!

I had been reduced from Gulliver to a Lilliputian in the blink of an eye. Even my older brother Lenny, an academic for Christ's sake, had more money than I did. And his offer to "help any way I can" was more than I could bear. I'm sure he sympathized to an extent, but his schadenfreude was showing, his joy in the universal criticism of bankers exceeded only by his glee in being reinstated as the big brother.

There were days during that first year when part of the Business Section in *The Long Island Advance* was missing because Amanda snipped it out "for a recipe I want on the other side." She knew that a story about any former Lehman brother who was still living large would send me on a pot and vodka bender. It didn't kill me if bankers at one of Lehman's former competitors were successful, although I didn't love it, but if one of my colleagues from The Firm (ha!) avoided my fate and found his way to success...this was intolerable. In any case, Amanda's censorship couldn't reverse the fact that my failure had become the massive center of my being, a curvature in space-time pulling me toward a depression no amount of smoke and alcohol could relieve.

Although my black hole-ish mood persisted most of that initial year, Amanda, from the beginning, was skipping about as if the changes were no big deal. And I came to realize that her cheery demeanor was not some facade she was affecting. She really did not mind our descent. She liked her new life! She was capable of spending hours making or fixing things, cooking, reading a novel about love during wartime or maybe some postapocalyptic dystopia.

As I think back to that autumn of nine years ago, it almost seemed as if she had been relieved of some burden.

Once she had us moved into our new hovel, she was constantly telling me how wonderful this or that little thing was. The coffee beans from Gristedes, some thrift-store object, our quiet little street. I didn't mind much as long as she didn't insist on more than a grunt in response. She let me be, allowing me to focus on my own *meshuggaas*. And I tried to see the wonderfulness, I really did, but the best I could hope for then was that in a moment of near sobriety, a little weed would enable me to taste food or take note of a sunset. I wanted to be happier, more light-spirited, if only for her sake.

A seminal moment in my arduous path toward an even keel was the day, about a year after we left the city, when I read that the former Lehman Executive Vice President William "Leafman" Crocker had declared personal bankruptcy. I didn't know Will enough to have an opinion on him, but the idea of a senior Lehman guy in even worse shape than I was cheered me immeasurably. Apparently, he had as high a concentration of Lehman stock and even more indebtedness than I did. I had scrambled to sell everything and succeeded in satisfying my creditors, but Leafman couldn't run fast enough to avoid a pack of angry fuck-ees who were all too happy to be quoted about businesses closed and workers laid off. Before The Firm's downfall, Leafman had a team of five guys with Craftsman blowers patrolling his vast Greenwich, Connecticut, lawn to make sure that when he circled back in from the West Side heliport he did not have to see even one lousy leaf on the expanse of green he called his "front forty." And now, he wouldn't be able to borrow enough to own a hot dog stand! I, at least, could likely buy a used car on an installment plan.

And soon thereafter, with the support of Amanda, the kids, and a cheap master of social work shrink, I began to discover ways to cope with my new life. The first sign that I might find a path back to what we'd called normal in Manhattan (i.e., attacks of depression every four months or so) came that afternoon of the Leafman story. When I returned home after an unprecedented walk, Amanda had a meat loaf in the oven. "How was it?" she asked hopefully.

"Nice," I said, and she walked over to hug me by the kitchen door. I felt her sweet breath in my ear, and we stood there, our bodies pressed together, enjoying the first moment of tenderness we had shared in months.

"Patchogue actually has a decent public library," I said, breaking away. "I got a card." I held it up triumphantly, stood up straight, and almost smiled. Soon, I began wandering over there each weekday afternoon at two, until Mr. Simpson and his pretty thirty-five-year-old assistant, Rachel, came to expect me. My new venue and Leafman's financial wipeout liberated me enough from self-flagellation to make room for a bit of self-investigation. I didn't dwell on the responsibility some might have me bear for the crisis of '08. I mean, nobody gets through life without a few mistakes, and now, thank god, I understand that blaming me for the mortgage crisis would be like blaming me for America's inequality or poor race relations. Sure, I had capitalized on certain contemporary realities. That's what you are supposed to do unless you're aiming for wealth and glory only in the frickin' afterlife, no? That said, I occasionally can't avoid seeing a connection between something I had done and some real-world suffering. And when that happens, I feel a kind of errant regret. Like when Greece cratered. Yes, I had been a player in helping them write a story everyone wanted them to tell. But does that make me a war criminal, a serial killer?

I spent most of my hours at the library reading math and cosmology books. But sometimes I just sat there watching the dust motes dance in the shafts of sunlight and asking myself: "How could you have been so fucking stupid?" I apportioned some of the blame to my mother (for her intimidating business success), my father (for his terrifying failure), and my brother (for his rivalrous goading), and I heaped as much as I could on Lehman CEO Willy "The Gorilla" Gould, the pusher who turned me into a greed-addled junkie with a jones for Lehman stock.

The library routine ended in January 2010, when Amanda sprang the news that an erstwhile friend of hers on the Board of Regents had helped finagle me a job teaching math at Patchogue-Medford High. The job paid only $800 a week. But she was typically ebullient when she told me: "It's a huge breakthrough!"

I Eeyored her an "Alright…if you say so."

On the first day of work she helped me dress, fed me breakfast, and drove me to school, where she deposited me at the curb like a swaddled baby she was set on abandoning. Thus, through no initiative of my own, I had a new daily destination. And soon, a new workday schedule. There I made my first new friend, Ron Beeman, the biology teacher. Sometimes after school was over, he and I would head to a local bar and down a few beers.

"Why the long face?" He had immediately seized the role of perennial cheerer-upper. I was The Kvetch.

"My students are stupid, and they don't give a shit." Read: "If I am so smart, how did I end up as the teacher of these blockheads?" And of course, what I really meant was, "*I* am stupid and *I* don't give a shit." To Ron's credit, he never pointed that out.

"Well, Jed, you've got to believe the credo this country's founded on: All men are created equal. Our job is to give them a fair shot," was typical Ron.

"We're teachers, not sorcerers. That credo is a myth. Maybe it was true when Madison wrote the Federalist Papers." I loved to goad him out onto a limb where he waxed poetic about human potential so I could begin sawing. He knew his optimism stimulated the cynic in me, and he was happy enough to let me saw away until some of my bitterness was released, whereupon he would flit to another branch.

We began to have dinner once in a while with Ron and his wife Becky. Putting aside the privileged life we'd led, Amanda and I were at a different stage than they were. We were grandparents whereas they had kids at home. So, the four of us had to struggle our way to some common interest.

"Any chance we could persuade you guys to learn golf?" Becky attempted one evening at d'Ambrosio's, an Italian joint they'd introduced us to, whose cheap carafes of Chianti enabled a buzz, helping one ignore their lamentable lack of fresh ingredients and cooking skills. (Becky taught phys-ed and shared an interest with Amanda in alternative medicine. She had a terrific figure!)

Why the hell not? I thought to myself. It's not like I'm so jammed with other obligations. In my fleeting fantasy, Becky rubbed her body against mine as she reached around me to demonstrate how to putt. We'd finish nine holes some afternoon and then spend a couple hot hours together at the local Days Inn. I was imagining the sounds she'd be making as I stood behind her in my golf cleats while she, who'd not had time to remove her blouse, knelt, pantyless, against the bed, but then Amanda's "JED, please pass the butter" snapped me back into the conversation.

Anyway, at age sixty-two I began to play golf. I couldn't afford lessons but picked up some tips on the internet. The public course was dry and poorly maintained, but green fees were only $15 on weekdays, fifty percent more on weekends, and the balls rolled forever if you managed to stay out of the rough, so, while I rarely broke a hundred, I added this super frustrating "sport" to a pitifully paltry list of activities I was determined to get better at. And, refreshingly, it gave me a reason unrelated to past mistakes to be disgusted with myself.

There is something about a paycheck, being paid for your time, which upends your understanding of money. It was difficult to get my mind around the fact that I was grossing $800 a week, an amount equal to about a fifth of what I made an hour in a run-of-the-mill $10 million year on The Street. And there, it would have been ludicrous to think of compensation in temporal terms; in fact, if you had told me my comp had anything to do with an hour, I would have laughed. Also, I had good tax lawyers who reduced my federal and state taxes to the level of a mere aggravation, while Medicare and other little nicks were unnoticeable. But as a working man, a teacher, the mandatory $83 social security contribution and the $20 for Medicare were no joke. After withholding, my monthly take-home pay was a lousy $718! Embarrassingly, Amanda's occasional income from cheffing jobs, a hobby in New York City, came to have a noticeable positive impact on our Patchogue budget.

Although I could not have foreseen it, it was Dalia, my favorite grandchild, who was to yank me back to my lifelong love affair with money. Of course, at the time of her birth, before the death of Lehman, no pulling was necessary. I was still in an accumulation mode. I had been giving heavily to presidential candidates of both parties and believed that, regardless of who landed in the Oval Office, I had a decent shot at becoming secretary of commerce. When I first laid eyes on her, she was wearing a onesie with a picture of a defecating diaper-wearing baby bull which read, "Trickle-down economics is BULLSHIT." Robby's wife, a bleeding-heart liberal, was clearly responsible for this incredible display of bad taste. You can't blame a newborn for what she's wearing, I reassured myself, and by Dally's fourth month, we clicked. That first time she looked me in the eye and smiled, I received a jolt I never recovered from. She was a bridge joining me with the past and the future, a connection at the soul level such as I had never experienced before.

I wanted her to have everything that money could buy, but she never showed interest in physical luxuries. She pushed away all the state-of-the-art toys I brought her. She favored simple objects, which she used to connect with people. When she eventually could speak, she said: "Gwampa, pway." And play we did. Her stuffed animals had many questions. At first, they were simple like, "Why do people shake hands?" But even then, it was clear that my, "Because it's polite," which would satisfy most kids, would lead her (and me) along a never-ending path of Whys. And soon I felt as if I, only I, was the fount of knowledge capable of satisfying her special brand of curiosity. In the early days, a giraffe named Claude (aka Cwowd) was her principal vehicle for questions. By the time she was two and a half, the baton had been passed to Katy the Kitten, who asked me why we count in tens. But by her fourth birthday, her rabbit, the formidable Floppalong, had become her Enquirer-in-Chief: "What does the earth weigh, Mr. Grampa?" Only Dally herself was permitted to call me "gramps." I did my best to explain the difference between mass and weight in Rabbit, and when Floppy (which I called him to put him at his ease) wanted to know why water gets bigger when it freezes, I was able to come up with an explanation I felt pretty good about. But even when I didn't do well, like with his "What is a flame?" question, my communication with Dally through him transported me into a joyous state. All this was before, at age seven, she spoke to me, without the intermediation of a stuffed critter, about pi, that mystical ratio of a circle's circumference to its diameter.

"How far out do the pi digits go, gramps?" she asked.

"No one knows," I replied. "People have run their calculations out to billions of digits."

"What do you think the last digit is?"

"I don't think there is a last digit." We looked at each other for a very long time.

The next two years of our visits were focused on questions having to do with endings and beginnings. Dally got us started that very day with "What does infinity mean?" which led us into a discussion of flavors of infinity and the concept that some infinities are bigger than others. Her math/philosophy period yielded to what I'll call her political period, the one she is in now. She must have been ten or so when it began, not long after I lost everything.

"Dad says you used to have lots of money."

"I did."

"Where did it go?"

"I lost it in the stock market."

"In the recession?"

"You know about that?"

"Mom says there are going to be laws to eliminate the unfairness of it all."

"What sort of laws?" I asked, glancing toward Katy the Kitten for help.

"Laws so that the people who stole the money and crashed the stock market won't do it again."

"Yeah, well. The economy is very complicated," I said. The scraping of my chair reproached me when I pushed back from the table. I had never before dismissed a subject this way, or implied that it was too hard for her to understand.

"Mom says they won't go to jail, though," and I could see that her manner was not accusing but genuinely perplexed. She looked to me for the clear and rigorous explanation she could always count on.

"Hopefully they'll change the laws," I said. "Sorry, honey, but I really need to...I've got to get to the bathroom."

And there were other questions I had to skirt. I thought maybe the day would come when she grew old enough, jaded enough, that I could level with her about my past and how I felt about certain rules. Even now I don't dare tell her how little I mind when bad things happen to people as long as I'm right in predicting them. Or how, when I notice the brutal murder of another innocent, the most I say to myself is, "Well, that's not nice." But I knew that if in her teens she could see into my mind, she would judge me inadequately empathic. And it certainly wouldn't do to share with her how much I had needed a growing net worth to confirm my superior intelligence.

I continued to conceal my cynicism in the remaining years of the Obama presidency, hiding how unmoved I was by her fervor for what she called "fairness" on issues like taxes, healthcare, education, the environment, and society's treatment of minorities. But her innocent zeal had begun to pull on me. Eventually, at her urging, I began writing checks aimed at alleviating some aspect of human suffering, checks large enough to force me to settle for a cheaper cut of meat or not to see a movie if we wanted to pay the rent on time. And, you know? For the first time ever, these donations, these little hardships gave me a new feeling...one of connection to those she was trying to help and, of course, to her. Undoubtedly, she was helping me become a better person. Each time I sent her back to the city on the LIRR, I was left with another phrase of hers that stuck in my mind, terms like "distributive justice," "universal healthcare," and "racial equality." I wanted her to love me as much as I loved her, and each time I agreed with her or gave her a small sum for her favorite cause, my battery was recharged by the direct current of her approval.

It was February of 2016 when I took the four forty-five into the city for her sixteenth birthday party. Amanda, who'd mistakenly believed we'd agreed to celebrate the event the following Wednesday, was away on one of her "larks," in this instance, several days in the Catskills with "the gang." This group, all ten to fifteen years younger than Amanda, included Peyton, the boys' former math teacher, who'd coincidently moved to Patchogue. This time, unlike all the previous larks, when as soon as she walked out the door I would board a cannabis-fueled train to Stoli, I limited myself to a bottle of Courvoisier brandy and two ibuprofens. I was damned well going to show her that I could handle a visit to Manhattan without her assistance. I wished she could have seen me before I left for the station, sitting in our best chair near the front door, calmly reading a book.

And then, having shaved and showered, I even found an almost empty bottle of Old Spice and slapped a splash on my face, just like any fully functional male adult leaving for his granddaughter's birthday party.

On the real train in, I was looking forward to delighting Dally with the news that, under her influence, I'd likely vote for Hillary Clinton in the 2016 presidential election. Alas, she was wearing a Bernie shirt and wasn't as pleased as I thought she'd be, but she said "I'm proud of you, gramps. You've come a long way." Her tolerance wasn't quite what I'd hoped for, yet we found increasingly common ground as the Republican field narrowed to one.

With the election of Trump last year as the nation's forty-fifth president, Dally's idealism took on an edge of militancy that hadn't existed before. She had become a beautiful young woman who would have been accepted by any of the great universities on the strength of her math prizes alone, before even taking account of her freestyle swimming championships and editorship of her high school newspaper. But the day Trump was sworn into office, she told her parents she would not be going to college. "There is something more important to do," she informed them. They had moved into a one-bedroom, expecting she would leave for Stanford or MIT, so, even if they had been more supportive of her decision, there was no question of her living at home.

I received an anguished call from my son Robby. "Please, dad. I know she listens to you. See what you can do." And the next day she came for dinner.

"My parents don't get it. I have no choice. I am needed in The Resistance."

"How will you manage?" I asked, thinking about the rent bills I was in no position to help with.

"I am founding a not-for-profit. If it works the way I hope, it can pay me and a small staff. Not a lot but a living wage."

"What will it do?" I asked.

"It will use every available technique to stop him from destroying everything our country has stood for."

"Like what techniques?" I had admired Trump as the brash private sector deal guy, but, in sync with her, suspected he would make a horrible president. I mean, president of the United States of America? A real estate promoter with little to no relevant experience? The guy was a liar and a narcissist of Olympian proportions. You might as well have some self-aggrandizing financial engineer like the one I used to be before all the self-improvement of my recent years.

She was so organized I wasn't surprised when she fired up her laptop and walked me through a PowerPoint, concluding with a look of joyous determination, "All right-thinking citizens must act immediately or the very concepts of Truth and Democracy will not survive this loathsome man."

And I thought, *Bad news for Robby*; there was no point trying to change her mind. Right then, without her asking, I wrote her a check for $50, which made me feel better than any six-figure donation I'd ever been pressured into. So, lest there be any doubt, my special relationship with and support for Dally was helping raise my self-esteem. I was feeling as "constructive" about myself as if I were a buy on the Lehman Proprietary Trading stock watch list. I reckoned that having lived for seven years in Patchogue, this town of families, first responders, hospital workers, and secretaries, I'd been successfully transmuted from bankster to respected teacher, a pillar of the community. Maybe I wasn't so bad after all.

As Dally continued fighting the good fight, I would receive periodic dispatches from the front, mostly in the form of texts ("We did it!" "It's working!") but as time and Trump wore on, the texts dwindled, and I was forced to follow her progress on Facebook. Throughout, I kept my support steady through the occasional check and voicemails that mostly went unanswered.

So, one Sunday afternoon, I was delighted when my phone lit up with Dally's number. She never called. Perhaps she had been arrested and needed bail. How much would that sort of thing be? By the time I realized that she wouldn't be using her iPhone from jail, Dally's endearing voice was in my ear. "Hey grandpa," she said.

"Hey there, don't sound so down! We've got them on their heels! Keep up the pressure!" Maybe I was being too eager, but I wanted her to hear my passion for her cause.

"Do you have a minute to talk?"

"Sure, sure." Perhaps she was in trouble after all.

"So, this is weird…" A sigh came through the line. "But when our team looked into money flowing in Trump's direction, they came across a news item saying you'd given a hundred thousand dollars to his execrable supporter Roger Stone. A hundred thousand dollars!"

There was a long silence that of course I was meant to fill, but after ten seconds, I just said, "Hello?"

"Hello."

"I'm glad you brought this up."

"Okay." The rush of background air (*was it on her end or mine?*) began to fill my brain. It wasn't that I didn't have an explanation. Of course I did.

"Well, you see, I…in those days, I...I thought, if whoever won the presidency, if I was appointed to…anyway, thanks to you... See, I was born right after this world war, and my mom and dad had reasons to feel insecure, especially about money. Once I'd made a bunch on Wall Street, though, I could do politics at a level they never dreamed of…But now, thank god, as I'm sure you see, I'm a different person. One who—"

"Got it, gramps," she said, cutting me off, "No worries. Gotta go."

I became obsessed with wondering what she meant when she said she "got it." Did her hatred for Trump extend to all Republican donors, and would it damage our relationship? I couldn't bear the thought. For weeks afterward, I kept up my program of regular voicemails and Facebook encouragement, but not even a "like" or an emoji was thrown my way. This was her generation's version of radio silence, and I was devastated. I spent the better part of my days dreaming of ways to win her back. Most of them involved showing up at her dingy headquarters and writing a jaw-dropping check. Other times the check was mailed in a discreet, white envelope with a note that said simply, "I'm proud of you. Love, grandpa." I imagined her bleary-eyed, phone-banking contemporaries jumping up from their chairs and lifting an astonished Dally into the air as a single tear ran down her cheek.

But I had nothing like that kind of money.

Back when I did, I could have made this daydream real in a snap. But there was no way I could fund such a fantasy. This reality diverted my dreaming to all sorts of get-rich-quick schemes, the kind my father was known for. My first idea was to resurrect the old man's Burial at Sea deal that Lenny had fucked up. In my pursuit of that first brainstorm, I spent hours schmoozing the captains at the Bellport Marina. But I ultimately concluded there wasn't one among them who was partnership material. Also, with the barrier to competition so low, it felt too much like a fair fight. A guy can get hurt in a fair fight, even if he wins in the end. What I needed was an idea that would give me an unfair advantage.

So, I dusted off and rejected a few other ones while I waited for true inspiration. One possibility was a quantum information idea that would give me an unassailable edge in automated trading. I would use entangled electron particles to convey trading instructions over long distances instantaneously, leaving the schmucks relying on the existing infrastructure a losing fifteen microseconds behind. But when I costed it out, despite the huge leaps in quantum computing, the expense of renting the dark fiber from New York to Hong Kong was prohibitive.

While I was struggling to come up with a sure-thing scheme, I saw my beloved granddaughter even less frequently than before, not because I was so busy but because she was. Or at least that's what I told myself. But I was desperate to be back to the special relationship that had become the lodestar of my life. Before the chill of our Trump/Stone conversation, she really had been successful in dragging me in the direction of her intense dislike of Trump. This guy who managed to kick every sacred cow from the Pope to dead war heroes, from the FBI to *The New York Times*, was having sex with the most beautiful women and hobnobbing with presidents and kings. He owned about ten different homes, including a palatial triplex on Fifth Avenue, where his name was on the fucking building, while I struggled to make ends meet in a backwater he likely never heard of.

Although my dislike of him had become genuine, I must admit that it was basically a derivative of my love for Dally. Because unlike her, I was not impervious to the possibility that all his lies and narcissism could yield some positive results. I mean, putting aside the robust economy (which he deserved more than zero credit for) and the spending he was proposing on badly needed infrastructure, the bravado he was bringing to our foreign policy could conceivably be good for the country.

In one of my I'M BACK fantasies, I actually imagined that Trump reached out to me for the secretary of commerce position. Maybe I could get to him through my landlord, who was Jared Kushner's sister. Unlike the rest of his cabinet, I would be well-qualified to do the job, but that might not be a reason to ding me in and of itself. In addition, based on his other appointments, neither my Wall Street past nor my age should be an issue for him. And I'd made no contributions to any of his opponents in the primaries. No, the real problem was I was no longer rich and hadn't been in the news lately. And of course, even if he could overcome those facts and I could use my new position at Commerce to funnel some big bucks Dally's way, it wouldn't be enough for her to forgive me for taking the job in the first place. Naturally, I kept these thoughts to myself.

One night around 10 p.m., when I had been thinking of how to square the Trump/Dally circle, she called me in tears. "Gramps," was all she was able to articulate before dissolving again.

"It's all right, honey. Tell gramps what the problem is, and we'll fix it together."

She composed herself. "He's won. I, we, will be out of business in three weeks. He's normalized his insane destruction of America."

"What? Why will you be out of business?" I asked, already sure of the answer. Everything gets back to money. A fact that, once she calmed down, she confirmed.

"By Monday September 11, I won't be able to meet payroll. And it's not like I can take a cut; I haven't paid myself for weeks."

After I asked a few more questions about her situation, I hung up badly shaken. My beloved Dally had been living in the apartment of a guy she couldn't stand and subsisting on food stamps. I experienced a moment of frenzy during which I considered the potential of redemptive sacrifice. I would get on with it, relying on the unlikelihood an insurance adjuster would discover I don't eat sushi.

But I knew I wasn't yet ready. Instead, I swung instantly into thinking of other ways to make some money. She needed me! And lo and behold, an idea popped into mind: a chain of high end all-you-can eat vomitoria! The upside was considerable and perfectly in tune with the sensibility of Trump's America. The stock market feels like it's in lift-off mode. The economy is growing at a solid three percent, but far from applying the brakes, the Fed is pumping the money supply like a sex-starved ex-con on his first hooker. And Trump's tax plan, more money for the corporations already sitting on $2.3 trillion they don't know what to do with, is Viagra for the stock markets. I would have to launch my business before the market's persistent erection sent it to the emergency room. People are buying yachts, opening stores that only sell caviar, bidding through the high end of the range in art auctions. Even here in Patchogue, everyone is borrowing and buying again. You can tell from all the construction sites and the decent condition of the crap that folks put out on the curb.

I gave myself over to a brief reverie. None of that cheap, family style, coupons, and kids-eat-free-before-six Golden Corral type establishment. No, we're talking haute cuisine, reservations, tablecloths, solicitous service, an extensive wine list. The best food money can buy until you don't want any more. Private Restorative Retreat chambers, well-ventilated and served by power-flush toilets. Spritzed after each use with a distinctive air freshener associated with our brand. Only lunch and dinner, one seating per meal. Minimum of $1,000 per person and a time limit of five hours. Valet parking. Complimentary back rubs at table.

But get real, I told myself, by the time I *schnorred* the initial capital off my brother, found the location, and hired the help, six more months would have gone by and then, best case, another six before I got to cash-flow positive. Face it, I thought, the most reliable way to make a quick buck is the one that got me to four units in the first place. Honestly, it never made any sense to me that trading on inside information was against the law. Everyone has the same fair shot at finding an angle. Take the guy at Antonelli's Auto Repair, whose obnoxious son was in my math class a few years ago. Maybe Antonelli *papà* notices a flaw in the ignition system of a GM car. All he has to do is call his broker and short the stock. We all have our opinions on who has better information. This is what makes markets.

Folks say stupid things like, "The market went down today because there were more sellers than buyers." No, jerk. If I sell, there has to be a buyer on the other side of the trade. There are always the same number of shares bought as shares sold. And everyone is starting from the same pole position when it comes to information. It's time to stop fucking around. The God of Present Value is whispering in my ear. I hear the garbage truck lumbering down the street toward my home, which means about three hours till the US markets open. Willem "The Throkster" Throkmorton over in London is still in the game; he owes me one. Bailey has a nice perch on Morgan Stanley's Abu Dhabi prop desk. Robert "Robber Baron" Baronstein is chairman of Mergers and Acquisitions at Jeffries. Kramer, who segued smoothly from Lehman to Barclays, would expedite my opening the account and execution of the trades. I'll have three days to settle and, in the meantime, with the hundred K I'm sure Lenny will loan me, I can swing about three million strike price of options on some no-brainer names. By the end of the week, I should have a gain of at least a million on paper, and I will be on my way! It will feel so fantastic to be able to call Dally from my standing exercise desk. I'll be walking briskly with the treadmill on a slight incline, looking at my three blinking Bloombergs, slightly out of breath, with the news.

"Hey honey. It's gramps. We're good—"

THE END

ACKNOWLEDGMENTS

I would like to thank my gifted editors Sarah Bernstein, Andrew Postman, Alexandra Shelley, and Andrea Chapin who schooled me as I transitioned from nonfiction to fiction writing. To editors Kierra Sondereker and Renee Rutledge, as well as Abbey Gregory, Brian McLendon, Keith Riegert, and their colleagues at Ulysses Press, a special shout out for the creativity, expertise, and industry knowledge they brought to the manuscript.

I could not be more grateful to my friends from law school, Fred Sherman, Marc Fasteau, Roger Lowenstein, and George Frampton, whose comments on early drafts empowered me to continue this project. Other readers whose support was invaluable include Barry Buzan, Lucas Cantor, John Chao, Michael Coffey, Brian Dailey, Ken Davidson, Ben Edwards, Shelley Finkel, the late great Jim Hoge, Peter Kaminsky, Hesh Kestin, Karl Klingbiel, Cher Lewis, Don MacKinnon, my brother Tom Miller, Julia Ormond, Yfat Reiss Gendell, Markus Dohle, David Roberts, Esmeralda Santiago, Melvyn Schoenfeld, Robert Smith, Scott Spencer, Jean Strouse, and Jordan Tamagni. My daughters Lily and Izzy are in their own category for their love and support through this process.

I am grateful to the contemporary artist Deborah Buck, whose Anna Force in *The Windows of Buck House: Fabulous Fictional Female*s was the inspiration for this book's cover image.

I also wish to express my gratitude to those who have helped me understand the publishing business and make connections therein: Michelle Aielli, Jane Friedman, Betsy Gleick, Allison Markin Powell, Jim Mustich, Jess Siegler, Cindy Speigel, and Jon Taplin. Kudos to Shannon Nacey, my Chief Operating Officer, without whose protean skills I would have accomplished little in the real world. Special thanks to Michael Pietsch, Chair of Hachette Book Group, whose support for me and my writing has been, and continues to be, invaluable.

ABOUT THE AUTHOR

Ken Miller is president & CEO of Ken Miller Capital, LLC ("KMC"), a closely held merchant banking firm that invests in early-stage companies. He is the former vice chairman of Merrill Lynch Capital Markets and Credit Suisse First Boston. Mr. Miller has served as a member of the Board of Directors of Viacom, Inc., Intelsat Corporation, KinderCare Learning Centers, CNA Surety, and Loews Corporation. He serves on the board of the National Committee on US-China Relations and PEN America and is an active member of the Council on Foreign Relations.

Mr. Miller received his BA with honors from the University of Michigan (1964), and, in addition to an MA in Chinese Studies from Yale University (1965), received his JD from Harvard University (1969). His articles on China, venture capital, economic development, international relations, and the merger market have appeared in publications such as *The Harvard Journal of Legislation*, *The Business Lawyer*, *The Far Eastern Economic Review*, *The New Republic*, *The Deal*, *The Nation*, and *Fortune*, *Foreign Affairs*, and *Time*. *High Finance* is his first novel.